UNSUSPECTING HERO

*****

Roland Ladley

the very first of the Sam Green novels

Steven,

Christmas 2015

love

Roland Claire
x

There are darker places than the Dark Continent

Prologue

'Well, Sam, you understand that this is the end of our consultations?' The psychiatrist looked directly at his patient who was sat across from his desk. She seemingly stared straight through him, her face emotionless.

Sergeant Sam Green remained very still, exactly as she had been at every session since she began her therapy. Her knees were together and her hands were clasped, resting on her legs. The only thing about her that appeared to move were her eyes, which darted around the room. Perhaps, he thought, they were looking for answers? Even her voice was level, betraying any feeling. Doctor Allen put a lot of that down to her military training. But he knew that there was a good deal of other business going on in her head, much of which he hadn't been able to access.

'Yes, I know that, sir.' A flat response. The "sir" almost a polite afterthought.

The ending hadn't come unexpectedly. They had talked about it over a number of weeks, of the best way to move forward with her rehabilitation. He had got as far as he could, and so, with her agreement, they had decided that the next leg of her journey would not be with the Army. Today she would be signed off, discharged from the Services and transferred into the care of the National Health Service. It was a big change, but one he thought was for the best. Sergeant Green needed a significant event in her world to help her break out from the traumatic and complex memories that fogged her mind. To unleash the demons and let them fly.

'Your medical release will be signed today. I believe you have a meeting with your consultant later on this afternoon?"

Sam finally stopped looking through him and glanced behind her at the clock on the wall.

'At fourteen hundred', she confirmed. Still emotionless.

When she looked back at him he smiled. Today was a big day for Sam Green. Her entire existence had been centred on the Army and suddenly she was no longer fit for service. Off into the civilian world, an event far more terrifying than a battlefield for a lot of his patients. A world which didn't recognise "fourteen hundred" as a time of day. A complicated place, without boundaries and often without rules. She would have to lead a life devoid of squads and platoons, without instant companionship and constant banter. An amorphous place where self-reliance was challenging and teamwork a rare discovery. He knew he was taking a chance letting her go, but something had to change.

'Before we finish, is there anything else you want to say, Sam?' Doctor Allen instinctively looked at his watch. He knew his patient would never run a second over time. Good military training.

'Nothing else to add.' Again, her tone was distant; her eyes now almost misted over.

After such trauma it was not unusual for a soldier to close down, to hide from the outside and look within. But Sergeant Sam Green had managed it to the extreme. They had talked, he had advised, but there had always been a wall between them. An effective wall constructed swiftly by her. And even now, after all the time they had spent together, their goodbye would be short and brief.

The clock hit the hour and Sam was on her feet without being asked. She met his gaze. 'Thank you for your honesty and support, Doctor.'

Doctor Allen nodded, 'Good luck with your next steps, Sam.'

With that she left. And that was it. Another soldier had come and gone out of his care. He had to trust that the NHS knew what they were doing with her. As he looked down at his discharge notes, he couldn't shake off the doubts that remained.

Psychiatrically Sgt Green has been diagnosed with Post Traumatic Stress Disorder. The attack which resulted in her abdominal injuries were savage, and notably, she lost close friends in the same incident. Our staff have worked hard with her and a separate report will follow. However it is clear to me that she has yet to come to terms with her psychiatric illness.

She has been distant, but pliable in all our consultations. She is prone to listlessness, impenetrable moods and sleeps often; although she has spoken of wanting to be reckless. She is in my opinion, a risk to herself but not to others, although there have been no incidences of self-harm that we are aware of. The transition from military to civilian life might exacerbate her illness. Alternatively her disposition could improve once faced with the reality of finding a job etc. Until her new consultant has full visibility of her condition we suggest she is placed on an 'at risk' register and monitored at least biweekly.

After a final look-over Doctor Allen felt that a few words should be underlined for emphasis. However, that wouldn't be professional. As of two o'clock this afternoon Sergeant Green would be a civilian and under the care of her local NHS. She'd be monitored and looked after to the best of their abilities. But thinking back on his time with this particular patient, even with the intense care she had received, Doctor Allen couldn't stop himself from thinking that Sam Green was a ticking bomb.

Chapter One

It had been a short cycle ride from her campervan to the far side of the loch. The wind had calmed down since the ferry crossing and the route she had chosen to cycle, whilst undulating, was flat enough. Now sat on a rock overlooking the water, Sam could pick out the road she had taken to get here. She couldn't see her van, which was tucked behind a rise further to her right, but she knew it was secure. You could leave your front door open on Mull with a neon sign saying 'thieves welcome' and nobody would go in. That was her experience of the island, anyway.

Other than what she was wearing and what she was carrying in her daysack, everything she owned and everything that was important to her was in her van. If it was lost, she would be too. And this time completely.

The twenty-five minute crossing had been monumental. She had stepped over a line in the sand to her new life and there was no going back. That may be a bit melodramatic, she thought, but that's what it felt like. The wind had whipped the sea into a bit of a frenzy and even though you could almost spit across the Sound, the dear old blue and white Caledonian MacBrayne ferry had struggled with the squall and heaved left and right as if dodging countless tackles. But that hadn't bothered her. Her focus had been on Mull. And when she drove tentatively off over the lowered metal doors she knew this was it. The break. The clean break. And the start of the new Sam Green.

She opened the drawstring to her olive green daysack and felt inside for the plastic container holding her lunch: ham sandwiches with a touch of English mustard. She had gone as far as using wholemeal bread, but in recognition of the 'new me' she had kept the lunch menu simple: ham sandwiches, a packet of crisps, an apple and a small bottle of water. To be honest it was also a reflection of her bone idleness when it came to food.

But now she only had to worry about herself. Now she could adopt a no-frills approach without others judging her. Tuffy had once remarked 'This stew is, ehh, *nice* Sam.' Nice. Damned with absolutely no praise at all by Tuffy. Colour Sergeant Tuffnell, a woman not to be messed with.

Soldier first, maiden second. She wouldn't recognise decent stew unless her promotion depended upon it. Still, Sam's mother always said that cooking well was nowhere near as important as 'being good in the other department'. Bless her. She would be disappointed to learn her daughter was rubbish at both.

'Great,' Sam let the word slip out between mouthfuls and smiled to herself. Ham sandwiches. You really can't beat them.

She savoured the view which, surprisingly for November, wasn't interrupted by rain. Greens and browns giving way to dark rock and the odd exposed small cliff. The mountains here were really just hills, but the weather made them treacherous for the unprepared. Mull, she always thought, was a much more welcoming place than Skye. She'd visited both on adventure training exercises and found Mull rounder, less spiky. But the island had its dark places. Mountains like Ben More, which would expose your weaknesses and sap your strength. Anywhere north of Blackpool was dangerous if the weather closed in.

She had felt the cold hand of exposure once whilst on a training exercise in Sennybridge and without the help of some of her pals she might not have made it. The thing about the Army is that there's always somebody willing to jump into your green maggot with you to 'warm you up'. Both sexes. Thankfully that time it was a real emergency and the warmth she selflessly stole from - she can't remember who - was purely to raise her body temperature and not her heart rate. She had quickly recovered, acknowledging that one way to fight hypothermia was to get very personal with a fellow human being for as long as it takes. She had given herself a really good talking to, put her boots back on and continued even though the Doc had advised against it. She knew where she had got it wrong and she wouldn't get caught out again. Ever.

As she cast her eyes up and down the shore, picking out countless seabirds she couldn't recognise, she saw something close to the water that looked out of place. She frowned, put down the packet of crisps she was eating and stood up. She hesitated and didn't walk to it immediately. It's just a brown package. This was Mull. It wouldn't be dangerous, it was unlikely to blow up in your face. But the training she had been put through refused to be ignored. She gave the package some space, deciding to study it just for a while.

Her resolve didn't last long.

'Oh what the hell,' she said out loud, announcing to the world that she was ignoring all previously taught protocol and went to give the small package a poke.

5

On inspection, and with a tap of her walking shoe, she saw that it was just a wallet. A brown leather wallet darkened to almost black by the damp of the loch and etched with salt where the wind had dried some of the seawater.

She shrugged, a display of contempt to a previous existence, picked it up and opened it. Inside were a couple of credit cards, something that looked like a driving licence and some other scraps of paper wrecked by seawater. No notes and no change.

Her attention then turned to the driver's licence. She noticed that it wasn't a standard British licence. It was blue with a photo ID of an older black man, some simple typing giving a name, address and the words 'Sierra Leone Driving Licence' across the top. The whole thing had been crudely laminated, not an etched-on plastic affair like a modern western licence. She turned it over and then back again, looking for clues.

She checked the name: Dr Joseph Tebie. The two credit cards were from the Standard Charter Bank, a bank she'd never heard of. One was a Visa account and she didn't recognise the other. The licence, the two cards and the paper in the wallet were a soggy mess. Although there was the remnants of a yellowed photograph in a see-through plastic pouch. What was left of the photo showed a late middle-aged black man (older than the licence photograph, but similar) what she suspected was his wife and a teenage child. She studied the photo for a couple of seconds and briefly felt something close to emotion, a connection between a washed up wallet, the owner and maybe his wife and child.

Words came back to her. 'Feelings will return. You will start to get them back.' Yeah, right Doc. Like I actually care how I feel. That I cannot raise a tear nor shout and scream. I know I should and I know I should want to, but it's still too early. I need some space. And don't ask me again. I really don't care. Sorry. I can't even think about it.

The fleeting emotion was lost and she folded the wallet and put it in the top compartment of her daysack. She would stop at the next police station and hand it in.

Room 425, Fourth Floor, UN Building, New York,

Pierre walked into the room without knocking.
'Bonjour Middleton.'
'Good morning Pierre.' Henry Middleton replied, though he inwardly thought *why must you use my surname? It's not as if we don't know each other.*

The Frenchman continued. 'I may be the only one who's heard this but my French contact at Langley thinks there may be some truth behind Report 1415.' The Frenchman smiled. Knowledge is power. He thrust his hands deep into his trouser pockets.

There was silence for a few moments. Henry played with his pencil and leant back on his chair, swivelling it slightly, looking out across to Belmont Island. The view was good, but the windows were dirty and the concertina blinds equally so. Austerity measures crossed every international boundary, even multinational ones.

'What are you trying to do Pierre? We have good evidence that the report is rubbish. Anything else must be conjecture, scurrilous scaremongering. It's a conspiracy. We've shown that?' Henry, if nothing else, was a realist. The report was a one-off from the tiny UN detachment in Monrovia, written by a new but enthusiastic desk officer who had heard and seen something whilst he was up country. There was nothing to corroborate the report from any of the West African Missions. The report had crossed a few desks on the fourth floor in New York and died a death. Quickly. If it had made the press it would have sent all sorts of hares running at a time when what everyone needed was a single focus - Ebola. Everything pointed to it being submitted by a member of the UN Mission in Liberia who was slightly unhinged. Or someone hoping to make a name for himself. Someone in the building very few people had heard of. Realism dictated that the report was rubbish. There was no conspiracy in Liberia. No cover up.

'My contact has the Americans in a bit of a, how do you British say, 'tizz' about the report. They have every reason for the details of the report not to be divulged and are worried that with its gestation in the UN - who knows what will happen? They think we will either leak it, probably from the hand of one of the senior staff here who would like to see the Americans squirm. Or it will get out because we are just full of holes. You have to admit it remains a good story.' Pierre smiled again. He couldn't really hide his own anti-Americanism.

Henry stopped himself from replying straight away. If Langley was 'in a tizz' then they might actually think there was something to the report. They'd known about it since the beginning. There were enough US staff on the key fourth floor of the building to have read and shared the report with the CIA. So why get excited now? Henry guessed that in order to deny the report they'd want to know the truth - good or bad.

'Let's take this upstairs.' Henry was standing now. 'Someone in the press department will need to knock up a line to take and maybe Plans will have something new, although I doubt it.' He looked directly at Pierre. 'I guess you've told Paris?'

Pierre nodded. 'Bien sûr!'

'That's fair enough. I'll talk to London later. Whether there's any truth in it or not, nobody will want this out. Well apart from one or two of the Islamic States and ISIS.'

As they walked out Henry muttered under his breath 'What a bloody nightmare'.

Tubmanburg, Liberia

The sweat was dripping down him. The trip from Monrovia had taken an hour longer than Victor had expected and with the air conditioning broken on his Land Cruiser the wet heat was intolerable. The roads were at best poor, often washed away and nearly always rutted. He had told his German boss that he was visiting schools in the area, part of the UNHCR mandate 'in country'. And that was partially true. But he also had another job. Victor's contact in Tubmanburg had phoned him, saying that he had more on the story. Much more. He knew his initial report would cause a real stink, so much so he had run it past his man in his capital, Vilnius, before releasing it. But he knew the story was true - he had seen the evidence for himself. The Special Representative to the Secretary General (SRSG) couldn't have cared less about the story, his mind was on 'other things', although the UN's top man in Liberia had had the good grace to warn him of the consequences of pressing the send button thus dispatching the report to New York.

The truth was nobody believed him and, just as important, nobody wanted to believe him. But there was some of his mother's journalistic inquisitiveness that burnt strongly within, pushing him to uncover what was really happening. He couldn't stop himself from responding to the latest call from his contact up country for a meeting. Even though he was scared witless and sweating buckets. As he pulled off the road outside the crumbling colonial building that doubled as a hotel in the town, he knew he had to see this through.

He opened the Land Cruiser's door and stood beside the incongruously white vehicle. He raised his damp neckerchief to his brow. As he reached behind him to open the rear door to retrieve his case he didn't hear the click as the bolt from a Fielding sniper rifle engaged a round and slid it into the rifle's chamber. He certainly didn't hear the smack of the explosion that sent the 7.62 millimetre slug on a straight trajectory to his temple as the bullet outpaced the sound wave. And he didn't hear the thud of his body hitting the ground. By then it was all over.

Sam didn't feel like a new woman. She felt different, a little liberated, but she knew she would struggle to lose the old and embrace the new anytime soon. She'd finished the cycle ride, having got as far as Lochbuie where she had stared out to sea for a good half an hour before heading on back. The good news was that the wound in her stomach was sore, but not painful - something to be pleased about. How they had managed to stitch up the mess that she had held in her hands before she had passed out was a piece of magic. If only her head was less troublesome.

She had chosen well with the bike she'd bought. It wasn't a bad road bike, she could have paid so much more. It had some give and, at just five-five in her socks, it was easily light enough to pick up and chuck on the bike rack. Getting the waterproof cover over it was another matter though.

'Short arse', she snorted out loud at herself.

She looked up from the paper at the others in the pub hoping nobody had heard her. Talking to yourself is one thing. The psychologists, and she'd seen a few since her discharge, might have something to say about swearing at yourself out loud.

She'd driven the hour or so down the coast to Bunessan and parked up in a small hotel car park overlooking the bay. She hadn't made it as far as the ferry to Iona where she was convinced there was a campsite, but with the weather closing in and her stomach making noises like a washing machine whose bearings had gone, she needed to eat. She was also tired. Dog tired. It had been an exhausting two months since she'd driven out of the barracks. Sorting out her life, explaining to her few close folk what she intended to do - trying to dodge the questions. Throughout sleep had been elusive. All that noise in her head.

'Bloody noise,' she sighed. Oops - there she goes again. She looked up and smiled at the old man sat across from her on the other side of the fire. He smiled back and nodded.

He probably thinks I'm a weirdo.

The food was good; homemade beef burger and chips. Big chips as well. Not those reconstituted thin things, photoshopped to look fabulous. Chunks of real potato fried to a crisp. Fabulous. She had picked up an old copy of The Scotsman, laid it out on the table and, between mouthfuls, was reading anything that caught her attention.

She didn't normally do papers. A quick look at the BBC News app on her phone kept her as up to date as she needed to be. Having recently been involved in making front page news (at some personal cost), she didn't really care for it. There was too much of it. Too much bad stuff going on for a normal person to get their head round. And too many celebrities. Far too many reasonably talented people stuck up on a pedestal and then asked their opinion on difficult subjects. What did they know about that stuff? Yeah, sure. Ask them about music, glamour or films. But, come on, who cares what rock star X thinks about the latest terror attack, or flooding in Bangladesh? She felt she had a better grip on real life than them. And nobody ever asked her.

But when Sam could be bothered and had the time she liked to read the newspaper. She turned the pages back to check the date: Friday 7 November. Just a couple of days out of date then. She leafed through the pages and picked up another chip with her fingers. 'Manners, pet'; she could hear her mother even now.

She skimmed the print and the odd photo. She nodded to herself. She was very good at this. Her training and experience had honed her skill of scanning documents and picking out salient facts. She ignored prepositions (God, there's a word she wouldn't have recognised at school) and adjectives, and focused on nouns and verbs. Get the gist of the thing and go back and look again if there's something there. The Devil would always be in the detail, but you needed to find the right page first.

She laughed out loud when she glanced through the story about the traffic warden who had given a parking ticket to a wheelie bin. And then she stopped herself abruptly. The old man was looking across at her again, smiling to himself. Ok, so she wasn't all there just now. She knew that. She just hoped that she didn't come across as a complete fruitcake.

She read on. Always looking for the nugget on the page, the thing that stood out, or that just didn't quite fit in. Look for the absence of normal, not for the abnormal. That's the key. She knew she was particularly good at photos. She could pick out a face in a crowd even if she had just glanced at it. She saw in aerial photography what others didn't. A heavily camouflaged vehicle here, disturbed earth there. She could spot what shouldn't be there, or what should be there but wasn't, when everyone else had moved on.

She was almost as good with words. Now. To be fair, her schooling had been an effort. She'd got a couple of GCSEs, including maths and English, but she never considered herself to be well educated. She knew she wasn't stupid, her results in her promotion to sergeant exams proved that. But she only learnt when she was really enthused, or when her future really depended upon it. Then she was sharp, at least she felt that way.

She could look at a page of type and whilst there were still words that eluded her and sent her scrambling for a dictionary, she now read well and could get to the nub, read the subtext and make, sometimes, one or two insightful conclusions. And she didn't get bored with big documents. She just ploughed on through. Tuffy had said she was thought to be the best in the battalion, and if she kept it up she might get an award at the end of the tour. She knew she had spotted a couple of Improvised Explosive Devices (IEDs) from photographs that, if driven over, would have spoilt everyone's day. And the work she did on the crowd photographs from that morning in the Kabul market had enabled a couple of arrests of high value targets. Yes, she was good at that.

Stop feeling so pleased with yourself she thought to herself. *You didn't always get it right.*

Then she stopped thinking and stared at the bottom right hand corner of the page. She looked hard. She felt her heart rate rise instantly, like it always did when she saw something, something different, out of place.

The face in the photo.

'I know who you are.' Out loud again. Shit. *But I do - I know who you are. You're the wallet man.* This time to herself. She was too engrossed to glance across at the old man to check if he was looking at her.

The article was headed - 'Doctor Ebola succumbs to the disease'. She picked out the following key words and phrases: Kenema; Sierra Leone; 5 November; Doctor Joseph Tebie; Ebola; specialist; pioneering; indefatigable; major loss; fight against the disease; funeral; Freetown; Saturday.

The combination of The Scotsman's article and the misplaced waterlogged wallet made her feel distinctly uneasy. She had found something unusual and the timing and geography were all wrong. It was like when she had spotted some odd markings near a culvert on a recently taken aerial photograph, only to hear that the patrol was already on the ground. She had made the discovery too late that time. And one lad paid for her lack of timeliness with his life.

Something, somewhere, made her feel the same way about this. Her heart continued to race.

Chapter Two

Jimmy knew he wasn't very good at this. He knew he wasn't contributing in the way that he should, the way that his boss thought he ought to. He just didn't know enough, didn't have that feel for where events might be going. Wasn't a quick enough analyst and couldn't quite see the big picture. Yes he knew he was intelligent. Having a first in History from Downing saw him through the first set of interviews for the Foreign Office fast track place. However, even after a year of visiting a vast array of countries, reading a catalogue of books on history and politics that he could recite word for word, he still lacked the ability to make decisions under pressure. That's why they had brought in more horsepower at the beginning of the crisis.

Over a couple of weekends he had written a paper ('brilliant' according to his boss' scrawled comment) about the likelihood of a return to civil war in Sierra Leone. He could do that, amass facts, stew over likely scenarios and come to some sensible conclusions. All well-structured and following Civil Service guidelines. Conclusions and recommendations at the front on no more than a page and a half, supporting documentation following on.

But it was the instant stuff he really struggled with. It was the crises that got him into a bit of a pickle. He so wanted to be able to take it all in and throw out snap instructions. It's just his brain wouldn't let him. It just wouldn't, no, couldn't work at that speed. He would have been no good in the Army or working for the spies.

Since the Ebola thing had kicked off his boss had asked for 'additional resources'. The chap they sent, Darren Rickman, wasn't an Oxbridge grad. He had a degree from somewhere in the West Country and had picked up five or six years' experience in the Navy before crossing over. Darren was brusque, sharp and, much to Jimmy's dismay, ambitious. 'Don't worry Charles, I'll get a grip of the desk'. He had overheard him in the corridor talking to his, now their, boss.

And he had. He couldn't take that away from the chap, He was good; very good. The Army deployment supported by the NHS staff to Freetown to assist with the Ebola crisis would have taken any other member of staff in the building twice as long to pull off. Getting those people together took huge reserves of confidence and charm. If Jimmy had tried to make it happen on his own they would still be twiddling their thumbs in the training bases in Kent. Yes, there was the odd loose end, like who was going to pay for it all. But Darren didn't seem to bother about that. 'You worry too much Jimmy. It'll sort itself out in the fullness of time.' Right. Probably when you've moved on and I'm left to pick up the fucking pieces. He didn't used to swear. Nowadays he just couldn't stop himself.

Darren was on leave for a couple of days. 'I need a quick break. Recharge the Duracells. Off to Cornwall with my board and wetsuit.' Jimmy wanted to say 'I hope you don't drown'. But knew that deep down a small part of him wished Darren would take a board to the back of his head and lose himself in the cold waters of the Atlantic. Glug glug. Jimmy didn't think he was an unkind man, just a bit lost and the last thing he needed was a patronising show off on his turf when he was trying so hard to get things right.

The phone rang. The image of Darren waving frantically for help from a far off shore was broken. It was Freetown, he recognised the number.

'Jimmy here.'

Jimmy knew the voice straight away. It was the High Commissioner. *Yikes, what does he want?*

'Yes sir. Ok. Sure. Sorry? Oh my goodness. You're serious?' Of course he was serious, he was Her Majesty's High Commissioner. He then listened without interrupting. And the longer he listened the more his mouth fell open. At one point he mopped up dribble with his tongue.

'Ehh, wow. That's, well, extraordinary.' Pause. 'I'll get this to Charles ASAP.'

There was more from the High Commissioner.

'Understood sir. Are you going to put this in your weekly report?' He knew as soon as he said it that it was a stupid suggestion. 'Of course. Special report within two hours. And get Charles to phone you straight away. Sure. Makes sense.' He tried desperately to think of a clever question.

'Let me know....' He stopped before the end of the sentence. The High Commissioner had hung up. 'Fuck.' Jimmy put his head in his hands. *What a day for Darren to be drowning in the Atlantic*, he thought to himself. This was going to create a bow wave of work like he had probably never experienced before. There would be so many questions and very few answers. Certainly none that he could think of.

He had a flash of inspiration. *Phone Darren - get him back. Yes, that's the trick. He'd love the cut and thrust of this. Get him back - now. Otherwise I'm screwed.*

First thing though, was to find Charles and tell him Victor Solzman had been murdered in Liberia. Shot in the head a few miles from where he had allegedly found the clinic. *Fuck, this is big. Bigger than me.*

Fidden, Isle of Mull

Sam had a hell of a headache. And when it was like this she didn't even have the energy to get out of her sleeping bag. She had pills for this, the only pills left after what had seemed like a chemist load recovering from the 'incident'. For God's sake, call it what it was. But when it was like this nothing seemed to matter; nothing seemed to make a difference. The pain was incidental to the 'why am I bothering with all this' feeling that seemed to engulf every part of her, making her motionless, immovable even. If the van was going to be hit by a train it wouldn't be enough to make her get up and out. *Best probably to go that way. Nobody would notice. Not sure about the pain of being hit by a train. Hell, maybe I would get up. It would be touch and go though.*

She tried to think through the fog that clouded her mind. She had finished in the pub, slept overnight in the carpark on the van's 'rock 'n roll' bed and made it through the day with the short drive to the campsite opposite Iona. She knew she had been for a walk along the coast and, with the light fading, had made herself beans on toast for supper and gone straight to bed, earlier than normal. It had been a non-day in comparison to the highs of the previous cycle ride, the find of the wallet and supper in the pub.

'Bugger. The wallet and the newspaper article; that connection.' She thought she said that out loud. She lifted her head off the pillow and rested on her elbow. She tried to focus. She had no idea what time it was, except the light was streaming in through the curtains. That would make it about nine-ish. Maybe later. Her mind drifted back to the wallet she had found; Doctor Tebie. She could picture his face exactly. Ebola expert succumbed to the disease, funeral in Freetown later this week - Saturday, she remembered the day. And yet his wallet had washed up on the shores of Mull, some God knows how many thousands of miles away. But what if the wallet was lost some time ago, maybe on a trip to the UK? She sat up. Her head thudded a bit, but she was already feeling slightly sharper. *Think, girl, think.*

She reached to her right to the work top that ran alongside the bed cum sofa. She found her daysack and pulled it onto her lap. She stopped herself from opening the drawcord.

'Open the curtains first you idiot.' Out load again; chastising.

She drew the curtains back that were behind her head, covering the Volkswagen T4's rear window and pulled the one to her left open as well. Brown, beige, butter and white gingham. Not a bad match with the blue and orange striped seat coverings. She had made the curtains herself using the sewing machine left to her by her Mum. They were all part of the therapy, the transition from invalid to unemployed and probably unemployable. All because of the 'incident'.

She took out the wallet and carefully pulled apart the soggy mass of paper and card that she had found unrecognisable a day earlier. It was pretty hopeless. None of it made any sense. Some pieces were typed, some hand written. She could make out the odd word, but nothing coherent.

And then, a light blue scrap of paper about A5 sized folded to fit in the wallet, covered in scribbled black ink, much of which had run. There was a title: *Notes*....unintelligible word....*case* and then some unrecognisable numbers. Below that is was all gobbledygook. But, on the top right was a date: *2 Nov 14.* Clear as anything. The case notes of something or somebody. With an exact date of just six (or was it seven? - her brain couldn't cope with that question) days ago.

Dead Doctor; one continent. His wallet; another continent, only recently lost from his pocket. Surely? And if that was the case, why? There was something completely out of place here.

What now? She could take it to the police here where it would almost certainly languish without thought and then it would end up in the lost property locker with a note on a database somewhere. Even if she remonstrated and made the connection out loud, she knew she would be seen off with some platitudes. 'Yes, lass. We'll see what we can do. Now you go and have a great wee holiday.'

Options? She could drive down south and take it into Scotland Yard. She wasn't in any way sure why that was different to handing it in up here, but she thought she might at least speak to someone who could see the relevance of the connection. The connection she had seen: dead doctor and recovered wallet, same time, two continents apart. A connection made by an early thirties, ex-Intelligence Corps sergeant who had been medically discharged and was currently under the watchful eye of a psychiatrist. Yeah, like they'd take her seriously.

Go to the press? Get some investigative journalist on the case. Ebola was still big and these journalists were bright. Yeah, that was an option. She knew she would lose control of it straight away and that would hurt, but at least somebody might do something. Or perhaps not. She might never know. Other options?

What about phoning Colonel Tim? He was still running the Intelligence Battalion and, if nothing else, he would give her some sound advice. She had the greatest respect for him. In Afghanistan he was always in the analyst's' room at the base (the pit), enquiring, pushing, advising. Always with a half-smile, always checking on morale. 'How's it going girl' was his stock opener. She didn't mind the 'girl' bit. He wasn't that much older than her, but had been through the mill. Ireland in the early days (some said he spent two years running agents), Iraq for two tours and now his second in Afghanistan. That made him much older in experience than her, and his direction and advice was always completely sound.

He had also been beside her at her short inquest after the 'incident', seen it all the way through. And had written a very strong reference for her when she left.

'That's what I'll do.' Breakfast, or phone first? Phone. Duty before sustenance.

She picked up her mobile and phoned the Adjutant, a number she had kept for emergencies when she was in the military wing of the hospital at Frimley. She had no idea who the new one was. Captain Smith, the adjutant she knew, had moved on promotion about the time she left.

'Hi. It's Sergeant Sam Green. Sorry, ex-Sergeant. Is Colonel Tim in?'

The new adjutant was Captain Hall, the old signals officer. Phew. She knew him well. They had a brief discussion about how she was and then Mike Hall asked her what she wanted the boss for.

'It's all a bit odd. I'm up in Mull and I've found something completely out of place. Something that could be significant, or important and I'm at a loss as to what to do. I sort of know that Colonel Tim would be able to advise.'

She listened and was surprised and pleased that the 'Adj' put her straight through.

The next ten minutes ran away with itself. As she expected Colonel Tim was polite (kind almost) and thorough. He kept saying 'that's interesting' and 'right'. He finished off with 'keep the wallet for the moment. I'll get onto some folk I know in London who will probably be interested in this. When I put the phone down give Mike Hall your mobile number and I will get back to you, certainly by mid next week even if I have nothing. Then we can have a chat about what to do next. Oh, and enjoy your convalescence in Mull. Fine choice.'

And that was that. She had done something. Something constructive. Something useful and not on the list advised by the Doc. She was hungry now and looking out through the gentle rain could just about make out Iona in the distance.

Eat, dress and get the ferry across to Iona for a poke around. Yes that would fill the day nicely.

Second Floor Canteen, UN Building, New York

Henry was nervous. What had he let himself in for?

He sipped his coffee and let his eyes wander around the ground floor cafeteria. A sea of races and colours. The UN: an expensive and wholly laudable experiment that was hopeless but better than nothing. Without it and a few well-placed competent staff who earnestly tried to make it work (and not milk the opportunity for every dollar, like the rest of them), the world would be lacking a forum that made very little difference and cost a fortune. But it still provided an essential, collective voice. A platform where everyone had to listen even if you ignored the words. A matriarch unable to stop the grandchildren from misbehaving, but still the voice of collective reason. It made a difference, albeit a small one.

Henry reviewed the past forty-eight hours. The latest report from Liberia that Victor Solzman had been murdered by an unknown gunman had to be linked to Report 1415. It had to be? The press could only report the murder as a 'random killing of a UN official'. Nobody at the UN had divulged Solzman's report to them and, therefore, no link could be made. Yet.

The press line to take was (it was indelibly etched into his memory): *Victor Solzman was a valuable member of the UN's Mission in Liberia, UNMIL. Working with the Liberian government he was at the forefront of expanding the 'get back to school' programme. This random killing shows that whilst much progress has been made in the country we all need to be vigilant against a return to violence. His death also reminds us of the risks that UN staff often face as they make a difference every day in sometimes dangerous and volatile areas. Our thoughts are with Victor's family and friends at this difficult time.*

They had held an emergency meeting of key staff on the Fourth Floor. They did the numbers. The whole world now knew of Solzman's death. On the other hand only fifteen staff in the building had read Report 1415, and about ten others knew of its existence. Nobody wanted to ask the staff in the UN Mission in Monrovia (who had remained remarkably quiet since the murder - other than assist Lithuania with the body's repatriation) about the content of Report 1415 for fear of spreading the knowledge of its existence. But they reckoned maybe three or four more staff there might be aware. That made a total of around thirty. That was a pretty close hold, but not close enough.

Henry had asked how far the Report had spread to other nations' governments. He didn't divulge that London was aware and that both Paris and Washington knew of its existence. Looking up and down the conference table he counted six nationalities: that would be three more capitals that knew. How long could they keep this secret before a link is made between the Report and Solzman's murder?

Typically they decided to do nothing. They all agreed to restrict discussion of the Report to the people round the table. The media rep took away the task of putting together and distributing to the group a draft press release, just in case the Report made the news.

Henry asked the Ghanaian chairman if someone from the building should go to Liberia to carry out an independent investigation rather than leaving it to UNMIL. The Mission would perhaps inevitably conclude that Solzman's death was 'murder not connected with Mission business.' It would be a convenient conclusion. He made the point that the Lithuanian government would almost certainly send a team to do their own investigation (should the Liberian government let them into the country) and it would be helpful to have someone from New York there to keep an eye until everything settled down. *Or, just as possible, blew up* Henry thought.

'You go Mister Henry.' Ebeke always prefixed everyone's name with the colonial 'mister', even though he was in charge and competently so. 'You go as soon as possible and find out what's going on.'

That's all there was to it. He was off to Ebola-infested Liberia. Perfect.

He was first to leave the meeting. Pierre raised his hand to wave and had a big, knowing smile on his face.

Henry sipped his coffee. He hadn't really thought this through, had he? A UN official had been murdered, almost certainly because he had written something that was true that someone didn't like. Or he'd written

19

something that was untrue, which they equally didn't like. He, Henry, had pretty much volunteered to fly to West Africa and find out why this had happened. He was neither a policeman nor a soldier. And he certainly wasn't equipped to investigate a murder on the edge of a jungle where malaria was prevalent and had recently been joined by its much more deadly sister Ebola.

What *was* he thinking?

Chapter Three

The Black Dog, Vauxhall, London

Colonel Tim ordered a couple of gin and tonics and made his way back to the table. He'd had an average meeting in the MOD Main Building discussing further cutbacks to the whole of the Intelligence Corps against more reductions in the Army's overall manpower strength. The Ministry of Defence had asked him to be the Intelligence Corps representative on a central committee whose remit was to lose another 3,000 soldiers from across the board. They had three weeks before they had to report options to senior staff. Today's meeting had looked at closer integration of Reservists into the ranks when deploying on operations. It was a complicated exercise, and the internal Army politics made it altogether more complex.

He needed this drink, although he also needed some exercise. Sat on his bum all day made him feel, well, like he felt. Flabby. He put one of the glasses in front of his old friend David and sat himself down. It was just gone six, they'd heard the bells of Big Ben strike as they had walked in. The pub was quiet, but not so quiet you couldn't lose a casual conversation in the background noise.

'It's really good to see you David - great that you could find the time.'

'No worries Tim. We haven't seen each other for over a year? Last time was in Bastion.' David sipped his drink. 'If I remember the G and Ts were stronger back then.'

They laughed at that and spent a few minutes going over old times and asking after each other's families.

'So, what's this all about then and how can we at Vauxhall help?' David asked, raising an eyebrow at his friend.

Tim, first checking that no one was in earshot, went over what Sergeant Sam Green had told him a few days earlier. It didn't take long. They both took another swig of their drinks. Silence followed. Tim closed his eyes for a second in thought. And then a little too impatiently said, 'Well David? Does this chime with anything you lot know?'

David ran his right hand through his hair. He looked Tim directly in the eye having checked himself that there wasn't anyone close enough to hear his reply.

'There could be something in this. I've never heard of this doctor until very recently but I'd picked up from the news that he was big in Ebola and had died of the disease up country in Sierra Leone; Kenema I think.' He paused, thinking for a moment before continuing, 'But there is something not quite right in West Africa, something odd about the Ebola outbreak. How it started and how it spread.'

David looked ready to add something, but stopped himself. He took a sip of his drink, leaning back slightly in his chair.

Tim wanted to press. He could sense there was more.

'So, what?'

David leant forward again, gathering his thoughts.

'I don't know. I need to take this back into the building. It's possible that this is a key bit of intel. But it might just be wholly erroneous. Whatever, I don't think I'll be able to back-brief you on this, certainly not until we get to the bottom of our investigations, or it all dies a death - no pun intended.'

Tim suspected this would be the case, but forever the analyst he had to ask a final question.

'If Doctor Tebie wasn't in that coffin because he was accompanying his wallet half way round the World, then who on earth did they bury on Saturday?'

David stared down at the bar table and then back up again at Tim.

'I've no idea. I really don't.' He replied. And that was the end of the conversation.

Outside of the Black Dog, Vauxhall

David made his way back across to his office. He thought through the last forty minutes in the pub with his old friend. What Tim obviously hadn't picked up from the news was the almost coincidental murder of a UN official in Tubmanburg, a town in a different country but less than one hundred kilometres from the reported demise of Doctor Tebie. From MI6's perspective and David's involvement in that organisation, it was all building into something very knotty. And Report 1415 was at the centre of it all.

MI6 didn't have anyone in Liberia and their only representative in Sierra Leone was an older operative working out of the High Commission. He wasn't the right man to take this further. They knew very little. Far too little. And there was so much more they needed to know.

Henry felt dreadful. It had been a Herculean effort to get his visas, prophylactics and necessary country and Ebola briefs together and get to the airport in seven days. His flight to Monrovia was via Brussels. It was due to take off in an hour's time. He had an Army style hold-all, half of which was taken up with a white protective suit that he was told to wear if he came into contact with anyone with the disease, or anytime he felt vulnerable. Fabulous.

To be fair his briefings had been thorough. Provided he stayed away from hospitals and medical centres the percentages of catching Ebola were miniscule. The small UN mission in Monrovia was trying to carry on with everyday business since the reported cases of Ebola had flattened and even started to fall.

All he would do was take up some office space and ask some questions. Keep an eye and report back.

The UN police had gathered in Liberia a small investigative team from across West African UN missions and were due to report in a couple of days. The Liberian police had issued their report: murder, motive - possible theft. Henry couldn't reconcile that conclusion with the fact that Victor was shot from a distance and no attempt was made to take anything from him or his car.

They hadn't found the bullet. It wasn't in what was left of Victor's head.

The Lithuanians had a team arriving any moment now. He guessed it had taken them a few days to organise themselves, deal with the possible Ebola issues and then get diplomatic clearance. As this was a UN related death, and not just a national concern, UNMIL would doubtless have expedited all of the necessary paperwork. But it still took time.

What had surprised him was that nobody, not even the Lithuanians, had leaked Report 1415 or made reference to it. Maybe they were waiting for their police to report back? After all they wouldn't necessarily want to link Victor's death with an erroneous document. Not yet anyway. Maybe the US had leant on them? Baltic State allies and all that.

But he did feel dreadful. A heavy cold, probably. If he didn't shake it by the time he flew home they probably wouldn't let him back into the States. Perfect.

He thought about making one last trip to the loo, but his ringing mobile stopped him.

23

'Henry Middleton.'

It was his UK contact, or colloquially, desk officer in the Foreign Office, Jimmy Choo (ok his surname wasn't Choo, but it had stuck in his head and was better than Charrington). What does he want?

The chap banged on a bit, almost at a canter. Nothing detailed, but enough to get his message across. Delighted he was travelling to Liberia. London needed to be kept informed every step of the way. He spoke in riddles, obviously because of the open line. The chaps 'across the Thames' had no one in country and they were asking him to keep in touch.

'Sorry Jimmy, you want me to report to you every so often with what's going on? I do that anyway. When I think there's something to report.'

He listened some more. Someone from 'across the Thames' would be in touch (Henry knew he couldn't say MI6 out loud. Thankfully he had made the connection earlier in the conversation). Maybe they would give him some direction and ask for answers to specific questions? The someone who would phone was called David. Nothing hush-hush, just helping out another agency.

Henry didn't know what to think. He was struggling with a thumping headache, had enough on his plate getting to Liberia and dreaming up what questions he might ask from a UN perspective. Now his country's Secret Service seemed to want him to act as one of their agents. He wasn't paid enough for this; he certainly felt, just now, completely untrained and a little overwhelmed by it all.

'OK, Jimmy. Tell them that's fine. But I'm working to my own timelines and once I'm clear that my UN work is done then I'm back to The Big Apple. No questions. The UN would hoof me out if they thought I was working in this way for my own government.'

He paused. 'When will I hear from this David?'

Apparently as soon as they finished this conversation.

'Great.' He tried his best to lace that with as much sarcasm as he could. He desperately needed the loo now. And preferably before James Bond phoned with his new mission, should he wish to accept it.

Just short of Fidden campsite, Isle of Mull

At least her headache had gone. It had been a steady couple of days just walking and sleeping, trying to unpick herself. Put herself back together. The plan, which she'd agreed with her latest psychiatrist, was to get away from the stresses of normal life. Focus on nothing in particular. Concentrate on getting in touch with her emotions; crying would be good, let it all out. Not that that had happened yet. Not since the 'incident'. As much as she'd tried, it wouldn't surface. But that's what she had to do, dwell as much as she wanted. Start to notice things around her. See life for what it was now, not what it had been for the past twelve months. Do all of this without the distractions that continued to put her on edge, the loud noises that made her instinctively duck. And away from the incessant, intolerable questions from folk that were friends, and those that she loved.

Those that knew of Chris: 'Do you miss him?' What sort of stupid, dumb-arsed question is that? From those that didn't know about Chris: 'I hope the Army is looking after you?' And the worst of all: 'How are you doing today'. Shit, actually. That's how I'm doing.

Too many questions. All of them cloaked in pain with answers that would only come with plenty of tears. Tears she wasn't yet ready for. Possibly never would be.

But the last couple of days had been slightly easier. She had written a list of things to do the following day. Put her alarm clock on (ok so it was for eight thirty, hardly sparrow's fart) and got out of her bag and followed some sort of routine. She had walked for miles, mostly over the same ground. She had crossed by the short ferry and explored every inch of Iona, secretly hoping that a bolt of religious lightning would flash down from the heavens and make it all better. Nothing like that happened, but even in the cold November wind which drove rain horizontally under her hood and stung her cheeks, she had managed without too many black spots. Without the dreadful 'couldn't really care what happens' feeling.

Colonel Tim's phone call a couple of days ago had helped. He had spoken to a friend of his who 'worked with another agency' (say no more; she got the drift). They were interested in her story, so much so they had phoned him back - asked him to pass on for her to keep the wallet safe. And 'could they have her mobile number?' They had both laughed at that point. 'Me and a spook,' she'd said. Well I never. They would contact her in the next week or so and arrange for the wallet to be handed over. 'Would that be ok?'

She said that was fine and would stay at the campsite until somebody phoned. The anticipation of meeting someone from MI6 out of the context of a major military operation would be interesting. She'd had a bit of a sweepstake with herself about what the person (might be a woman?) would be wearing. And whether or not they would turn up in a sports car with a passenger unfriendly ejector seat. In her mind's eye it would be a man in his mid-thirties, probably with a slight paunch and wearing sturdy clothes - no tie. That was her bet.

She was about half a mile out from the campsite, coming in from the north. The scrubby light green grass and white sand was the perfect foil for the dark blue sea which rushed towards the shore carrying wave after wave of white horses. The wind was strong, but not unbearably so and the sun stole a glance through thick white clouds. Yes, she could get used to this. The wind naturally blew away some of her darker thoughts, the light sand brightened by the inconsistent sun lifted her mood just a touch.

'This might just be working. Early days, though.' Nobody to hear her this time, but so much more reassuring out loud.

As she turned the corner of a big dune she looked up to spot her campervan. She stopped dead and then immediately dropped to the floor. Her training had kicked in, giving her no time for actual thought. She had no idea why she had done that. She gave her head a violent shake, lying still for a second as her heartbeat pounded in her ears.

After a moment she stuck her head up, just enough to barely snatch a look before quickly lowering it. She crawled slowly backwards behind the dune, sat up with her daysack pressing against the sand and tried to take in what she had just seen. There was a man stood by her van facing out towards Iona with a pair of binos up against his face. Looking. Searching. And the van's sliding door was open and she was sure she could see somebody inside. They couldn't be standing up (unless they were vertically challenged) as she'd pulled the elevating roof down, but she was confident a pair of heavily booted feet were sticking out of the door, as if the person was on his knees. And there was stuff on the floor outside the van. Her stuff. All over the place.

'Come on Sam, think clearly.' Through gritted teeth. She moved position, just in case her previous exposure had been seen. She popped her head up. Yes, sure enough the guy with the binos was scanning South away from her and there was (almost certainly) a man in the van thrashing about. She spotted a silver car just behind where the van was parked. Looked like it could be a newish Mondeo. No, no...it was a Focus. But definitely a Ford. She could tell by the nose.

She dipped down again, quickly. The campsite was empty. Actually it wasn't a conventional site, just parking with electric in the dunes. The lady who owned it didn't live on site, but visited early evening to collect the fee. There was an adequate shower and a loo, but no one else. It was mid-November after all. These hoods had all the space and all the time in the world to go through her things. To wreck her fragile life.

Sam's jaw hardened; how she wished she had an SA80 in her hands. She knew then she would have absolutely no concerns about taking a couple of well-aimed shots. Breath in, hold your breath. Grip the trigger closing your forefinger to your thumb slowly. Bang. Finish squeezing the trigger. Release. Breath. Next target. She was a good shot. That would teach the bastards.

They were hoods, thugs, crooks of some kind. Not spooks. There's no way MI6 would treat her this way, surely? These idiots were looking for something, possibly her. Strangely she wasn't scared. Not at all. Her life seemed pretty pointless. She'd been badly injured and mentally scarred enough for any further abuse to seem inconsequential. She took her daysack off, moved further along the dune again and had a quick look. She dipped back down immediately. The man with the binos was looking her way. She moved again, a good ten metres dragging her daysack with her, and looked again. The binos hood was looking back towards Iona. The other guy was out of the van and on his mobile.

She dropped down. 'What now?' A whisper. She needed to get a better view of both the car and the men. Certainly clearer than 'two blokes in warm clothing and boots driving a silver car'.

She crawled to the right. Then with a foreground of bushes between her and the blokes she got up on her haunches and scrambled more quickly. Eventually she found herself in a position behind the van, with the sea just beyond it. She saw their car just twenty metres away, and noted its registration, make and colour. She'd never forget that. Impossible. She rested for a while. The crawl had taken it out of her. She was breathing deeply. Her stomach hurt; somewhere deep inside something had rubbed against something else. There were plenty of scars that shouldn't be there. Plenty of damage that could still be done. She needed to be more careful.

Suddenly the two men appeared from behind the bushes on the left and made their way to the car. She drew back but couldn't stop herself looking again. She had a good gawp at one, and a glance at the other. Then they were off. Gone. Bouncing down the track in their Ford. She sat back and literally drew breath. But then a scent wafted up her nostrils that made her pause.

Fire? She sniffed again. *Oh God! No!* She picked herself up, not before checking that the car was out of sight, and ran as fast as her healing stomach would let her into the clearing where her van was parked.

But she was too late. Her van was on fire, not quite engulfed, but far enough gone for her not to go anywhere near it. There was nothing she could do.

Everything she owned, any hopes she'd had for a future, everything, was in that van.

She instinctively looked down at her boots and walking trousers. She still had those. She felt reassuringly for her daysack which she was carrying limply in one hand. It was still there. She placed her free hand on her chest, feeling for her Goretex jacket. Got that. And then she looked to one side of the van. Her bike, which she had locked up against the fence was parked where she left it. Unaffected by the fire. Small mercies. Very small mercies.

She looked back to her campervan, the heat of the fire now warming her. At that point Sam's expression crumbled as something inside of her snapped. The sight of her van, of her things and her hope of a fresh start, burning wildly out of control. The questions about Chris from probing relatives, the concerned looks from knowing colleagues, the strength it had taken to get this far - all built into a well of emotion. Opposite the restful tranquillity of Iona shattered by the destruction of fire, it became too much. Far too much for her. She sank to her knees, her shoulders shaking as she realised it was gone. Everything was gone. And she had no idea why. She reached up and touched her cheeks. Dampness. Wet fingers. She was crying. And she couldn't stop. After everything that had happened she was finally crying, crying endless bucketfuls   of   tears.

Chapter Four

Henry had had an uncomfortable flight. As part of the cutbacks the UN mandated that all their staff fly cattle class. This was all well and good for people travelling without any particular ambition or purpose on short haul flights. Across the Pond they're a blooming nightmare. He'd lost four hours of his life by travelling east and had sat next door to a nervous wreck of a man whose method of coping with his agoraphobic tendencies was to talk incessantly to his neighbour. And when they weren't listening, to himself. Because of this, even though they flew through the night, Henry had not slept a wink.

But that wasn't all. His short telephone conversation with David the Spy prior to his departure from JFK went along the lines of: we know about Report 1415; we think there's truth in it; its contents would be very damaging to us and particularly our allies the US (he had emphasised the word 'allies') if they were disclosed; we - he said it in a way that Henry was included in the word 'we' - need to keep ahead of the game and influence outcomes where we can; Henry was to stay in touch and report back if he found out anything new that wasn't included in Report 1415; and we would be interested in the outcome of the murder investigations concerning Victor S, the Lithuanian.

It was all very surreal. Henry had made the point that he was working for the UN. Any unofficial conversations with one's own country over codeworded material was at least strongly frowned upon, if not a sackable offence. Yes, David the Spy knew this. And did David understand that 'he was not trained to work undercover on behalf of....'. He was stopped at that point by David the Spy and reminded that they were talking on an open line. But yes they appreciated this and were grateful for anything he could do. He was then reminded that in many ways he was perfectly placed to help, in the centre of it all and with an authority to ask any questions he pleased, and go anywhere he wanted. He was the UN's man from New York, after all.

'And what if I let you down?' It was a pathetic question to ask a member of MI6, but he couldn't stop himself. He felt weak and feeble the moment the words passed his lips.

'Just do the best you can. That's all we can ask.' Was the rather patronising response.

Henry felt himself sweating, even though it was cool in the terminal. He had a three-hour transfer window before his flight to Monrovia and his mind raced. This was ridiculous. He was flying to West Africa, to a country he had never stepped foot in before, a country which, as well slowly emerging from a civil war, was known to be a dangerous place - particularly for white men. And especially in Monrovia after dark ('comme Harlem' Pierre had said, smiling again. Idiot Frenchman).

On top of that, whilst the official line was that Ebola was under control, the UN Mission was still reporting a further fifty cases a week 'that they knew of'. And now he was jeopardising his short, but reasonably effective career with the UN by agreeing to act as a conduit for MI6.

With that last thought he felt for his mobile phone. David the Spy had said he would phone him daily at five o'clock Liberian time. If anything else more urgent came up he had given him his own number, but to remember that the lines were not secure.

He couldn't afford to lose the phone. He breathed out audibly. It was there, where he left it - in his jacket pocket.

He wiped his brow with his blue spotted handkerchief. He was wearing a brown pair of chinos, a simple cream cotton shirt and a green linen jacket, which already looked like he had slept in it. No tie. He had decided not to pack one. He was travelling light; an official, but an observer. 'Here to help where I can' would be his stock phrase.

'....and spy on you whilst I'm at it,' he huffed under his breath. What was he playing at? Oh well.

Henry made his way to a small Belgian style cafe before looking over the menu to find something that would cool him down - and hopefully calm him at the same time. As he was fingering the card, translating the French with his rusty schoolboy knowledge, he failed to notice the casually dressed, medium-build black man take a seat on one of the red sofas about ten metres from him. The man looked directly at Henry, raised his hand to his chin and rubbed his stubble. He then sat back, took out a can of Diet Pepsi from his tatty leather briefcase, pulled the ring and took a long swig.

Edinburgh to Kings Cross Train

Sam's phone rang again. She looked at the number. It was the same number that had phoned twice this morning. Like the last two times she held the phone directly in front of her face and studied the number as the device vibrated against her palm. A combination of fear and bloody mindedness had stopped her from connecting before. An unknown number trying to contact her after two men had burnt down her campervan. Ruined what was left of her life. But she was alone and the person on the other end may have answers for what the bloody hell was going on. And she needed answers.

Her resolve shaken, and in a moment of what she thought later was weakness, Sam pressed the green button to connect the call.

'Hello.' She withheld her name, hardly trusting herself to talk let alone give out personal information. It was a woman called Jane. Was this Sergeant Sam Green? 'Go on,' was all she could muster, not confirming the stranger's inquiry.

Jane was calling on instructions from her boss who knew Colonel Tim Brand. A flicker of relief flashed through Sam, though this was accompanied by a thread of caution. Jane continued, talking about Tim's discussion with Sam about what had been found. And would she be prepared to meet up and hand it over? Sam's mind raced, but a red flag flashed when Jane said, 'I hear you're on Mull?'

She knows. Sam panicked, her heartbeat racing. She took a breath and calmed herself. She closed her eyes, rubbing at them with her free hand; how much information should she disclose? Who could she trust? For now, no one. She was in a busy carriage and so couldn't continue the conversation there.

'Hang on, it's loud in here, I need to move.' Sam slung her daysack over one shoulder (she wouldn't, no couldn't, leave it anywhere on its own) and made her way down the train to where the loos were. There was no one else with her. She stopped, leant against the carriage wall and took a deep breath.

'Are you still there?' 'Yes' was the reply. 'Good. Listen to me, I haven't got the energy to go through this twice...please.' She added the 'please' in recognition that, despite everything, she hadn't lost all her dignity. But she needed to be listened to. She deserved to be listened to.

Sam continued. 'I was waiting for your phone call on Mull. Whilst I was waiting two men ransacked my campervan and set fire to it.' She paused just for a second, the image of her burning campervan flashing through her mind. She pushed that to one side, chastising herself. She had rehearsed this. *Get back on track Sam.* 'I'm guessing they were looking for the wallet I found, the one I spoke to Colonel Tim about.' Jane wanted to interrupt, but Sam wouldn't let her as her frustration flared.

'I said listen.' Her voice was firmer now, an edge rising to her tone. 'The only person other than me who knows about the wallet is Colonel Tim.

No one else. That means between my conversation with him and now with you somebody has decided to forcibly try and find the wallet.' Sam let out a shaking breath, her emotions beginning to creep to the surface. Jane wasn't going to get a word in until she'd had her say.

'I've had a tough year. Further compounded by all this.' Sam waved her free hand about, gesticulating to nobody who was watching. She was tired and felt her guard slipping, tears rising to her eyes once more. She was just one person and she could only handle so much. Pacing now, 'who do I trust...who would *you* trust?' It was a rhetorical question because she hadn't finished the prepared speech.

Her finger pointed at no one in particular.

'So, no, I'm not going to meet you, nor anyone else until I get my head around what's happening. And you should look to your own staff and ask yourself what's going on and how you've let this come about. I am pissed off, really really pissed off.'

Sam drew breath, letting that hang for a second before she pressed the red button. The line went dead.

She stared out of the window, her shoulders heaving and adrenaline coursing through her system. The scenery flashed by but she didn't take any of it in as her mind raced, confused and erratic thoughts founded on the last ten minutes.

West Africa Desk, FCO - King Charles Street

Jimmy had the Observer laid out on his desk. He was taking a breather. The 'hired help' Darren had, thankfully, got on a military plane and flown to Freetown to run an eye over the Army/NHS effort to contain the Ebola virus in Sierra Leone. The news was that the epidemic had flat-lined and it looked possible that the combined efforts of the UK's involvement, the Red Cross and various other charities might have made a real difference. The country, however, was still in meltdown because of the disease. The slight progress they had made over the last twelve months, the improvement in the judiciary, the combat effectiveness of the Sierra Leone army (and their low-key involvement in the UN operation in Sudan), and the reconciliation programme between the former rebels and their victims had all been put on hold. He knew how important momentum was to keeping these programmes on track.

But it was the economy that had been hit hardest. Jimmy couldn't recall the figures off the top of his head ('poor on his feet' was the phrase that leapt out at him from his last written appraisal signed off by his boss,

Charles), but he thought he recalled that the country's GDP would take a thirty percent hit when the figures were in for 2014. Mind you, he said to himself, that's thirty percent of not very much, so it's probably no great loss.

So whilst Darren was out saving the world, Jimmy was just keeping things ticking over. The Solzman murder seemed like a flash in the pan now. MI6 had taken the lead in London on the murder and with it, thankfully, Report 1415. He had neatly brought together MI6 and the British UN chap, Henry Middleton, after he discovered that Middleton was travelling to Liberia. So the spies would now have their own eyes and ears in country. The British Embassy there was threadbare, hardly coping with in-country UK nationals and the threat of Ebola, so using their resources to support MI6 was a nonstarter.

As soon as he knew Middleton was travelling to Liberia he had phoned his opposite number in Vauxhall and they were onto Middleton like a shot. 'Very good work, Jimmy. Well done,' Charles had said. That seemed like a first - a 'well done'. Middleton, however, didn't seem very pleased with the connection, but that wasn't Jimmy's concern.

He looked up at the clock on the wall. Eleven fifteen. Still time to read some more of the old rag before he added a few lines to the report that was due.

The Observer was short on news today. He glanced over a couple of articles and read the title of a small patch on page five: 'Fully clothed man washed up on Oban beach.' He read the short paragraph in full. Apparently an elderly, unidentifiable black man had been washed up on a beach near Oban. He was fully clothed. The local police were investigating, but a 'police source' had said that it was likely to have been an accident or suicide as there was no apparent trauma to the body.

Jimmy's train of thought was along the lines of: fully clothed Scotsman pissed out of his skull, falls off a ferry and gets washed up on the local beach.

'Bloody Jocks,' Jimmy snorted. He moved on to the next page.

Nearing London, Kings Cross Train

Sam had the bones of a plan. Just the bones.

She had expected Jane to phone back but she hadn't. Instead twenty minutes later her mobile rang and it was an Aldershot number. It took her less than a second to work out it was from the Battalion and whilst she didn't recognise the whole number she guessed it was Colonel Tim's, or the adjutant trying to connect them. She didn't pick it up. She didn't pick it up when it rang five minutes later. Nor five minutes after that. She had merely gripped the phone and stared straight ahead, waiting for the train journey to end. A thought crossed her mind, *I should probably get myself a new SIM*.

Her mind went back to the fire. She had unlocked and moved her bike out of danger, using a free hand to protect her face from the heat of the flames. Then she had slumped to the floor, turned away from the burning van, staring at the sea and Iona in the distance. She was utterly lost.

It hadn't taken long for the police to arrive. Someone on Iona had probably seen the fire and called 999. The policeman had been kind, asking 'Are you alright wee lass?' followed by 'How did this happen?'. She'd responded in a detached, uncommitted way. 'I probably left something plugged in'. She'd wanted to say 'her hair straighteners' but even your average Highland copper would have soon worked out looking at the state of her that that was very unlikely. Her auburn curls, attractive to some, a mess to others, couldn't be straightened with a steam iron. She'd taken some comfort from the fact that she'd found something amusing. She still had some strength.

The fire service had turned up after most of the fire was out. The van was already a dark brown mess, all gooey like burnt sugar. 'Not much more we can do here,' one of the firemen had said after they'd doused it all with foam. 'We'll call Sheamus' Recovery to pick it up as soon as possible.' The policeman had issued a force accident number so she could deal with her insurers and asked if she'd needed a ride anywhere. 'No thanks, I'll book into the pub down the road until I get my act together.' She needed space. Lots of it.

The police had then left and Sam paid little attention to a small crowd that had appeared, trying to be casual but unable to hide their gawping expressions. Almost on autopilot and with the start of a thumping headache, she had thrown on her daysack and cycled down the road towards the pub.

She was surprised at how quickly things had coalesced in her mind. Her life had moved swiftly from decent career, a budding, strong and passionate relationship with a man she thought she loved, through major catastrophe which cost her lover his life and tore open hers (both physically and metaphorically). Then onto a slow but seemingly effective rebuild. And suddenly a smack in the face with a shovel. The loss of almost everything she had. Everything falling apart again.

She'd hurt. All over. But through all of this the few remaining threads of her life had come together and had cemented into a determination. She remembered thinking to herself; I am going to do something. I need to do something. And what she had decided to do was reckless, no, probably stupid *and* reckless. But at least it was an action, something to focus her mind on instead of reflecting on her rubbish life.

Her thoughts had been clear. What else did she have to stay for? The only thing of significance left was the wallet that had somehow washed up into her life and turned her world on its head for the second time. Men had come and burnt down her van in search of this wallet. It had to mean something. She had known as soon as she'd seen it that it held some significance. And because of her random arrival on that beach her life had gone from a therapeutic rebuild on a remote, Scottish island with the hairy brown cows, to some sort of spy thriller.

It had become personal. Those men had taken everything from her. They had reached into her life, poked about before lighting a match with little regard to the effects it would have. But she had something on them. She had the wallet. And now she had a purpose. They'd lit a fire. Not just in the van, but inside of her. And she'd decided then, over a pint of Guinness, that she was going to try and get to the bottom of all of this.

She would travel to Sierra Leone and find the Doctor's family, dig around and try and establish what he had been up to; see if she could throw any light on this mess.

There. That was the plan. She had come to that conclusion in the pub, as quick as that. She had money (about fifteen grand in the bank - the insurance pay out should replace that if it all went) and a small medical discharge pension. She'd had all her cards and passport on her when the van was torched. She would need to get some more clothes. At this time and with her tastes that should take less than an hour in TK Maxx in the red label section of the 'Women's Active' row.

She had used the pub's poor Wi-Fi to research travel options (she was completely ignoring the Ebola question, although she knew she would need some anti-malaria pills). What she thought she knew about travel to Sierra Leone turned out to be true. There didn't appear to be any civilian flights in and out of Freetown at the moment - she had remembered hearing on the news that BA had cancelled their scheduled flights. She then looked at the geography of the region. Left and right of Sierra Leone were Guinea and Liberia. Both, she knew, were suffering with Ebola.

She ran through their overview using Wikipedia. Both countries looked like basket cases, but Guinea seemed the less inviting of the two.

An ex-French colony run by an ageing dictator; early on in the blurb they mentioned torture by security forces. Her French wasn't that hot, so that wouldn't help. Liberia, on the other hand, was a country set up by the US to house freed slaves, it had been through civil war but Uncle Sam seemed to be keeping an eye on it. And English was the first language. That worked for her. Decision made.

She'd found Doctor Tebie's home town of Kenema in Sierra Leone. Kenema was in the north east and close to the Liberian border. She'd thought there was a road that ran from Kenema into Liberia. Well it looked like a road on Google Maps. Of course there was no way of telling whether the road was useable, or if the borders were open. And then there was the small thing of a visa. She had checked the Liberian Embassy in London's website and it seemed that getting a visa might just be possible. Flights to Monrovia (an odd, East European name for a city founded by the United States she thought) were possible via Brussels. She would need some form of cover story, so she'd have to work on that. But at least it would get her some of the way there. And away from all of this rubbish.

Sam paused, looking down at her laptop as a question ran through her head, 'Is this really a good idea?' Her lips pursed in thought, trying to figure out who she could contact to gain more information on the area, to help her understand what she was really getting herself into. Deciding on an old Army pal, staff Sergeant Linda Ross, Sam reached for her phone. She knew that Linda had spent a year in Sierra Leone helping train their soldiers. Linda, as far as she could remember, had had a ball and would be a mine of useful information about that part of West Africa.

And that's where she found herself. She'd organised to meet Linda in London, not giving any reason other than a catch up. She was now left with the puzzle of how to broach the subject, 'So Linda, crazy story, I found this wallet...' Sam shook her head. She'd surely think of something? Still the truth might be an option, that is if she couldn't think of something more believable.

Chapter Five

Second Cross Road, Twickenham, England

As Sam expected there was a lot of catching up to do before getting round to talking about anything of significance between two old friends. Her predicament was always in the back of her mind, but for now she enjoyed just chatting to Linda. They spent an age going over the two years they'd been together in the Battalion. The countless training exercises, the other members of the Warrant Officers' and Sergeants' Mess (some friends, some not) and the hijinks at the formal dinners. They did not get round to the Afghan tour, it just didn't seem appropriate - too raw, too near. So instead they stuck to amusing anecdotes.

'Do you remember when Tuffy snuck out of the Officers' Mess with the silver statue centrepiece under her mess kit?' Linda chuckled with a broad smile. 'She looked like she was pregnant!'

'Yes, of course.' Sam enthused, also breaking into a huge smile. 'She stole it with a group of lads, took it out the back door, dug a hole in the Mess garden and then sent a ransom note to the 'Adj' for two thousand pounds.' Sam laughed, probably louder than she meant to. The reasonably expensive bottle of red wine she'd bought from Tesco was beginning to have an effect.

Linda was laughing too, and continued the story. 'The Adj, bless him, set up a midnight exchange for the statue for the following night. And we all turned up wearing black balaclavas...where was it?' Her expression shifted to a frown in thought but Sam perked up as she remembered.

'Outside battalion headquarters, remember?' Sam added, her eyes full of humour and fond memories.

'Yes, I remember!' Linda slapped her legs with her hands, almost knocking over her wine glass. 'And the officers turned up in black tie, looking all James Bond. They had a briefcase with Monopoly money in it and...'

'The bastards had water pistols and a fire hose and we all got a huge dousing!' Sam interrupted with a laugh. Such good times, she thought. Such good times.

Sam's Chris had been one of the lads in black tie, she remembered. He wasn't the most handsome, nor the fittest of the young officers, but when he smiled, to her he was the most attractive man on the planet. The difference in their ranks, that between an officer and a sergeant, wasn't a problem, not nowadays. It was complicated. It was tricky. But it wasn't against the rules and the longer they spent in close proximity to each other the more their being together seemed inevitable.

Linda was nodding her head, seemingly agreeing with Sam's thought process. She stood up then, pulling at the hem of her skirt to smooth it down. 'I must pop to the loo. Could you put the kettle on Sam?'

'Sure.' Sam responded. But she sat still just for a second to take in her surroundings. Linda had done well. Only a staff sergeant. Couldn't be on more than thirty-five grand a year, but somehow she had scrimped and saved and found a deposit for this small but tidy and well decorated flat in west London. There were nice feminine touches. Like blue and cream striped covers for the sofabed and all the chairs, complemented by cream curtains decorated with blue flowers. *Yes, she's done good has our Linda.*

Linda was her immediate boss in the battalion, running four analysts overseeing a discrete area of operation. They could manage anywhere: Iraq, Afghanistan, even Northern Ireland. The processes were the same. Gather and review, analyse and report. Always looking for the absence of the normal. And then be prepared to stand on two feet and report their findings to a senior audience. The small team was good, possibly the best. Mostly because Linda was excellent at what she did and a brilliant boss. She never once lost her temper, never once raised her voice. But she did work the small team hard and would pick up mistakes quickly and point them out, which they all accepted. Sam had learnt a great deal from her.

Linda was a little different of course. The flat was all female; no hint of a man. Linda 'batted for the other side', an awful euphemism used so often in the Army. But being gay was ok. Nowadays. This generation really didn't care and, as there was no longer a rule banning lesbians from serving in the Armed Forces, one of the last pillars of the old-school had been removed.

'Thank God for that.' Sam, almost spat the words. Out loud again, though. She wondered if Linda had heard her.

She stood up and walked over to the kitchen door. As she was filling the kettle, Linda came into the small kitchen and asked 'So, what's this all about then, Sam?'

Sam turned to her, kettle in hand. Those words brought her back to why she'd come here; why she'd called Linda in particular. With it, a wave of emotions flushed through her and she was surprised to find that tears were threatening to rise and spill. If she let them. But she shut them down, swallowing and forcing a smile for Linda's sake.

'Let me make the coffee first and then we can sit down. I think this is going to take a while.' Turning her back on Linda, Sam was thankful for a moment to get herself back together. She didn't want to break down, not here. She'd pour them some coffee and then they could discuss what was going on.

Back in the small lounge it took Sam about an hour to finish her story. The truth, pretty much unabridged. She had tried so hard to put a cover story together. She'd even dreamt up an ageing relative who had stayed on in Sierra Leone since independence and was now on her death bed. *You see, I have to go and see her, whatever the risks.* But in the end she knew Linda well enough, and trusted her implicitly, to just let it all come out.

Linda didn't respond straight away, but her expression said it all; it was damn complicated. She licked at her lips, looking down at her coffee. She let out a long breath.

'Well, wow.' She shook her head, 'Sam, that's a bit of a mess.'

'Tell me about it.' Sam agreed. But she did feel better sharing everything that she had been through over the past couple of weeks. Linda shifted her hands to cup her cooling mug of coffee.

'But I suppose there's no talking you out of this, then? Going to Sierra Leone?'

Sam shook her head, sitting back in her chair as she did.

'No, Linda. I'm not sure what else I have. I have already booked my flight to Liberia for this Tuesday. And I am due at the Embassy on Monday to pick up my visa.' She looked up at the ceiling, her eyes searching for who knows what. 'I need to do something. Something to bridge what happened in Mull to where I am now. I can't reconcile the gap without some form of explanation.'

Linda sighed but didn't argue with Sam; she had her mind made up. And knowing Sam, when she had made up her mind to do something, you couldn't budge her. Arguing with her would be more of a hindrance than a help. Instead Linda decided to share with her knowledge on the area.

'Well, let me give you some of the recent history as far as I remember it, and see if I can help put some flesh on the bones as to what it's like out there, and what to look out for. Kenema, in particular, requires very careful consideration. Medium sized town based on an ageing colonial centre, surrounded by a few brick buildings, and further out mostly huts. Cut straight out of the jungle. If Ebola doesn't get you, and you avoid malaria, Lassa Fever is never far away.' She paused. 'I'll go and make us another cup of coffee and we can talk it through.'

Linda was relentless and thorough. It was one-thirty before Sam managed to pull down the sofa bed and prepare herself for sleep. Linda had shown her where everything was, but as is nearly always the case with Army people, she didn't make a fuss. Sam had a tongue in her head and a pair of eyes. She could sort herself out.

In the only bedroom, just before Linda turned off her light (thankfully tomorrow was a Sunday so no early rise to catch the train to Aldershot), she took out her notebook from her bedside drawer. She pressed down on the top of the propelling pencil and, under a list of eleven points, wrote down: *12) Phone Colonel Tim ref Sam.*

She fell asleep almost immediately. One of the Army's greatest training lessons; take the opportunity to sleep whenever you can.

Headquarters of the United Nations Mission to Liberia (UNMIL), Monrovia

Henry had already taken a dislike to Liberia. He was, even by UN standards, well-travelled. Post Bristol University, where he had studied for a degree in Politics, he had spent six months exploring the Far East. His short spell with the Department for International Development, DfID, had seen him working in Bangladesh and latterly Sierra Leone. From both of these he had travelled locally and to neighbouring countries.

From Bangladesh he went to India and Nepal. From Sierra Leone to Guinea, Ghana and Nigeria. Working for DfID was fun for a while - you weren't allowed to abbreviate the title to 'Dif-ed' even though that rolled off the tongue, it had to be pronounced phonetically: Dee Eff Eye Dee. Why they were so fussy about it Henry would never know. But after a bit he found it too left wing, run by too many 'do gooders' and giving too much of the wrong sort of love. Sometimes, Henry thought, the recipients of aid just needed a good shaking.

It was his Sierra Leone tour that had alerted him to jobs with the United Nations. He was, by his own admission, a drifter. He wasn't particularly ambitious but always wanted to do the right thing and do it well. And that had singled him out in DfID. He had taken a 'field promotion' in Bangladesh, ending up running a small team working on improving schooling standards in the south of the country. His potential was quickly recognised and he was moved to Sierra Leone where DfID were concentrating on the Judiciary and the jail system across the country. In the capital Freetown he had come into contact with the United Nations Sierra Leone Mission, UNAMSIL, at the very end of their reasonably successful mission. He had quickly fallen for a Swedish woman who was fairly senior in the Administrative Wing. Their love affair was passionate, but short lived. Henry soon learnt that a good number of western women in UN missions were either lesbians or running away from a broken relationship. The latter was true with Eva. She had left a fiancée in Stockholm whom she couldn't face spending the rest of her life with. And now all she really needed was sex and not much else. By the time their relationship finished, however, he had caught the UN bug.

Henry felt there was something truly altruistic about the UN. Yes, the money was good and the working conditions in the Missions weren't that bad, but so often this attracted the wrong type of person. For him the money was not the attraction. The UN's purpose, in countries where help was needed most, was laudable and worthwhile. Each of the Mission's mandates signed off by the Security Council were very well meaning and mostly gave the civilians and troops on the ground more than enough clout to deliver peace and rebuild nations. He wanted to be part of that.

Unfortunately the troops were nearly always provided by second and third world countries desperate to be paid the huge sums offered by the UN for participating nations; countries were paid in the region of $35 a day for each soldier deployed. For a battalion's worth of soldiers for a twelve-month tour that could be in the order of $7,000,000, a huge sum for countries like Zambia and even Kenya. However, their operational effectiveness and that of their civilian counterparts was barely competent. Often seven or eight competent staff officers held together a multinational Mission headquarters that may have a staff of well over a hundred. One or two companies of soldiers on the ground doing the work of a couple of brigades.

But Henry had found his niche. He enjoyed the multinational feel, the good and the bad. He loved the notion of being involved in an organisation that was big as the world. An organisation that was meant to represent the very best of mankind, even if at times it displayed its worst traits. He applied for and was accepted for a minor position working in the transport wing of UNAMSIL and moved from DfID to the UN whilst he was still in Freetown. It didn't take him long to make his mark and be offered a post back in New York working on the operational side of the organisation. He loved his current job, in the thick of overseeing all of the Missions in Africa - and he loved New York.

But he didn't take to Monrovia. Not initially anyhow. It was everything Freetown wasn't. The Sierra Leoneans, when they weren't drugged up to the eyeballs and macheteing each other to death - that's how they were often conveyed by the world media, were happy, friendly, colourful and very welcoming. Music and dancing was central to who they were. The women were reportedly the most promiscuous in West Africa, but they weren't trashy - they just enjoyed their often short lives. He had read that the average life expectancy for the Sierra Leonean woman was forty-seven years. It's a different life, led a different way.

He never felt threatened in Freetown, nor up country in Sierra Leone. It helped that he was English. Sierra Leone was one of the few African countries that remembered British governance with any affection. 'Hey, white man. You English? Come back now and govern us again. We really need you.' The small, 'show of strength' beach landing in May 2000 by the Royal Marines onto Lumley Beach had reaffirmed the British as their saviours. The landing had stopped the rebels' advance into Freetown in its tracks and rescued Sierra Leone from the ravages of civil war.

Monrovia, Liberia's capital, was different. He'd only been in the country for less than thirty-six hours but he'd already experienced that. Pierre was right - it was just like Harlem. The black men here appeared tougher, more threatening and less inclined to engage in conversation. He may have imagined it, but they strutted more. He didn't expect any, but there was no deference, no recognition that most westerners in Liberia were there to help the country beyond the ravages of civil war and assist with rebuilding their nation. The men hang about in groups on street corners, furtively and rebelliously. The music was all rap, a loud beat and dark, lyrical words. It wasn't a light hearted place. It wasn't colourful. It was oppressive, dark and, at night, sinister. The incessant damp heat didn't help.

He had spent the first full day getting to know the staff in UNMIL headquarters. He hadn't managed to have an interview with the top man, the SRSG, but had spoken to most of his senior staff. Importantly he had a meeting with the lead UN policemen, Sergeant Richards, a Canadian who was investigating Solzman's murder. He hadn't pressed. It had been their first opportunity to talk and Richards was noncommittal. 'We still have a number of interviews to complete'. He also told Henry that he had left an officer up in Tubmanburg and was waiting for her report before coming to any conclusions.

So after his first full day in country if there was a story, other than murder linked to theft, it was not forthcoming.

Henry spent his second evening in the confines of his hotel. He'd sat alone at one of the hotel's dinner tables, ordered a couple of beers and steak and chips. He tried to sum up what he had learnt so far. Report 1415 might well have not been written. Very few of the senior UNMIL staff seemed to have heard of it, and only one admitted to have actually read it. That was the SRSG's chief of staff, a German, who dismissed it as 'irrelevant'. The German had acknowledged that he had allowed Victor Solzman to post the report, but their hands were full with the Ebola epidemic. The Report was a distraction when they were at full stretch. The chief of staff further assumed that Solzman's murder was probably nothing to do with the Report, nor the Ebola crisis, but the actions of some deranged African who had it in for the United Nations.

He reviewed his meeting with the UN police. They were probably not going to uncover anything of note. And the Lithuanian team had only just managed to arrive in Monrovia. As he understood it, they were under strict instructions to stay in Monrovia due to the Ebola crisis, so were unlikely to add anything to the pool of knowledge. It seemed that both Report 1415 and the Solzman murder would both be swept under the metaphorical carpet and be lost forever. If there was a conspiracy it wouldn't be exposed. It would die a death in the jungles of Liberia.

As a result he had nothing to report back to David the Spy. Earlier on in the evening David had pressed him on the phone, asked him if he was 'holding anything back?' Henry had told him everything he knew and said rather forcibly (it must be the heat...) that he had never before had his integrity questioned - by anyone. And was a little affronted at being asked.

David finished their short conversation by asking Henry 'if he were intending to head up country to Tubmanburg?' The question had caught Henry off guard. He knew he should probably travel, just to get a feel of where the murder had occurred, so that he could talk about the incident with some authority. But for that he needed to find some inner strength (to be honest with himself - some courage). David the Spy's question tested that courage. Poked at it with a sharp stick.

'Yes, of course.' Henry had spat out the reply, not hiding his lack of confidence as well as he would have liked to. 'Good, good,' was the response. Now he just needed to get himself into the right frame of mind to make that happen. He'd think about that tomorrow.

As he was getting up to leave the restaurant and head off to his hotel room, the waiter arrived silently at his table and placed a folded note by his left hand.

Henry looked up at the waiter and said 'Thanks'. The waiter made a half bow and backed away from the table. Henry unfolded the note. What he read made him take a sharp breath.

'VS was murdered because he knew too much about Ebola. Phone me.' And on a separate line was a Liberian mobile number.

Aldershot, Battalion Headquarters

Colonel Tim Brand was rarely lost for ideas. He was trained both as a professional analyst and as a decision maker. Attendance at the Joint Services Staff College had honed his ability to accept information from many outlets, assess all the options and rationalise everything into the most acceptable decision, whilst always noting the risks and planning for several outcomes. He'd done well at Staff College. Being asked to command the battalion, a huge honour, was partly down to how well he had performed.

But for now he was lost. His conversation with Linda Ross had thrown him completely. He assumed that when he'd walked out of the Black Dog ten days ago that would have been the end of Sam Green's 'walletgate'. He had trusted David Jennings' staff to deal with Sam Green professionally, courteously. He knew that Sam was unhinged, or prone to be. Her injuries, both mental and physical from the horrendous mortar attack in Bastion, were enough to plunge any sane person into a maelstrom of anxiety and depression. The fact that she had made such a quick and positive recovery was testament to her inner strength, strength she had shown in spades within the Battalion well before the attack. He couldn't believe for a second that she was telling Linda anything but the truth.

But Sam was alone now. Out of the reach and the care of the Battalion and the huge resources of the whole of the British Army. She wasn't his responsibility, nor was she the Army's. That would be the official response. The question he had to answer was, what should he do now with what Linda had told him - that Sam's campervan had been arsoned and she was now going to travel to Sierra Leone to find some answers?

The only person in the Battalion who had spoken to Sam Green about the wallet was him. And the only person he had spoken to about their conversation was David Jennings. Should he go back to MI6, speak to David again and update him? Could he trust them? Surely he could trust them? Or should he use the relative short reach of some pals in the Army to try and keep an eye on Sam? He knew they had no soldiers in

Liberia, but there was still a small detachment in Sierra Leone. Maybe he should dig out their staff list and see if he knew anyone on the team?

He scratched his head and then reached for his sports holdall. As was always the case, when he had a tough decision to stew over he would go for a run.

Chapter Six

Jane Baker was a hard worker. She thoroughly enjoyed her job, especially as she worked for David Jennings. As she walked towards his office, she tilted her head to one side in thought. David was a straightforward man. It was something she actually admired about him. He didn't faff about and in their line of work that was important. Time was of the essence with everything they did. Uncomplicated and uncluttered analysis was key and David provided that atmosphere. He had incisor like intelligence, cutting through reams of information and always giving clear instructions.

When she reached his office, seeing the door was ajar, she poked her head around it.

'Hi sir, you wanted to see me?'

David glanced up from the red folder that was on his near empty desk. He looked tired. From what she knew he had a lot on his plate. Their resources were stretched and the threats they were dealing with were widespread, often irrational and at times unfathomable. But even with the stress and the worn lines around his eyes, he had kept his desk as tidy as ever: laptop, telephone, simple old-style wooden in-tray. Uncomplicated and efficient.

'Yes, Jane. Come in.' David gestured for her to sit down and she took the invitation, tucking her skirt underneath her as she did. 'Have we got any more on the Sam Green case?'

Jane's expression strained and she shook her head. 'No, not much. We've lost her I'm afraid.' David sighed, though she knew the expression wasn't directed at her but at the situation. Jane continued, 'The last I have is from GCHQ who have traced her phone. It was talking to a number belonging to a Linda Ross. She is an army staff sergeant who served in the same battalion as Green and lives in Twickenham. Clean record. Since that call we've had nothing at all. Certainly Green hasn't booked to leave the country through any travel centre. She may well have turned off her phone, or bought a new SIM.'

It was better than coming back with nothing, Jane thought. But she was frustrated that she didn't have more information to help clear this up for David, who seemed to be lost in thought. His eyes were distant, calculating and thinking. He looked down to the open folder.

'So, let's recap.' David said, not looking at Jane as he began to speak. 'We believe Green found a wallet belonging to Doctor Tebie, a world leader in the fight against Ebola, which she discovered on the shore of a loch on Mull. As far as the world is concerned Tebie died of Ebola and was buried in Freetown a week ago last Saturday.'

Jane nodded in agreement, a frown bunching up on her forehead as she listened. David continued without a pause. 'There's the uncorroborated UN Report 1415, which links the States with the outbreak of Ebola in West Africa. And the UN staff member who posted the report was murdered in Liberia shortly afterwards.'

David's hands moved as he spoke, seeming to map out and section each part of his investigation and Jane was his audience. She didn't speak; he was in his zone, and a word from her could break it all down. Besides, it was useful for her to hear all this back. There was a lot to keep track of.

'In addition we have a heightened security alert, yet to be disclosed to the British public, of a terror cell in the UK linked to a biological agent threat - but nothing substantiated. Back to Green. We agree to meet up with Green on Mull, by which time her campervan has been searched, ransacked and burnt by unknown parties, but she survived. All of that, or none of that, could be related?'

David paused and for the first time his eyes stopped searching his folder for an answer and engaged with Jane's. Unfortunately I have no answers sir, she thought but waited as he spoke again. 'And to top that all off, she thinks we might have had something to do with the torching of her van?'

It was a bit of a pickle, Jane mused but nodded, giving her boss a sheepish smile. 'I think that's what we have sir, yes.'

David frowned and looked back down at his red folder. There was silence as he leant back, crossing his fingers in front of his mouth as he did. Jane shifted in her chair, waiting for the next question. 'What have you got from your contact in Langley?'

Jane shook her head in response. 'Nothing further. They're understandably jumpy about Report 1415. I've not mentioned the issue with Sam Green since my initial disclosure to them. I've sort of left it as if we'd met up with Green and retrieved the wallet. No point in washing our dirty laundry just yet.'

'Do you think we ought to pursue Green? And, have you any thoughts about who the chaps were who went for her campervan?' Two questions from David.

'Second question first, if you don't mind sir?' David nodded, indicating for her to continue. Jane swallowed, thinking through her response as she spoke. 'Somebody obviously thinks the wallet is important. Why is unclear. They, whoever they are, probably don't want any distractions concerning Doctor Tebie's death. They want people to believe that Tebie died in Sierra Leone.' This she was pretty certain of. She'd been thinking this through and this was the only conclusion she could come up with. 'The timing of the Report, the murder, and the find of the wallet is all too close to be a coincidence. So, noting that I can't answer your second and to answer your first, I think we should pursue Green. But possibly in a much wider context. Try and establish why Tebie is important to this, especially to some third party. If we find Green she may lead us to them.'

David studied her, dropping his hands from his mouth and nodding. Jane relaxed at that, seeing that he obviously agreed with her. 'Well, that's settled then, Jane. Keep at this. Get into Tebie in much more detail; speak to whoever you need to. And try and track down the wallet. As far as we know it's with Green, so find her. If I were you I'd keep our powder dry with the Americans at the moment. Let's work this on our own, but keep the channel open with regard to Report 1415 and the Solzman murder.' He stopped, glanced sideways and then added. 'If I get anything from Middleton in Liberia I'll let you know ASAP.'

'Thanks sir.' Jane stood up and turned to leave the office. However, she found herself stopping. Something was bothering her.

'What is it Jane?' David asked from behind her.

She smiled to herself, turning back with a small shake of her head. 'It's nothing really.' She paused, 'But my contact at Langley. He's an odd fish.'

'How's that?' David asked, almost humouring her at this point.

'When I was over in the States a couple of months ago we had lunch together. Business of course,' Jane quickly added.

'Of course, of course,' David ushering her along with his hands.

'It was all very Christian. We said grace before the meal and in conversation his hatred of Islam and all Muslims was never far from the topic of conversation. At times it was almost venomous.' David raised an eyebrow, but said nothing, letting Jane go on. 'And subsequently every time we finish our chats on the phone he always says something along the lines of 'and may the good Lord bless you'.' She paused again, touching her cheek with a hand and frowning now. 'It's all a bit Da Vinci Code, if you get my meaning. Very odd.'

David shook his head. 'I wouldn't concern yourself too much Jane. We've not been through 9/11 and we don't seem to have the religious zeal that affects many over there. And in some ways you need that single mindedness, that...' he stopped, finding the right word, 'fanaticism - to get results in this very complex area.'

'You're probably right.' Jane said, though she wasn't convinced. Something was bothering her, but not something that her boss needed to concern himself with. Her oppo at Langley gave her the creeps. But that wasn't a threat, was it? Giving David one last smile, she turned and left to further her investigations into Doctor Tebie, and the errant Sam Green.

UNMIL Headquarters, Monrovia

The heat was getting to Henry. He hadn't been able to shake the cold he had picked up before he had left New York, and whilst it wasn't so bad that he couldn't make it out of the hotel, he felt lousy. After the hiatus of the note left by the waiter and his frantic telephone call to David the Spy, he had made it as far as the UN transport pool to try and book a vehicle to drive up to Tubmanburg. David's people had run a trace on the mobile number at the bottom of the note. He'd told Henry that the number had turned out to be a monthly pay-as-you-go with Comium, a West Africa-wide cell company. David had added that by pulling in various favours they were close to being able to 'monitor' the number. David had given emphasis to 'monitor' making it clear to Henry that this meant eavesdropping.

Whoever was trying to contact Henry knew where he was. David had advised that Henry do nothing with the number until he could guarantee that they could trace and intercept the call. Henry had assumed that in the day and age of Mission Impossible they could get live satellite coverage of his every move, so surely listening in on a phone conversation should be easy? Obviously not. In the meantime David had suggested that it was probably best if he went up to Tubmanburg to get a 'feel for the ground'. Henry, grinning to himself, imagined being on all fours 'feeling the ground.' In any case, they agreed that waiting to phone the number until he got to Tubmanburg was probably the safest approach. Should anyone be interested in him and be using the phone as a trigger, he'd be out of Monrovia and on his way up country and out of harm's way.

'Oh, and try and check to see if you are being followed,' David had added, almost as a throwaway line.

'How on earth do you expect me to do that?' Henry had blurted out. He was pacing around his hotel room at this point, his free hand rubbing the top of his head.

David had told him that he should just keep a gentle look out for people who might be following him, or cars that stayed behind him for extended periods of time. 'It's a bit like the movies, really it is.' David had said.

Henry's mood turned, the absurdity of the situation becoming clearer by the moment - he had to stop himself from screaming down the phone. All of a sudden he was furious. He was very quickly losing what little control he had had in the first place. He was, he reminded David at the end of their conversation, not prepared for, nor very good at this. David had reassured him that he would be fine. And that was that. End of phone call. It had all been wholly unsatisfactory.

Henry entered the transport pool's office and immediately the cool air-conditioned atmosphere made him feel slightly less on edge. The prefabricated metal building was just big enough for three desks and a number of filing cabinets. Not much else. Sat at the central desk was a large-framed black man in a lumberjack shirt and jeans, but wearing a light blue UN emblazoned baseball hat. Henry noticed on one corner of the man's desk was a small cloth Stars and Stripes hanging from a thin gold metallic flagpole. *American - good*, Henry thought.

'How can I help you, son?' An American southern drawl dragging out the 'you'.

'Hi. I need a car please for a trip to Tubmanburg. I'm from New York.' Henry showed the American his UN identity card. 'And here is a letter signed this morning by the Deputy SRSG authorising my travel.'

The American looked closely at Henry's ID and the letter.

'Yup, looks dandy to me,' the American said, again extending the 'yup' from one syllable to two. 'You'll need a driver, son. Have you got one?'

'What? Why?' An unnecessary diversion. Henry wanted things to be as simple as possible just now.

'You don't have a license to drive UN vey-hicles, not here, no sirree.' The American smiled. He wasn't necessarily enjoying the exchange, but he was making the most out of his position of authority. 'I kin get one for yer, boy. D'you want me to?' The American winked, knowingly, as though he was about to do Henry a favour, albeit an illicit one.

'Sure, sure. That would be great.' Henry would take anything at this point.

The American turned his head to the left and over his shoulder bellowed 'Mo-hammed! Come in here, ye hear?!'

Almost immediately a young black lad, in Henry's eyes almost certainly a Liberian locally employed civilian, came scuttling into the prefab and stood upright to attention next to the American's desk.

'Yessir,' the young lad said, quickly, eager to please.

Without standing up the American put one hand on the young man's shoulder. 'This gentleman needs a driver to go to the Burg. You ready to go?'

The man hesitated and then said, 'Yessir. Ready now.'

The American turned back to Henry, then looked down at his laptop screen. After a short pause he wrinkled his nose and with all the methodicalness of a man whose life depended on accuracy, he typed on the keyboard using his two index fingers, reading slowly out loud as he typed. ''U..N...Land-cruiser...14.' He paused, licking his lips. 'Monrovia to Tub-man-burg...twenty first November.' He carried on like this for a couple of minutes until he was satisfied that he had recorded everything correctly.

He then looked up at Henry. 'It's got a UN radio which Mo-hammed here knows how to use.' Mohammed nodded. 'It's just been serviced. And it took us a while to get the blood out of the seats, so we don't want you spilling no more!' At which point the American laughed the loudest laugh, rocking back on his chair and then forward again. In between snorts he continued, 'Only kidding, boy. Only kidding. There was no blood on the seats, just on the paintwork,' to which the American guffawed some more.

Henry looked at Mohammed who wasn't laughing. He just stood there looking slightly nervous.

'Priceless.' Henry muttered under his breath.

Aldershot, Battalion Headquarters

The adjutant had left a copy of the staff list for the Sierra Leone International Military Advisory Training Team (IMATT) on Colonel Tim's desk. Tim had just finished writing a number of confidential reports on his junior officers, a critical annual document for these young men's posting and promotion chances. He took the reports very seriously.

He gathered the draft reports together in two hands, banged the ends gently on the desk so that they came together neatly as a set of papers. He put them in the beige folder marked 'Staff in Confidence - Officers' OJARs.' The adjutant would collect them later and check them for errors.

He reached forward across the oak and red leather inlaid desk, a desk that stayed with the office and had seen countless commanding officers before him. He picked up the IMATT staff list. IMATT was a multinational, multi-Service team designed to reshape the Sierra Leonean Army, taking it from an ill-disciplined and badly led group of 'rebel bashers', and turning it into a competent force designed primarily for defence. The 'International' title was a bit of a misnomer; the team was ninety-five percent British and nearly all of those were Army officers and senior ranks. The list showed only twenty-two names. Last time Tim had been briefed about IMATT the team was over one hundred strong.

Tim studied the short list, using his finger to hover over names.

'Ahh, good.' Tim said out loud. 'Captain Bomber Brown.' He checked Bomber's regiment. Scots Guards. 'Mmmm,' Tim was nodding, acknowledging that he had found someone in the Sierra Leone team that he knew.

It looked from the staff list as though Bomber was IMATT's quartermaster, the man responsible for keeping the organisation running by providing the right resources. *Bomber would be good at that*, Tim thought. He remembered him as a Colour Sergeant instructor at the Army Officers' training establishment at Sandhurst. Tim had been an officer instructor at the same time as Bomber and they had served in the same company. He knew Bomber well. He wasn't surprised that the man had been commissioned into the officer corps later on in his career. He had been outstanding at Sandhurst, training officer cadets hard, but always with a compassionate and humorous slant. If he remembered rightly Bomber had returned to his unit on promotion, just a couple of ranks short of being the senior soldier and knocking on the doors of a Queen's commission.

'Adjutant!' Tim raised his voice slightly so Captain Mike Hall could hear him through the open door.

Captain Hall came quickly into the office. 'Yes, sir?'

'Thanks for the IMATT list. See if you could get Captain Brown, the quartermaster, on the phone please. I think they're the same time zone give or take, so you could try now.'

'Right away Colonel.' The adjutant accepted the list, turned smartly and walked out of the office.

Tim stood up and stepped to the window, staring out across the parade square. He was taking a risk by not informing his pal David Jennings in MI6 that he had spoken to Staff Sergeant Ross. That Sam Green was aiming to travel to Sierra Leone, probably via Liberia. He trusted David implicitly, but there must have been a breakdown somewhere for Sam Green's van to have been ransacked and burnt. He prided himself as an officer that looked after his soldiers above all else, no matter what the cost. He had decided that the best way to do this in Sam Green's case was to leave MI6 out of the loop - if they were worth their salt, and they wanted to find her, they would. But it may be that alerting someone in country might be enough to give ex-Sergeant Green a bit of help when she needed it most. It was certainly worth a try.

His phone rang. It was the adjutant.

'C.O.' His preferred response, short for commanding officer.

'I've got Captain Brown on the phone sir.'

'Brilliant. Thanks Mike. Put him through please.'

Liberian Embassy, Fitzroy Mews, London

Sam was next in line. It hadn't been a long wait. There weren't many people queuing up to travel to Monrovia. She was surprised at the simplicity of the system, how smart the small embassy was, all wood panelling and leather, and how keen the staff seemed to be to process visa applications. Linda had warned her of the Sierra Leonean High Commission in Holborn. She had gone there once to expedite a visa application for a senior civil service visitor whilst she had been on leave back in London. The office was at the back of a rundown street, near a group of garages. Linda had said that at first she thought she had made a mistake but the wooden plaque on the half-glazed door had made it clear that she was in the right place. Inside it was no better.

It seemed that the Liberians took their Embassy responsibilities slightly more seriously.

'Number four please.' A large black lady behind the left desk called her forward. She was wearing what Sam thought must be national costume, a highly patterned cream and brown dress with matching scarf, her hair black as coal and just as shiny. She was beautiful, even if she was almost too big for her chair.

The fact that her number had been called made her heartbeat pick up. She was going to have to lie. Well, the form was lying, though she had filled it in. The lie was under the heading 'Sponsor in Liberia'. Here

53

she had used her uncle's name and found an appropriate address in Monrovia that was close to the main university. She had given her uncle the title 'Professor.' She thought this might work, but there was always the chance that it wouldn't. And she really needed to go to Liberia. To get to Sierra Leone. She needed to take this wallet back home.

Sam made her way to the desk and sat down opposite the black lady, with her desk between them.

'So, dear. How can we help missy today?' A strong Americanised accent with a beaming smile.

Sam explained that she needed a tourist visa. 'I'm hoping to fly tomorrow, so I'm sorry if this is a bit of a rush.'

'No problem,' the 'no' extended warmly. 'Can I have your application, photos and passport please.' Sam nodded, handing them over. As she did so she could feel the adrenaline building in her system. The lady ticked her application against information on her computer screen. She stopped towards the bottom of the form and Sam's stomach knotted. 'Sam Green. That's you?' A question to the computer, not to Sam. 'I see your money has been transferred to our account. Good. Now missy, what's the purpose of your visit?'

Now it was time to lie out loud. Sam licked her lips but recited what she'd planned before coming here. 'I'm meeting up with my uncle. He's a lecturer at the university. He's been there for some time.' She was speaking too fast. *Slow down girl. Slow down.*

'I'm studying for a masters in tourism in post-conflict countries. He has agreed to put me up for a couple of weeks whilst I have a look around your lovely country's coastline.' Nice touch the word 'lovely', she thought.

The black lady's smile broadened further. 'Well isn't that just dandy. You must go to Elwa Beach, way down from Monrovia, a good ten miles. Such a grand beach. Quiet and secluded. No boys playing football. I can see that's what you need.' She tipped her head on one side and smiled again. Then she took a pen to a self-adhesive visa which sat on top of a pad of them and wrote Sam's details on it. Sam relaxed, though tried not to let it show. She was going to go to Liberia and get this all sorted.

The woman carefully pulled off the visa, opened Sam's passport and gently pressed the visa onto a blank page. To finish the transaction she took an Embassy stamp and, having pressed it onto the ink pad, transferred the embossed authorisation onto the visa in Sam's passport. The black lady lifted the passport checking the visa intently. She closed it and offered it back to Sam.

'That's it?' Sam asked, raising her eyebrows in surprise. Another wave of excitement flushed through her.

'That's it. There's a leaflet here about the Ebola regulations.' The woman handed over a folded piece of paper covered in type. 'And, now, you go and have a lovely time in our great country.' The black lady was big smiles again.

'Thank you. Thanks very much.' Sam replied. And with a relief she hoped wasn't that obvious, she gathered her belongings together and headed out of the building into the cold and wet late November day.

Chapter Seven

Tubmanburg, Liberia

Mohammed was a good driver. He had negotiated his way out of bumper-to-bumper traffic in Monrovia and then avoided most of the potholes on the city's outskirts until the tarmac had run out. The sand and mud road, wet in places after the late summer rains, seemed to have held together well. Even the bridges, whilst reminiscent of World War Two tank affairs, were all intact. More accurately Mohammed was a cautious and meticulous driver, which meant he drove slowly, a little too slowly for Henry's liking. Out of the corner of his eye he could see Mohammad's hands gripping the wheel with such commitment that it would seem that if he dared loosen them there was a risk of an unexpected drop into a nearby ravine. Henry didn't know if Mohammed was a naturally vigilant man, apprehensive at the world he lived in, or was just plain scared to be driving the same UN vehicle to Tubmanburg where only a couple of weeks earlier his predecessor had been shot dead.

Either way, the man wasn't very good company. Even though Mohammed understood most of Henry's questions, he just chose to ignore them. English was common tongue between the two men as it was the first language of Liberia. But, like in Sierra Leone, it had been bastardised throughout the generations and most of the population spoke a version of Creole, or pidgin English. Either way communication was possible, but the most Henry got from Mohammed was that he was married with a daughter, he lived in Monrovia and was very lucky to have a driving job with the UN. 'Very lucky, Henry sir. Very lucky.'

In a rare moment of chattiness Mohammed did try to explain to Henry that Tubmanburg was named after a Miss Tubman, 'a very important lady in America...escaped being a slave and took others from slavery, Henry sir.' Mohammed was beaming now. 'Big lady. Important lady. Town is named after her, Henry sir.' Henry had enjoyed the history lesson, but hadn't enjoyed the moment that Mohammed had jerked the car across the road to avoid a truck-sized pothole, throwing Henry against the door of the Land Cruiser.

So in summary, a short history lesson was all Henry had managed to get from the Liberian. That and a large bruise.

Henry had been keen to engage Mohammed in conversation from the start and was disappointed at how little he had wanted to talk. Henry liked people, they interested him. A country is just a piece of land. The people make it what it is. Henry guessed from his name that Mohammed was a Muslim, but there were no outward signs of his religion. He had half expected him to pull over at one point in order to pray. But Mohammed had just kept driving. Henry was also keen to keep his own mind off what he was doing, or more accurately what he was being instructed to do from London. He had kept checking to see if they were being followed. There had been a beat up red car that had tailed them from the UN compound until the outskirts of the city, but it had pulled off next to a ramshackle garage and that had been the last Henry had seen of it.

On the brown dirt tracks that makes up the national road from Monrovia to Tubmanburg they had been followed by a number of cars, overtaken by a few. But, Henry thought, nothing suspicious - that's what he had surmised with his well trained eye. He had raised his hands to the heavens when that thought had passed through his head. What on earth was he doing? Who did he think he was, Tom Cruise?

They arrived at Tubmanburg late in the afternoon, but the sun still had plenty of strength and the early afternoon shower had evaporated making the humidity levels very high. There was no air conditioning in the Toyota and they had had both their windows down for the whole journey. Henry's dark blue cotton shirt was drenched down the back and under the arms. Every nook and cranny was damp, from between his toes upwards. And where there was dampness, the fine sand that had lifted from the road stuck to his clothes. He had got used to the warm damp climate in Bangladesh and Sierra Leone, but he wasn't anywhere near acclimatised after just three days in the country. It would take him some while yet, by which time he really hoped he was on a flight home.

Tubmanburg had a small colonial centre, nearly all of it run down and the remainder of the town was metal and brown clay huts. There were lots of dwellings made good with plastic sheeting many bearing the acronym UNHCR in big black letters. They stopped outside The Lincoln Hotel, the same hotel where Solzman had booked in to stay. Mohammed pulled over but kept the engine running. They looked at each other, but neither said a word. Mohammed had made his own arrangements for accommodation and looked like he had no intention of getting out of the four-by-four, nor turning off the ignition. He was ready to move on quickly. Henry looked around, swivelling in his seat to get the best possible views from each direction. He had absolutely no idea what he was looking for, but looked anyway.

'Nine o'clock tomorrow morning please Mohammed. If I need you before then I'll phone you on your mobile.' Henry gave a curt set of instructions. Bizarrely mobile coverage in West African countries was very sound. Most locals had at least two phones with different SIMs using each one to make cheaper calls depending on company rates.

'Very good, Henry, sir.' Mohammed nodded, an impatient look to his features. He clearly wanted Henry to get out of the car so he could drive away.

Henry reached onto the back seat and grabbed his holdall. He opened the door, got out and stood still on the uneven pavement. He closed the Land Cruiser's door and waited. Nothing. Mohammed drove off a little too quickly for a beat up blue Mazda that was coming from behind. It hooted its horn.

Still nothing. Yes, lots of noise, an exuberance of colour and that dark, musky smell that pervades everything and everywhere in Africa. Scores of people walked past him, some brushing against him (he held his holdall close), loud, heavy music beat out from a local electronics store where TVs and old washing machines spilt out onto the road. All manner of cars and trucks negotiated the main street hooting their horns and driving erratically to squeeze past other, slower vehicles.

But no shot, no bang. No blood.

Henry's thoughts were broken by a ping to his mobile. Still determined to stay rooted defiantly to the spot, he fished out his phone from his pocket. It was a SMS from David the Spy: *we have number covered. you can phone it now.* With his thumb he pressed 'reply' and spelt out*: booking into hotel now. will phone in an hour*.

Feeling slightly more relaxed and rather pleased that nobody had tried to kill him, he took another long look around, up and down the bustling street and a quick glance onto the roofs of the shops across the street.

Everything seemed clear, nothing untoward. *According to his well trained eye*. He sighed and then made his way into the hotel.

Roberts International Airport, Monrovia

The plane landed exactly on time. Sam felt a sense of relief mixed with something like excitement, but much deeper. Something verging on fear. But as she genuinely felt that there wasn't a great deal left in her life worth worrying about, it was more a deep sense of adventure, like the moment just before the roller coaster launches itself from the highest point of the ride.

She'd experienced something like it a couple of times before. Her first flight into Bagram in Afghanistan had set her nerves on edge. But that feeling was different. It was anxiousness stemming from the need to do the job well. To not let anyone down. How would she cope in the cut and thrust of real operations where soldiers' lives depended upon her ability to analyse and report in a timely manner? How would she deal with the shift pattern, the long hours, the cold, the heat, the rarefied air and no breaks - no weekends? They had trained hard and she had experienced extended periods of sleep deprivation, but then, when mistakes were made (and they all made mistakes), it was just training. No one died.

But getting off that flight was different to this one. Then she was part of a team, with a hierarchy, with somebody else ultimately responsible. There were medics, accommodation and food, all provided for. This time she was on her own. Completely. Only Linda Ross knew where she was and she had told Linda that she would text her every couple of days to let her know how she was. Anything longer than a week and Linda was to worry. She'd not spoken to her Dad, not that he would have understood; he barely recognised her when she saw him at the home. She'd spoken to no one else. Everything was up to her. Any mistakes impacted only on her and that, in a way, was a relief. She may be on her own, but nobody was looking to her for answers. There were no operational deadlines, no senior staff to brief.

So it was different to Bagram.

The flight had been uncomplicated. Five hours in the air on a half-full flight. Most of the passengers were black men and women boarding the plane overloaded with all sorts of hand luggage. M&S, Tesco, Lidl and even Harrods shopping bags. Seemingly full of goodies. Most of the men were dressed smartly; many were wearing ties and a good number in highly coloured, long dashiki. Many of the women wore African dresses with their strong colours, like the lady behind the visa desk at the Embassy. Bright green and turquoise dresses, shimmering, catching the light. Many were patterned in what Sam thought was probably tribal stripes and twists. They were happily dressed, with matching head scarves and big gold jewellery. Sam thought that most of it was probably costume stuff. But they all looked fabulous.

It was a fun flight. There was none of the protocol Sam had experienced before on international flights. Everyone sitting still, calmly like professional fliers. Here, once the seatbelt sign had been turned off the passengers were on their feet, talking over a row or two to a friend, walking up and down the aisles, looking out of the windows by peering over the laps of other passengers. It was like riding a bus in Lewisham, but for a lot longer and without the opportunity to get off. It was one big party with everyone being everyone else's friend.

Except for a couple of stern looking western men dressed in khaki outdoor trousers, olive green cotton shirts and leather belts with big silvered buckles. The two of them had short cropped hair. Sam noticed that they drank quite heavily and, after an hour, had slept for most of the flight. She imagined them to be mercenaries on their way to provide security for the diamond mines. They did not look like they wanted to join the party, nor did they engage with the locals. They ate, drank and slept. Their demeanour speaking volumes: *do not disturb*.

There were a couple of other white folk on the plane. Sam had sat next to a middle aged Dutch woman who worked in an orphanage. Her name was Margaret and she was lovely, if slightly austere. Sam thought she was probably in her fifties. She had explained that she had left Holland a number of years ago having been a primary school teacher. Even there she had felt that she wasn't contributing enough and so had made her way originally to Ghana having seen an advert in a paper. One thing led to another and she now worked full time at Elizabeth's Orphanage for Young Souls just outside Monrovia. It was Christian based, but Margaret had emphasised that it was low church and they looked after about thirty young children; the eldest was seventeen, the youngest just five. They had lost a girl to malaria a month ago and one of the staff had succumbed to Ebola when in central Monrovia a few weeks back. Apart from that they were unaffected by the disease, but took special care with visitors making sure they were checked for coughs and colds before they came onto the premises.

Sam had spent a good two hours talking with Margaret and, as she stood up to take her daysack from the overhead locker, she was close to asking her if she could spend some time at the orphanage helping out. In many ways it seemed like a much more sensible proposition than what she had set out to do. As it turned out Margaret gave Sam her mobile number and said she was welcome at the orphanage at any time and that there'd always be a bed for her provided she was happy to mix with the children. Sam had held the small piece of paper with the number on it very tightly and then stuck it in the small velcroed pouch in her waist belt where she kept her passport. Elizabeth's Orphanage might just be a much needed place of refuge.

As she waited for the queue of passengers to disembark, she began to feel the heat of West Africa slowly moving down through the cabin. She did not really know what to expect. Bagram had been freezing when they arrived on the first tour. But by the height of the summer when the dry heat was overpowering to the uninitiated, she had become acclimatised. Tonight, as she stepped off the aircraft, the initial sense of heat and damp that had seeped into the cabin when the doors opened became a wall of hot humidity. It was almost nine o'clock in the evening but the sense of steam bath was strong.

Then there was the smell. She'd heard that people say when you get the smell of West Africa into your nostrils you never lose it. She immediately understood that view. It was a hot, damp smell. Wood smoke, a bit of body odour and she didn't know which, but maybe a garden herb or two. Something agricultural.

The terminal building was a poorly lit affair a couple of hundred metres in the distance and looking left and right, there were only two other planes on the apron. One was a small white jet with the black letters U and N on its tail. The other looked like something out of the fifties. A prop plane, a dull silver but with little else to identify it. She had without doubt just arrived at the airport of a third world country. She gave an involuntary shiver, despite the heat.

This is it she said to herself. *Best foot forward.*

HQ IMATT, Leicester Square, Freetown, Sierra Leone

Bomber Brown met Brigadier Lester Sembe in Bomber's office. The Brigadier, a Sierra Leonean officer destined to become the next Chief of the General Staff, was a good acquaintance. He was currently based in Kenema where his brigade headquarters was located. Bomber knew all three brigade commanders well. His post, IMATT's quartermaster, was a key one. As well as keeping the IMATT team ticking along he worked alongside the staff of Sierra Leonean Army supply chain and had a remit to check that it worked well, particularly with regard to fraud and theft. The brigade commanders knew which side their bread was buttered and were keen to keep Bomber sweet.

Bomber was standing behind his desk. He moved to its side. 'Morning Brigadier, how are you?' Bomber asked with a big smile, bracing up to attention almost in a jocular way.

'Very well. Fine, thank you Captain Brown. And you?' The Brigadier returned the pleasantry, reaching for Bomber's hand and shaking it firmly.

'Good, Sir. Thank you. It's very decent of you pop in. I know you don't come down to the city that often, although, as we both know, it may soon be your hometown.' Bomber smiled. The compliment wasn't lost on the Brigadier.

'Let's not count our chickens yet Captain Brown. There'll be no announcement until February and my brigade has got your stores inspection to get through first. But, you're right, it would be good to move back into Freetown and out of Kenema. I am a city boy at heart.' In one motion the Brigadier gestured to the soft chair in the corner of Bomber's office and without waiting for an offer sat down. He made himself comfortable and looked across to Bomber who had sat back down at his desk. 'So how can I help you?'

Bomber ran his hand through his very short hair. He recounted some of what Tim Brand had told him. He didn't go into too much detail save a brief description of Sergeant Sam Green - he had a recent Sergeants' Mess photograph of her emailed through which he had had printed out and laminated. He explained to the Brigadier that Sam was an old friend of Bomber's (a small but helpful white lie). She was hoping to meet up with a pal of hers in Kenema and was likely to try and enter Sierra Leone from Liberia. She wasn't in any trouble, but it would be helpful if his boys could keep an eye out for her in the Kenema area and let Bomber know if they came across her. She was harmless, but prone to accident (another white lie). He just wanted to know that she was safe.

'Does your friend appreciate that the borders are closed?' The Brigadier asked.

'I'm not sure, sir, but she's a canny operator and might just make it anyway.' Bomber replied, again making up some of the detail on the hoof.

'That's fine then. I will distribute this photograph among my soldiers and they will do their best. I hope from this I can expect your best attentions at my forthcoming inspection?' A clear quid pro quo.

'Of course Brigadier. I am confident that everything will be in order.' Bomber stood up and offered his hand by way of a contract. The Brigadier's supply system was always in good order and he knew that the inspection would pass without any issues. Helping out a friend of a friend in this way would not contravene his sense of duty and doing the right thing.

It was coming up to eight thirty. Henry approached the bar with some trepidation.

He had phoned the mobile number that was at the bottom of the slip of paper he had been given by the hotel waiter the previous evening. He had spoken to, what sounded like, a Liberian man. His English was good, but it was thickened with a Creole twang. The conversation had been short. 'Meet me at Spud's Bar, just three blocks south of your hotel at eight thirty tomorrow night. I will be wearing a baseball cap with the letters USA above the peak.'

Henry had wanted to ask a question, but the phone went dead. Immediately he called David the Spy and asked if they had been listening to the conversation. 'No, not personally.' It was an exasperated and slightly sarcastic reply. Henry knew it was late but expected his contact in London to be slightly more pleasant; more interested. David immediately apologised for being sharp, said that other people would be listening to the call and he would be briefed later. But, whilst he was on, could Henry give him the bones of the conversation.

Henry made the point that there were no 'bones' and pretty much quoted the conversation verbatim.

David remained silent for a few seconds and then said, 'Go and meet the man as requested and see what he has to say.' The line went quiet for a couple of seconds and then David had added, 'By way of precaution book out of your hotel tomorrow and find another. Try to do it discreetly. We're just ringing a few changes, that's all.' Another moment of quiet. 'Use tomorrow to do your UN stuff.'

Henry acknowledged everything and the phone call ended.

He hadn't slept well, but the good news was his cold had started to clear. More and more nervous at the prospect of the evening's meeting with his contact and very uncomfortable with his own Mission Impossible, he had tried very hard to fill the day. He asked questions about Solzman's booking amongst the hotel staff and quizzed local shop proprietors about the day of the murder. This had unearthed nothing of importance. But it had taken a couple of hours and with Mohammed contacted to say he wasn't needed, Henry had booked into another hotel just down the road and spent the afternoon in the new hotel room drinking coffee. His effort to meet the UN policewoman who Sergeant Richards had said was still in Tubmanburg completing her enquiries, had come to nothing when he found out she had returned to Monrovia that morning.

So a day of not a great deal as a precursor to an evening of what? Henry thought. He checked his watch. It was eight twenty-five. He looked up at the neon sign above the door. 'Spuds All American Bar.' Clear as anything.

One meeting, Henry thought to himself. *And then back to Monrovia.*

He took a deep breath and pushed the door open. He was greeted with a typical scene from any American bar he'd been to in New York, although it was darker especially at the sides and in the corners, away from a small set of central lights. At the far end of the room there was a long wooden bar behind which a young black lad was serving drinks. A fluorescent light on the top shelf of a full drinks cabinet added a bit more light to a gloomy scene. All manner of liqueurs and whiskies filled the shelves. The bar wasn't quiet, but it wasn't noisy either. No music, just the chatter of men talking to each other. The odd loud laugh; a single harsh word from one table to his right - maybe the start of an argument, but nothing came of it. Around the outside of the room the walls were segregated into wooden booths - two benches facing each other across a table. They were all dark.

Henry stopped in the middle of the floor and looked around. He was nervous, almost shaking. He closed his eyes for a split second and then opened them. The bar had twenty or thirty customers, mostly black men but there was a table of three white men off to the left hand side. They were playing cards. *Probably aid workers*, Henry thought to himself. They ignored him. In fact nobody seemed to give him a second glance.

He looked for a single man wearing a baseball cap with 'USA' above its peak. No sign, anywhere. He tutted to himself. Actually this could be good news. If the man wasn't there, there would be no meeting. He could get in the Land Cruiser tomorrow and return to the safety of Monrovia. Yes, let there be no man wearing a baseball cap with 'USA' on it. Please.

He walked up to the bar. The bartender met his eyes and nodded.

'Have you seen a guy wearing a baseball cap with 'USA' on it?' Henry asked, making a sweeping gesture with his hand across his forehead as he spelt out the three letters.

The bartender didn't say anything, he just tipped his head to the left and offered directions with his eyes to the far corner of the bar.

'Thanks.' Henry said. *Bugger* he thought to himself.

He made his way over to the corner of the room. It was dark here; *this guy knows how to arrange secret meetings*, Henry thought.

Just as he approached the booth in the corner with a single occupant, Henry noticed something strange. Something out of place. The man was slumped at the table, his baseball cap laid in front of him, the 'USA' staring up bold as anything, a sign of recognition that he was at the right spot. But the man was still, his face turned away from him, resting on his arms. As if he were asleep. He was wearing a black leather jacket, but it was lifted up on one side by a slim object. A silver and brown object, shaped like big pen. It was partially metallic, a slither of it caught the light from the distant bar and flashed.

Henry stopped. Perfectly still. His heart racing and his stomach twitching. He looked down to the bench where the man was slumped. His blue jeans darkened below his jacket, the patch catching what little light there was and reflecting a dark red hue. It stained the wooden chair where the man sat. A crimson pool. He knew what he saw. And he knew it meant trouble.

The blood drained from his face and his legs turned to lead. He tried to move them but couldn't. He tried again. This time they moved. Turning slowly he walked like a zombie towards the door he had used to enter. A flash of inspiration from some part of the very small bit of his brain that seemed to be working, altered the short route to the front door. He moved left, staying away from the glare of the light from the bar and the small dim set of lights in the ceiling in the middle of the room. He made it to the door, almost tumbling through it onto the broken pavement. He quickly looked left and then right. His hotel was a couple of hundred metres from the bar. He turned to walk in that direction, but again his legs held firm. All he could think about was the fact that he needed to pee. He closed his eyes, trying to gain some strength but all he got for his efforts was the sight of the dead man, the knife and the blood.

He couldn't stop himself. His stomach gave an involuntary lurch, he bent over and threw up all over the pavement. He remained bent double, breathing deeply, keen to regain some composure. Staring down he couldn't help noticing that his vomit had sprayed all over his shoes.

'Bugger.' He said under his breath. 'Bugger, bugger.' He stood up and tried to move his legs, this time they did what they were told. Unceremoniously he staggered in the direction of his hotel still desperate for a pee.

Just as he moved away from the entrance to Spud's Bar the front door opened again. Out walked a medium-built black man. He stood at the door and watched Henry leave. He then reached into his pocket and pulled out a can of Diet Pepsi. He pulled the ring and took a long swig.

Chapter Eight

David popped along to Jane's desk first thing. He was keen to talk to her about last night's conversation with Henry Middleton so that the two of them could put a few things in train to keep ahead of the game.

Jane looked up from her PC. 'Hi, sir.'

David sat on the corner of her desk. He sighed a little, letting his shoulders drop.

'We have a bit of a problem. Henry Middleton arranged to meet his contact last night in a pub in Tubmanburg. My hope was that his contact, who I'm assuming was the same chap who had arranged to meet with Solzman before he was murdered, would shed some more light on Report 1415. We spoke about this?' David asked.

'Yes, sir, that's right.' Jane replied sitting back in her chair resting her hands on her lap.

'Well, he turned up at the bar and found the guy dead in a booth. Killed with a knife apparently.' David stopped for a second, letting Jane take in the latest news. 'Anyway, he was understandably anxious when he contacted me last night, not helped by the fact that he couldn't get me for half an hour because I was at the theatre.' David raised his eyes to the ceiling and paused.

'Wow, well, that'll be tough on him. You gave me the impression he wasn't happy to be coerced into helping us in the first place?'

'That's true.' David shook his head at the situation. 'After I had calmed him down I told him to stay put. He was really keen to get hold of his driver and head back down to Monrovia and catch the first plane out. He had left the bar without speaking to anyone. He thought he might now be connected with the murder.' He paused, breathing out loudly. 'We need to find out who this dead informant is. If we have that bit of the jigsaw we might be able to fathom out what's going on, or at least have another lead.' David thought for a second. And then a bit sheepishly he said, 'I managed to persuade him to stay in Tubmanburg for now to see if he could find out who the dead man was. Use his UN credentials, throw his weight about a bit. I said I would speak to the Embassy and get him some sort of cover.'

'Bloody hell sir, you're asking a lot of him, aren't you?' She raised both hands almost defensively expecting him to come back at her. It was unlike Jane to be quite so forthright with her boss, but all of a sudden she felt a pang of sympathy for Mr Middleton even though she had never met him.

'You're right Jane. But he's the only contact we have on the ground. We can support him through the Embassy if things go belly up down there and I'm on to that. He said he would see what he could do, but he would book his car for three o'clock this afternoon and would leave then no matter what info he had for us. He did add *if I'm not in jail by then.*' David smiled a half smile. He dealt with life and death matters most weeks and this was only different because the chap they were dealing with wasn't on his payroll.

'And how can I help sir?' Jane asked.

David sat for a few seconds, his stare caught by something moving down the Thames looking through one of the windows of the shared offices.

'Get yourself a visa and all the jabs and pills you need. I don't think it will be necessary for you to go out there, but if Middleton gets into trouble then we might need feet on the ground. Clear your decks with the Embassy, but be prepared to move within twenty-four hours. Oh, and what about Green?'

Jane grimaced a little. She knew what she was about to tell her boss wasn't going to help his mood. 'Assuming she caught her flight she arrived in Monrovia last night.'

'What?! What the hell is she playing at? Bloody hell.' David paused for just a second collecting his thoughts. 'Are you sure?'

'We have confirmation from the Border Force. I asked them to do some background checks and put a tag on her name. They let me know this morning.' She almost winced.

'Middleton and Green both up to their necks in murder and mayhem and both potentially out of our reach and control. It's a disaster waiting to happen.' David thought some more, clenching his teeth. 'You better get on the flight whatever. This is developing into something which could reverberate across the whole region and undermine our credibility with so many parties. Get yourself on a plane. ASAP.' David almost barked out the final sentence.

'Yes sir. Will do.' She was already starting to clear up her desk at this point. 'Should I speak to the US? Liberia is very much their territory and they won't thank us if we're not upfront with them.' Jane knew that she would make that call if the decision were hers, but just now that fell to her boss.

'No. No.' David shook his head, rubbing his fingers across his chin. He'd calmed down a little. 'Not yet. Let's see if we can find the name of the murdered man from Middleton and get him safely out of the country. Then we'll be down to just one errant Brit. We can make up some reason why we didn't follow her, should Langley find out that Green is running around their backyard.' He paused and then reinforced his decision. 'No, not yet.' David's final comment seemed to Jane to lack conviction, but it was firm enough for now.

Joseph's Guest House, Monrovia

This is amazing, Sam thought. What a place. She was leaning out of her window looking directly onto one of the main streets in downtown Monrovia. She had had a good night's sleep despite the humidity, the lack of air conditioning and the rotational 'whooshing' of the ancient ceiling fan above her bed; yet it did provide some relief from the blanket of heat that enveloped her. Just before she had dropped off she had lain naked and motionless trying to absorb the cooling effect of the fan whilst recounting the events since she'd got off of the plane.

It had been mad; even without the damp heat that instantaneously made her clothes stick to her as if she had stood in front of a garden sprinkler. The airport terminal had intermittent lighting, the queues for passport control were chaotic and noisy, passengers arguing with the officials and unidentifiable men coming forward from the other side of the desks and joining the fray. Sam had struggled to find the correct entry form and was confused as to which colour (blue or green) she needed. A man in a vague uniform had kept an eye on her as she had scribbled her details down on the green form. Feeling self-conscious with the uniformed man still throwing the odd look at her, she had tried to hide behind a large group of black women standing next to the carousel, all looking fabulous in their multi-coloured dresses.

Surprisingly she wasn't given a second glance through customs but was near on assaulted when she entered the arrivals lounge. Four or five men had rushed up to her and fought, almost literally, to take her bag to a taxi. She had been relatively prepared to be pressed with offers for help, but the intensity, almost ferocity of the barging and pushing to be the one to help her was close to overwhelming. But she was unlike other tourists who might be completely phased by the attention, worried that once they'd let go of their bags they'd be gone forever - lost to a thief in the maelstrom that was the airport lounge. Sam simply wasn't that bothered.

She knew the locals wouldn't go that far, not at the airport. It was too exposed and these men needed the work and the tips. She had been more worried that her luggage might be tampered with by staff at the airport between the plane and when it arrived on the carousel. She had secured her suitcase with a couple of additional luggage straps and some cheap padlocks. Any expert would make light work of it all, but it might be enough to put a casual thief off.

On inspection off of the carousel, they looked untouched. That was a relief.

A twenty-something strapping black lad in jeans and a Man United football shirt had won the battle for her bags. 'Follow me miss. You want taxi?' Sam nodded and the young man had driven a path through the crowd, Sam following on behind. The taxi driver sat nonchalantly on the bonnet of his beaten up Mazda 323 (Sam always the observer) as they approached. He stood up and triple shook (shake-grasp-shake) Sam's suitcase man as if they were old friends. He smiled at Sam and the big smile remained on his face after Sam had given the Man United supporter five dollars for his troubles, a note he accepted with delight.

Sam had told the taxi driver to take her to Joseph's Guest House, a small hotel she had picked off of the internet hoping that it would look like its electronic descriptions and the service bear some resemblance to the few reviews posted on the website. The taxi driver hadn't batted an eyelid when she told him the address, so that had been good news. The shortish drive into the heart of the city was just like driving in Kabul; two and three lanes accommodating five or six columns of traffic at times, horns hooting and every third vehicle a beaten up truck, every fourth a battered motorcycle and every fifth a wooden cart pulled by either a mule or a man. The taxi driver had negotiated the conditions with ease, only nudging another car once on the thirty-minute drive.

Sam had struggled to take it all in. Afghanistan is a brown place, arid and lacking in colour. There are splashes, but overwhelmingly it's a two-dimensional, albeit beautifully two-dimensional, vista. On first inspection Sam had found Monrovia, even in the dark - maybe especially in the dark - a vibrant and eclectic place. Colour was everywhere. Even the noises were colourful with loud blues and sharp reds. Neon lights lit up scores of ISO containers which had retained the advertising logos of a previous past, even though they had been made into open fronted shops; Maersk here and Hapag-Lloyd there. Some shop fronts had glass and these were piled with goods of all descriptions, lit by bright lights, many of different colours.

Bars and eateries forged from poor bricks, metal sheeting and large plastic tarpaulins, were full of punters. Handwritten 'Sky Sports - Live Premier League' billboards were commonplace, with many bars topped with a big satellite dish awkwardly pointing to the dark sky. People spilled off of the block pavement to avoid deep puddles left from a recent storm. And Sam was able to pick out the sea between buildings, inky dark, lit by a few lights out in the distance. It was crazy. Crazy because of the complete lack of familiarity, amplified by inescapable heat.

Joseph's Guest House was comfortable. A two up, two down in central Monrovia which had been converted into a boarding house with five rooms and one shared bathroom. It was clean although worn around the edges, and for twenty dollars per night was just what Sam needed. The proprietor was another large black lady called Michele. Sam had not been able to guess her age. She could have been between thirty and fifty-five, but she had instantly taken a motherly approach to Sam.

'Well, what do we have here then?' delivered in a Huckleberry Finn accent followed by a broad toothy smile. She fussed over Sam, showing her to her room and puffing up her pillows and explaining very slowly and clearly how the light switches and ceiling fan worked. She escorted Sam to the bathroom and pointed out the idiosyncrasies of the shower and toilet cistern.

It took Sam a while to thank Michele enough for her to busy herself back downstairs. But that wasn't before 'Now Miss Sam, don't you hesitate to call me if you need me anytime, night or day. I'm just down here.' She had pointed to the bright green door on the bottom floor behind the stairs. She had smiled again, all white teeth, and had given Sam a small wave.

And now it was a new day. Michele had provided Sam with a breakfast of fresh fruit, some bread and coffee. She ate in a tiny dining room fitted out with a small table and two chairs. Sam was excited, most of her inhibitions and nervousness from the night before had disappeared. Not a single thought to her past. Something was blocking all of that. Somebody had pressed the 'override' button. She was currently in a different place, physically and metaphorically.

She looked out on the scene below, a bustling street where cars, trucks, wooden carts, motorbikes and people were moving around as one. The noise was incessant, horn hoots indecipherable from engine noise, people arguing and chattering, and generators humming in the distance. No colour was missing. And the smell. That wood smoke, the damp, the heat and that unmistakable whiff of hot people. It was an assault on her senses.

She loved it.

Now all she needed was a plan. In some ways she thought she would be happy to stay at the guesthouse for a week and acclimatise. Get to know Monrovia. She felt safe at Joseph's and could easily pop in and out as she got to know the lie of the land. But something was nagging her. Her military training didn't allow for time stood still, time for reflection. She had been trained for action, for decision.

So what to do? She had to find a way to get to Kenema. She thought the borders might be closed, but she wasn't sure. On interrogation, the taxi driver, who she thought understood the question, had replied in Creole along the lines of 'no possible. Might de bus to Tubmanburg. Den ask.' She hadn't bothered to enquire if Monrovia had a bus station, but Michele had given her some instructions on where she might pick up a bus to go 'up de country'.

That's what she would do. Go to the bus station and check out what was possible. Yes, she would do that this morning.

Tubmanburg Main Police Station, Liberia

Henry was in a dark place. He was sat on a plastic chair in the main police station in Tubmanburg surrounded by, in his mind, all manner of crooks and thieves. The place was steaming, dirty and unpleasant. Just now he hated Liberia and really missed the comfort of his UN office and his small flat in Brooklyn. He must look awful to the casual observer. After his conversation with David the Spy which, really frustratingly, had taken an age to connect because the man was 'at the theatre', his mood had turned from fear to loathing. *Why had he let himself get into this position? Why had he let MI6 talk him into this?* Recurring thoughts that had no answer.

He had very reluctantly agreed to stay on in the town for a day to see if he could identify the dead man he had seen the previous evening - every time he thought of the poor man his stomach turned. But he had been insistent that he would leave Tubmanburg at three and he had called Mohammed and made the arrangements, including being picked up from the hotel and driven to the police station. He hadn't slept at all. Or that's what it felt like. His mind kept revisiting the events of the evening and every creek and knock from the hotel sent his nerves on edge. Whoever had killed the man was obviously just as capable of murdering him in his bed.

71

He had tried to piece together what had happened, stepping back from the whole situation - trying to make some sense of it all: Report 1415, murder of Solzman, him travelling to Liberia, a local man furtively contacting him, MI6 involvement, him phoning the contact, him arranging to meet the contact and the finding the contact dead.

But when he tried to piece it together all he could think of was the sight of the dead man, the congealing blood, the knife - and his own safety.

His thoughts were broken by a hulk of a policeman who was beckoning him over from the other side of the counter. The policeman looked stern, almost arrogant as he caught Henry's eye with a pointing finger and summoned him with a wave of his hand. David leapt to his feet and moved quickly across to the counter fumbling for his UN identification card as he did so.

'Yes, sir,' there was no emphasis on the 'sir' from the policeman, it was spat out, 'What do you want with the police?'

'My name is Henry Middleton. I am a senior UN official from New York and I, eh, I need some information.' Henry emphasised the word *senior* knowing that power was everything here in Africa, especially among the police and military.

The policeman didn't say anything, he just gave a curt nod. Up close Henry could see that he was a huge man, with a big neck and massive hands. He was a monster and looking into his face he thought he saw a hint of menace. He certainly didn't seem like a man to be messed with.

The policeman took his ID card and studied it up close, turning it round two or three times. Henry waited to let the information digest.

'I'm here in an official capacity. There was a murder last night, as I understand it, at Spud's Bar. I'd like to know, if possible, the name of the man who was, um, murdered.' Henry's sentence tailed off towards the end. Listening to himself weakly ask the question it all sounded impossible, a pathetic inquiry from a man who, even with his UN credentials, didn't really have the authority to ask. His lack of confidence came across with his stance; his shoulders were rounded and his head hung slightly forward. He tried his best to maintain eye contact with the policeman but found himself looking down at the counter.

All of a sudden there was a kerfuffle behind him. Henry looked over his shoulder and immediately he recognised the man at the centre of the ruckus - it was the bartender from last night. He was screaming at two policemen who were manhandling him towards the counter. Henry moved to one side, his large policeman now distracted by the noise. Henry didn't pick up much of what the bartender was shouting but it was clear that he was proclaiming innocence against some crime or other and he certainly heard 'white man' a couple of times in the tirade.

As the small jostling party reached the counter, Henry tried to duck and move backwards, feeling incredibly self-conscious and, at that point, very white indeed. But he moved too late. The bartender spotted him immediately and screamed 'Dat's him. Dat's white man, dere. It him - he did it. I saw him do it. Dat's him.'

Henry stuck both hands up defensively and shook his head. *This can't be happening, surely?* he thought. He tried to say something official and authoritative, but nothing came out. His mouth was dry and words failed him. He knew at that point, tired, worn and probably unshaven (he suddenly couldn't remember if he had bothered this morning) he looked guilty. He was the man who had murdered an innocent in Spud's Bar. He'd even gone to the police and made an inquiry about the death. It all made sense. Back in the States the police might not have missed the absurdity of him, a potential assailant, walking into a police station to ask about a crime he was meant to have committed.

Here the wrong penny dropped into the wrong slot and before he knew it the two policemen had released the bartender and quickly grabbed him by the arms, seemingly with some relish, holding him firm.

His large policeman, still standing menacingly behind the counter, looked directly into Henry's eyes, eyes now alive with fear. 'Take him to the cells.' he growled.

Monrovia's Central Bus Station

Sam had queued for almost an hour by the time she made it to the only open ticket window. She was, and she'd had time to work this out, the only white person in the depot. There were hundreds and hundreds of black men and women, along with goats, chickens and other fowl she didn't recognise. Some were in cages, others alive but held tightly together with twine. The noise was even louder than out on the street and she held onto her daysack as if her life depended on it.

On the way in she counted all of two buses, neither of which looked like they were in any state of repair to go anywhere quickly. Both were already overfull, with cases, boxes and animals in crates strapped to the roof. How they remained up there when the bus was static was a mystery Sam thought. God knows what will happen when the bus starts to move and hits the first pothole.

She came to. The man in front of her had got his ticket. Through a small window which had small round holes cut to allow conversation and a gap under the glass to afford money and tickets passage, the ticket vendor said 'Hello miss. How can I help you today?' Perfect, clear American English.

Sam cleared her throat. 'I need to get to Kenema in Sierra Leone. My aunt works in an orphanage there and I think she is not very well....'. Her words faded as she looked at the man. He was shaking his head, but smiling at the same time.

The man didn't say anything for a few seconds but reached to one side, grabbing hold of a pen and a scrap of paper. 'That's not possible, I'm afraid. The borders are closed. I can give you a ticket to Tubmanburg? That's as close as you will get from here.' He said this slowly, pedantry almost, whilst looking downwards, jotting something on the small piece of paper. He stopped writing and looked up at Sam.

He repeated himself. 'That's not possible miss. I can only give you a ticket to Tubmanburg I'm afraid.' At the same time he pushed the piece of paper under the glass. He was still smiling, a genuine smile.

Sam looked down. The ticket man had written: *Go to Tburg. Phone the number below. He's my uncle. He will get you to Kenema.* A mobile number followed.

Sam looked at the man, smiling to herself, reflecting the man's warmth back to him. 'Thank you. Thank you very much. I'll have a ticket to Tubmanburg please. When does the bus leave?'

'There's one tonight at seven o'clock. Or there's one leaving tomorrow morning at eight. It's the big green bus out front. Make sure you're here an hour early to get a seat. Otherwise you might be on the roof.' The man was still smiling. Sam didn't know if the man was joking or that she might actually be sat on the roof if she was late.

'Thank you so much,' Sam said, opening the zip of her waistbelt and putting the scrap of paper safely inside.

Zero Seven Hundred tomorrow morning it is then, Sam thought to herself. *Let the adventure continue.*

Chapter Nine

A bus, en route to Tubmanburg

Sam was comfortable enough on the packed bus, despite being squeezed between two total strangers. One was a slim, aging man wearing an ancient pinstriped suit, an equally worn white shirt (browning round the collar) and a striped tie. The other was a rather large young man who was perched on the edge of her seat - one cheek on, the other off. The bus was overflowing so it didn't bother Sam that the young man had sat down next to her on a very small piece of spare cushion.

She had made the bus in good time. Others had made a bigger effort though; it was half full by the time she got on. The windows that could open were permanently ajar - but it was still sweltering. And the more people got on the hotter it became. Now she was sat between the fat and the thin men, she was warmer than ever. Sweat trickled down her chest and stained the front of the cotton shirt she had bought from Millets a week ago. Her back was drenched. She hadn't thought twice about putting her daysack in the luggage rack, although she had kept her precious bits and pieces in plastic bags in her waistbelt, which was also drenched. She had left her suitcase at the guesthouse. She had told Michele she was exploring the country for a week or so, so wouldn't need the room. 'Would she mind keeping hold of her bag?' Sam hadn't wanted to travel overloaded and also needed anyone who was interested to think she was coming back to Monrovia. Michele was delighted to help 'Yes, Missie Sam. Of course. I'm so looking forward to you coming back and staying for a while.'

The journey so far had been uneventful. If you consider being driven by a bus driver who thinks he's in the front seat of a racing car, takes every pothole at fifty miles an hour and is constantly singing to himself, uneventful.

The passengers were much more subdued than those in the aircraft, Sam thought. There wasn't the room to move around, but she guessed that people on buses were much more workmanlike than those on aircraft. Money was probably in shorter supply and life generally tougher.

But the chickens made up for the lack of chatter from the occupants. The seven or eight inside the bus, accompanying a stern looking man on the back seat, squawked and spluttered in their rickety cages. The thirty or so on top of the bus were equally noisy, although difficult to hear above the banging of the suspension.

Probably scared to death, Sam thought.

But Sam was relaxed. Actually she felt content. At ease with West Africa. Not quite in love with Liberia, but completely comfortable with her surroundings. She was surprised at how at home she felt. The people seemed kind enough, although Michele had warned her about walking out at night. Nobody seemed to be bothered that she was a single white woman travelling alone. One or two of the men had looked her up and down and, she felt, mentally undressed her. In the bus station this morning a young black man had propositioned her. 'How 'bout it, white girl? Want some black man?' She had stuck her middle finger up at him and put on her sternest face. The man had arrogantly tutted and walked off. That worked then, Sam had thought.

She hadn't given the past couple of months much thought. There hadn't been a right moment to reflect on everything. She did know her new-found confidence was based on a 'what the heck' attitude, hewn from being at the lowest point in her life when, surely, things couldn't get any worse. As she pondered Sam focused on the dirty red and orange stripes of the headrest in front of her, feeling her mind drifting off as the smell of stale sweat, cheap deodorant and chickens sent her into a daydream.

She was in Bagram. She was walking between the single storey, sandy coloured accommodation towards the Intelligence and Information centre where she worked. It was a dull light, about six-thirty in the morning. Her shift started at seven and her routine allowed her enough time to get a quick snack from the mess before the start of the eight-hour slot.

She was smiling. It had been a great evening. Chris and her had snatched a couple of hours together, sitting outside of the NAAFI on one of the wooden benches. They both wore combat trousers and t-shirts, their body armour and helmets down by their feet just in case there was an attack. Their weapons were in the armoury - there were enough people on guard to keep everyone inside the base safe from direct attack. They had held hands and discussed their future. Neither of them had used the expression 'in love', not yet anyway, but Sam was very confident that their relationship was strong. Especially as they were now talking about renting a flat and moving in together when they got back to Aldershot.

She gave a little skip. The sand, which covered much of the whole base, puffed up in a small cloud around her feet. She was a happy girl, she thought. Her work was highly regarded - she'd had one or two notable successes - and the man of her dreams was now very much part of her life.

But it was in that moment of pure happiness that hell was unleashed. Her very real fantasy was broken by a flash of light off to her right hand side. Almost immediately afterwards a wall of heat lifted her off of her feet and flung her like a paper towel in a stiff breeze to her left. A massive explosion followed. The sound was so extreme that her eardrums felt as if they had burst. She was on her stomach, her head pressed against a cold, sharp metal object. Another flash, this time a little further away and then more sound. Objects were flying through the air, landing around her, filling the air with sand, thrust up from the floor.

She knew she had to get up. She knew she had to get to safety. She had been carrying her helmet and body armour, but she tested both hands and they were empty. *Where's my stuff?* She lifted her head, but then pressed it against the floor again as a fourth and fifth explosion echoed around her. More heat, more sand and more dust.

Then there was a moment of calm. Eerie, complete calm that seemed to drag on but in reality only lasted a couple of seconds. The silence was pierced by gunshots. And following that there was shouting.

Sam lifted her head again, looking back to where she thought she must have been when she was knocked down. Her helmet and body armour were on the floor a couple of metres away. She brought her hands to her shoulders and pressed her palms to the floor and lifted her torso. Flash. Bang! Another explosion. She didn't flinch. She had to get herself better protected.

Move now girl, come on. She pushed on her hands to lift herself off the ground. But it was then the pain started. Indescribable pain. Sam's mouth opened with a yell of agony that moulded into the backdrop of war. Her teeth clenched and her body trembled, but even at that point she focused on her survival. She had to deal with the pain and move to find cover. With a grunt she lifted her torso again and focused on her middle, where she thought the pain was coming from. For a moment she didn't understand what she was seeing.

Her brain refused to recognise it. She could see red, grey, colours that blossomed out from the slash in her brown and cream combats. A haze came over her as she stared at the mess of her body. She had been well trained; trained in combat, trained to deal with these situations. But her brain had never had to deal with the image of her insides hanging out of her body. A delirious part of her thought about reaching down to push whatever was hanging out back in, but the numbness spreading through her prevented her from any movement.

It took all her willpower not to faint. The echoes of explosions carried on around her and she hissed a breath through her teeth. *My insides are not hanging out of me. I am fine.* She knew that was far from the truth, that she was in serious trouble. She couldn't move and she couldn't drop down or she'd squash her insides. She felt sick now, queasiness adding to the light headedness. But she couldn't hold this position much longer. What the hell was she going to do? She could hear the explosions continuing, and the cry of someone else in pain. Fury swelled inside of her; she wanted to help - she needed help. An unvirtuous circle.

Thud. 'Ah!' Sam's trance was broken as her head hit the seat in front. The bus had stopped suddenly. She and the two men had all been thrown forward, but no harm seemed to have been done. Neither of them spoke, they just shuffled themselves and sat back again in their seats. Sam, still in a bit of a daze squeezed in beside them, confused and shaken.

She felt the old man looking in her direction. Their faces could not have been more than a few inches apart. He had reached into his pocket and was holding out a handkerchief. Sam frowned, but then felt the cool touch of tears on her cheeks. They were dripping down her face and onto her already wet top below. She smiled at the man and took his handkerchief which, thankfully, was whiter than his shirt.

Headquarters MI6, Vauxhall, London

David reread the UK/US EYES ONLY TOP SECRET email on the screen of his secure computer. They had been following a pan-European terrorist threat for about six weeks. The threat had begun with information from his opposite number in the States. It was different from the usual threats of bombs and potential shootings in public areas, and targeted assaults on prominent people and members of the Armed Forces. Whilst they were difficult to track and seemingly indiscriminate in their nature, for those threats he and his team felt they could get inside the mind of the terrorist. Apply some rationality to what they might try and do, mix in a bit of logic and get ahead of the game. They also knew where to look. Which addresses to monitor, which phones to tap and with some very good signals intelligence overseas and a number of well-placed good agents, reach far into countries known to provide support for terrorists based in the UK.

This latest threat was different in that they, the Special Intelligence Service, or MI6, had no leads other than those provided by the Americans. And the nature of the threat was just behind a nuclear briefcase in terms of severity. Biological warfare. Anthrax (the easiest biological weapon to manufacture and transport) was the likely vehicle for mass terror and was top of the current list, but recently they Americans had added bird flu. He had no idea how a terrorist would release bird flu in a way that could undermine a local health service and start the spread of a major epidemic. But it was written in the email on his screen. He must, David thought, get one of his team onto that.

The threat, as was nearly always the case, was nonspecific in both time and place. The Americans weren't keen to release their source, but the opening statement included the line 'from our agents in the Arabian Peninsula'. This would include terror cells in Yemen and Saudi Arabia, among others. Attack locations included all major cities in the UK, France, Spain and Denmark. Timing was slightly more specific: attack likely within fourteen days.

David and his people had pushed their contacts hard both in the UK and overseas for any evidence of a planned biological attack. GCHQ had not picked anything up of note on the signals and telephone side. On his instruction they had put additional analysts onto the case. Everyone had drawn a blank.

Which surprised David. He couldn't remember a single incident where the US had notified them of a European terror threat without his people either corroborating the threat, or actually knowing about it before they were told. It didn't make a great deal of sense, but there's always a first time.

Of course a biological threat was probably the worst kind. Even chemical weapons, whilst extremely effective in very small quantities, have a limited life once dispersed and people affected cannot spread their ailments. Mustard gas will mess up your lungs and probably kill you. But in the meantime you can't infect anyone else, no matter who you sleep with. Once the attack is over, it's a case of containment and mopping up.

Many biological threats are contagious. Like a pack of dominoes, once one person goes down with the flu, all those they come in contact with are likely to fall soon afterwards. And then an epidemic becomes a pandemic. Chaos quickly follows.

So they had an unspecified biological threat against major UK cities (but it could be France, Spain or Denmark - *I wonder if they know*?). It was due within two weeks and they, MI6, only had the Americans to rely on for further updates. Unless they had a lucky break. Soon.

Tubmanburg Jail, Liberia

In the past twenty-four hours Henry had been through every emotion known to man. He'd even felt a feeling close to affection for his current warden, an elderly black man who seemed to have taken a shine to him. His cell was a one-person affair - at least that was positive. Three white walls, a single barred window and a wall of black metal bars and cross members, with a small metal gate affair for entrance and exit. He was in the Wild West.

His warden sat on a small stool in the corridor just opposite Henry's cell. He had kept an eye on Henry, providing water and the odd cup of disgusting coffee, as well as cheese and bread on a regular basis. He had accompanied him in a discreet way to the very poor shower this morning which didn't come with the luxuries of soap, and stood outside the loo when Henry needed to go. Every so often he'd asked Henry 'you ok mister UN man?' with a smile and a thumbs up. Henry had replied with his thumb and half a smile.

The cell was bare, but it had a bed and a wash basin. It was clean enough, but poorly decorated. Paint was peeling and the walls were damp to touch below anything short of two foot. No air conditioning and no fan. It was not a healthy place to be. It was hot and wet and Henry's clothes were damp and dirty. He smelt as if he needed another good shower - and that's because he needed a good shower.

He was in the loathing stage now. Almost insolence. He hated everyone and everything. He had been in the cell (he'd been allowed to keep his watch) for almost a complete day and he'd not heard from anyone in authority. *That's not strictly true* Henry snorted to himself. He'd seen the Deputy of the police station this morning. He had pleaded his innocence, giving a full account of what had happened in the bar (but as yet didn't disclose why he had arranged to meet the dead man; he'd kept that up his sleeve). He had made the point that he wanted to speak to his Embassy and the UN staff in Monrovia. In no particular order. The fact that he'd been left alone in the cell overnight without recourse of talking to Embassy or UN staff had incensed Henry and he had made that point to the Deputy.

The Deputy had listened intently, made a few notes and had left saying 'I will speak to your Embassy in the next hour. In the meantime Mr Middleton I would hope you could come up with a good story as to why the bartender strongly believes you murdered the man in the bar. This doesn't look good on either you or the United Nations.' He had walked out of the cell without giving Henry a chance to add anything further. Since then, apart from his warden, who had just recently brought him a further cup of coffee (bless him), he'd not seen nor spoken to anyone.

Where are you? Where's my Embassy protection and, if it's not too much to drag you away from the theatre, where's my MI6 Godfather? It was close to hatred now.

The warden stood up, looked to his left and nodded. Another policeman who Henry didn't recognise came into view followed by a white man in a pale cotton suit and open necked shirt. The white man looked harassed, a little dishevelled and tired.

'Henry Middleton?' The man in the pale suit asked with a very English accent.

Henry shot to his feet. 'Yes! Are you from the Embassy? Have you come to get me out of here?' All delivered quickly without a pause.

'Maybe. Look, my man, could you let me into the cell?' The question was aimed at the policeman who was already reaching for his keys. He opened the lock with a big key, pushed the door ajar and let the man in the pale suit in.

'Twenty minutes. I'll be back.' Short and direct. The policeman walked away and the warden sat down again. Henry noticed he was looking a little sad.

'Well. Have you come to get me out?' Henry asked anxiously.

'Hello, Mr Middleton.' The man ignored Henry's question, which irked Henry immediately. 'My name is John Tweedle. I'm the relationships manager at the Embassy. It has taken me a whole day to get here. It's not been easy, I have to say.'

'It's not easy for you!? Well excuse me for not getting my violin out.' Henry was almost shouting. 'I'm here, in this bloody hell hole, because I was asked to do a job by some of your people...and you're complaining about a three-hour drive?'

'Yes, well, we were only informed of your presence here a day ago. And it's highly irregular and rather uncomfortable for us.' Tweedle was still standing and Henry was stood right next door to him. The smell of his own unwashed clothes, Henry thought, would make this appear all very *Midnight Express*. 'We don't have the authority to remove you from custody just yet. It would have helped if the Ambassador had known about your trip. Then he could have spoken to his Liberian counterpart and smoothed things over. We do feel a little on the back foot.'

'You know about my contact with "David" in...' Henry had the sense to look beyond Tweedle and see if anyone was listening '...well, you know, London?'

'Yes, we're aware. But as I said it's highly irregular and we don't have the authority to remove you from custody until we know the facts of the case and can put a plea into the Liberian Government. It may be that the UN would have more clout? But I'm not sure how that works. Do they know?' Tweedle was keeping himself calm, although he was now pacing a little around the cell, his right hand rubbing his forehead.

'How the bloody hell am I meant to know? I've not been allowed to call anyone, to leave the cell. It's like bloody Colditz in here. You have to sort this out.' Henry's anger dissipated. He was tired now. Tired and emotional. He sat down on his bed and put his head in his hands. He manfully held back tears.

'Yes, yes, of course. I will remonstrate as appropriate, but they work by slightly different rules here. I will also contact the UN and let them know what has happened. I'm not sure they have much reach in the case of a murder enquiry...' Tweedle was cut short, David was on his feet.

'It's not a bloody murder enquiry that involves me as a suspect. I am a British citizen tasked by a sodding faceless bureaucrat in London to do something I didn't want to do. You get me out of here or, at the first opportunity I'm going to the press. This is bullshit. And you know it is.' Henry's anger was back now. It masked fear. A fear of staying in the jail for another night. Maybe longer.

'I'm afraid the press have beaten you to it. I've already had The Telegraph on the phone for tomorrow's edition. It could be quite a story for them. We have, of course, made it clear that we think you are innocent. But it will run for a while.' Tweedle put one hand up in defence.

'What. What do you mean by "you think I'm innocent". What the hell are you lot playing at?' Henry held nothing back. His words were accompanied by spittle which sprayed on Tweedle in a way that made the man in the pale suit reel back ever so slightly.

They were interrupted at this point. The new policeman was back and making it clear that the twenty minutes was up by pointing at Tweedle and gesturing for him to leave the cell. Tweedle was quick to get out of the cell. Henry turned to face the small window. He had resigned himself another night in the cell and sat down with a thud, like a teenager who had been grounded for the night.

'I will be staying in Tubmanburg until we clear this up. I will talk to the UN Staff in UNMIL. I hope to see you tomorrow. Keep your chin....' But the last word was lost as Tweedle was manhandled down the corridor away from Henry's cell. Lost and deafened by the whitewashed walls. All that was left for Henry to cling to was the sight of his nice warden.

He was looking at Henry with his head on one side. 'Coffee Mister UN man?'

Hotel Washington, Tubmanburg, Liberia

Sam lay on her bed staring up at the ceiling. She had turned the air conditioning down; it was too cold in her small room. The hotel was inexpensive by European standards, but probably the best in the large town. She chose it on a whim. It was close to the centre and not far from where the bus had finished its journey.

What a journey. It had been more than just getting here. More than the bumping and lurching as the bus negotiated its way along the rough, part tarmac, part clay road. More than getting very close and quite personal with her two male neighbours. More than the next leg of her journey; her journey to who knows where? She had re-lived the dreaded mortar attack for the first time in graphic detail. She had felt the pain, smelt the dust and the cordite. She had connected the attack, her injuries and Chris' death. Death at the hands of the enemy who had tried to kill her and others around her.

They weren't all Taliban. Not really. Many were men, just men. Inspired to fight because they had nothing else. Their dignity destroyed by years of oppression from the Russians and now NATO. Further disassembled by stronger men than them, men with charisma and religious zeal. Frightening men who demanded their support. Who killed those who didn't obey. Who used God as their weapon, their word. Who murdered their brothers and raped their sisters. In a world such as this there was only one option: fight. Islam was a banner under which those who lived with fear as an overriding emotion, were forced to kill. Sam couldn't stop herself having sympathy with the average fighter. She guessed many 'uld prefer to be tending their goats or tilling the fields.

And she had cried. Not about where she was now, but where she ﹍t she had been through. It hurt so much. But at least now ﹍ was a long way off, but something had happened to her in the past few days. Her absolute desire to put some sort of jigsaw together with Tebie, his wallet and his death had sent her on a journey. Her arrival in Liberia and the overpowering assault on her senses, the sights, the sounds and the smell, had unpicked something in her brain. Had made it all unravel. Maybe, just maybe, what she was doing was part of a cleansing process? Maybe now she could begin to piece it all back together.

She didn't know. She just knew she needed to sleep. To wake up tomorrow and phone the number she had kept safely in her waistbelt; get herself into Sierra Leone. Now she had started, she needed to keep the momentum going.

Chapter Ten

Hotel Washington, Tubmanburg, Liberia

Sam had slept well. She woke with the rising noise on the street below, showered in the communal washroom and was dressed by eight o'clock. Walking down the central staircase she turned left at the hand written sign 'breakfast'. The entrance to the restaurant was a half-glass double swing door which she pushed open revealing fifteen to twenty tables set out for breakfast, half of which were occupied. Taking a quick look round the room she spotted an empty table to her right and a buffet style breakfast.

Suddenly she stopped in her tracks, her whole body tense. She blinked and her head involuntarily jolted backwards, as if she walked into a stiff wind. There at the breakfast bar was someone she recognised. No doubt about it. She was caught between turning away, hiding - or checking, reconnoitring, working things through. She was stood like a prune in an open space and not ten foot from her was one of the men who had torched her van. Sam knew. She didn't forget a face. It was Binos man. Just under six foot, dark wavy hair, Roman nose, pallid complexion (Northern European or American), angular cheekbones. Mid-thirties. An unhappy face; a serious face.

She was about to turn to her left, having made a snap decision to leave before he looked up and saw her. It was too late. It was fleeting, but eye contact was made. He didn't blink - not a sign of recognition. He went back to talking to the man behind him in the queue, a medium build black man. Both were casually dressed, open neck cotton shirts and lightweight hiking trousers with plenty of pockets. Binos man was wearing a brown gilet. Sam thought she saw a bulge under the gilet - pistol size. But she couldn't be sure.

The glance had taken a split second and in that time she had changed her mind. She decided to stay in the room. It was a risk, but he hadn't seemed to recognise her, unless he was an extremely good actor. It was possible that he didn't know what she looked like, or had an old photograph. She had dyed her hair before getting on the plane - more ˈˈ now.

ˈ mental process which raced through her brain for staying was ˈˈ out, having just waltzed in, would draw attention to ˈ not. Half the guests were white, and whilst she might be the only single woman in the hotel, with a low profile she could be lost in the crowd. More important, leaving would ruin her chance of working out what the bloody hell was happening. Mull, her, Tebie, Binos man. Now, just ten days later and three thousand miles away, they were all reunited again. This was no coincidence. She had, serendipitously, arrived at the right place at the right time. Or possibly the wrong place at the wrong time. She would stay and try to establish what Binos man was up to.

She walked over to the buffet. Both men were finishing off, pouring themselves a coffee. Sam walked close to them. American. Strong east coast accents. Educated, and looking closer at the clothes, reasonably expensively dressed. The black man had a pair of Wayfarers sticking out of his chest pocket. She picked up '…it's got to be done. I'm working on ten thirty…'

She sat down three tables from the pair, Binos man had his back to her with Wayfarer man facing her obliquely. Their conversation was quiet, not in a necessarily secret way, but too quiet for her to pick up anything else. She made up her mind to follow them as best she could. If nothing else she might be able to find out who they were, or who they had signed into the hotel as. Sam mused over how the next couple of hours might pan out - she needed to go to the loo; should she go up to her room and pack her stuff? Should she wait in the small foyer? How do spies do this for real? She realised that she was enjoying this. She had no fear, no nerves. She gently praised herself, 'Well done girl', at such a volume nobody else could hear. She was excited, buoyed by the fact that she might have a chance at getting back at Binos man. Unravel what he was up to and maybe create her own little piece of havoc for him and his friend.

She walked back over to the breakfast bar, passing within a few feet of their table. She didn't pick up anything they were saying, although she noticed two additional things. On the table was a set of car keys. She clocked the fob - it was a Nissan (likely to be Terrano four-wheel drive in this country - I'd go for a dark one if I were up to no good); the keys glistened, they looked new. New, brown Nissan Terrano? Second, perhaps strangely for breakfast, Wayfarer man was drinking a can of diet Pepsi. *Mmmm, that's odd.*

Tubmanburg Jail, Liberia

Henry was amazed that he had slept so well. His dreams had culminated in one of those irrational scenes where he needed to run away from someone but his legs wouldn't allow him to. Everything had been in slow motion, no matter how hard he tried.

He woke in a sweat, finding the nice jailer placing a bowl of cornflakes on the small wooden table in the cell. Accompanied by yet another cup of coffee. Which Henry could smell: instant and made predominantly with chicory. He lifted his head slightly and smiled at the man.

It didn't surprise Henry that nobody had been in touch with him overnight. He had dwelt on the visit from Tweedle and the more he thought about it the more his confidence in the system had diminished. His mind pursued the worst case scenario. To the British government he was now an embarrassment. There's no way that MI6 would publically accept that they had any involvement with him. All their conversations had been over the telephone and whilst he might be able to make a bit of noise about how he'd been used by them, it would probably be lost in the cacophony of the murder enquiry.

He was stuck with what to tell the UN. Why did he go to the bar? Why was he working for the British Government whilst he was on UN business? His brain ran over what he remembered about previous UN staff involved in criminal cases abroad. He thought that responsibility for them reverted to national governments. If that was the case he was back where he started with Tweedle, the Embassy's embarrassment with his involvement, and MI6's tardy contact with them. Which they weren't happy with. From his perspective, as a man who mostly saw a glass half full, he was in a difficult position.

Surprisingly his mood wasn't one of complete dejection. OK, he'd hit a low directly after Tweedle's visit, but last night he'd developed a bloody-mindedness. He was comfortable enough, he was allowed to shower and was fed adequately. This wasn't *Midnight Express*. And this morning he was feeling strong enough to make a bit of a stand. Actually the more he thought about it, the stronger he felt. He was ready for a fight. He had done nothing wrong. He had followed instructions from his country's Intelligence Service to the letter. He would stand up for himself. Be considered and calm. Just now he had guts. He was feeling audacious. Nothing would stand in his way for justice.

He smiled at his kind warden and raised a hand in thanks, nodding as he did. Today would see Henry Middleton at his best. Upstanding and fearless. Somehow, somewhere the system would kick in and look after him. Between now and then he wouldn't flinch.

Sam set her breakfast pace to that of the two men. As they were finishing off, so did she. She saw them readying to leave, Wayfarer man taking a final swig from his can, and then cautiously followed them out. They went upstairs and she luckily overheard Binos man say 'twenty minutes?'.

She looked over to the reception desk, a small wooden enclosure with a marble effect top. Standing behind the desk was the man she had got to know last night; he had welcomed her with a smile and they had a conversation about Tubmanburg, the sites and what to see.

He looked up at her and smiled, giving her a quick wave. He was dressed in the same white shirt and black waistcoat. She walked over to him, thinking on her feet.

'Morning Denzel,' she had asked his name at the end of the conversation last night, 'I'm meeting with the two men who have just walked upstairs later this morning - did you see them?'

'Yes, Miss Green, I recognise them.' All smiles.

'The thing is I've rather embarrassingly forgotten their names and I don't want to have to reintroduce myself to them. Do you remember who they are?' Sam smiled. Every step she was taking was into the unknown, fraught with danger. She loved it.

Denzel tilted his head on one side, a bit puzzled. There was a conflict within him, but it didn't last long. He looked down at a big paper document open on the desk below the height of the counter. 'That's Mr Lightman and Mr Schulz. They American.'

Sam smiled broadly. She had absolutely no idea if those were their real names, but she had something. 'Thanks Denzel. See you later.'

As she bounded up the stairs to her room, she reminded herself of her plan. Which was, in essence, to remain as flexible as possible. She needed to pack her bag (she had no idea if she would be staying in the hotel this evening) and book out. Then she had to get in a position to follow Lightman and Schulz as best she could. She knew this would quickly unravel if they drove away in a car, but this place did have taxis. She'd always wanted to say 'follow that car.' She had to keep ahead of them.

Once in her room she popped to the loo (*they don't do that in the movies*, she thought) and threw all her stuff into her daysack, but not so quickly that she didn't check she had everything. A scan of the room and then she walked back to the foyer. She reckoned that had taken seven minutes.

'Could I pay please Denzel?'

'Yes, of course Miss Green.' Another smile. Denzel was efficient. The hotel had an old electronic cash machine and, Sam noted, receipts were hand written. There was a PC in the corner but it wasn't turned on. With sporadic electricity, relying on computers wasn't always sensible.

'Is there a hotel carpark?' Sam was trying to find where the Nissan might be. *Ten minutes since breakfast and counting* she thought.

'Round the back Miss Green. You have to go out of the front door and turn right and right again. There's no customer entrance out through the back.' Denzel looked up from his receipt writing to match his words with hand gestures.

'Thanks Denzel'.

Sam paid her bill, smiled at Denzel and walked out the front door. The reasonable cool of the hotel foyer was overtaken by a wash of hot damp air. Even at just gone eight thirty in the morning the weather was debilitating. She walked round to the hotel car park which, Sam was surprised to find, was full of cars. The Nissan, a black (not brown - but close) Terrano, was easy to spot. It was dirty with a layer of dust up to the level of its wheels, but it did look new. *Fifteen minutes* she thought. *Quicker girl.* She looked for any obvious identification markings, clocked the number plate which was Liberian registered, and had a quick peek in through the windows. A bit of rubbish on the back seat. The boot was covered with a black horizontal boot blind. Nothing in the front seat. Except, under the passenger's seat was a leather looking folder, its corner just sticking out, visible from the side window. *Seventeen minutes.* The folder had a badge on it, she couldn't quite make it out. Gold, blue, red and white. She looked across to where she had entered the carpark and then up at the back wall of the hotel. Nobody coming and no one looking out of the hotel windows.

She took out her phone. With a dexterity that surprised her she had the camera ready in a couple of seconds. *Click.* Tap on the screen for zoom. *Click. Click.* She put the phone away and walked nonchalantly back out of the car park.

As she reached the main pavement she looked back to the entrance of the hotel. Lightman and Schulz exited the hotel and turned towards her. They were deep in conversation, not looking at her.

Three choices. *Make a decision now.* She took the middle one and stepped out into the road between two poorly parked cars. So intent was she on getting out of the line of sight of the two men that she almost walked into the path of an old truck. She stopped herself, pulled back, and when it was clear made a dash across the road. Looking quickly behind her she saw the men had gone into the car park. *Where's a taxi?* She glanced up and down the road on tip toes to look over a high sided van just down from her. Spotted one. She jogged along the road and put her hand out in front of the battered Mazda to stop it from moving off. She bent down to the passenger window. 'Are you free?'

'Yes. We d'you wanna go white lady?' The taxi driver had a reasonable command of English. That was good.

'This is going to sound a bit mad, but can you follow a car?' She paused; the taxi driver's look was close to incredulity. 'Like in the movies?'

He smiled. 'Ok miss. If that's what you want.' He raised his eyes to the roof of the taxi. 'Get in.'

Sam got in, just in time. The Black Terrano was pulling out of the hotel car park turning left.

'Follow that black Nissan. Please. Keep a distance. I'd rather lose it than the occupants realise they are being followed.' Sam was looking directly ahead, keeping an eye on the Terrano.

'You're the boss.'

Petersville Street, Tubmanburg, Liberia

The Nissan had driven a couple of miles and parked outside a brick house on the edge of the town. It looked like a residential street, slightly more upmarket than average for up-country Liberia, with two and three storey houses, a potholed but tarmacked road and a number of cars. There were no front gardens, the houses started where the broken pavement stopped.

All the properties looked tidy, although a couple had the first floor windows bricked in and nearly all had iron railings over their windows. Sam noticed a black man was waiting outside of the house where the Terrano had stopped. On first inspection he seemed to be guarding the house, but there was no sign of a weapon. Further down the street there was a compound type place, with shards of broken glass on top of the walls. It had thick metal entry gates which looked firmly locked. On one corner was a raised guard post which Sam noticed was occupied. *People in this road take their security seriously* she thought.

The two men entered the house, leaving the Terrano giving a single bleep to say it was locked and alarmed. Sam asked the taxi driver to drive past the house and then pull up round the corner. She was surprised at how easily she was settling into the routine of being a spy and equally delighted that her driver was playing along.

'Bad place here, miss. Street is fer de rich. Men who have made it any way they could. Not like it here.' The taxi driver mood had changed a little. He was more sombre, less relaxed, but he did what he was told. They had agreed earlier that he would stay with Sam all day for fifty US dollars. No questions asked. He looked at this point as though he might regret that commitment.

As they drove past Sam nonchalantly looked the house up and down. There was nothing that seemed untoward about the place, except the guard who was now leaning against the wall smoking a cigarette. Wait….no she spotted something. The roof of the house was crammed full of satellite dishes and antenna. She craned her neck for a better look. There was a microwave dish, two satellite dishes (much bigger than your average TV dish) and four or five antennas. The microwave dish must be pointing at another dish on another building somewhere; if she remembered rightly that's how they worked. And the satellite dish looked like it was capable of sending as well as receiving data. *That stuff is not cheap*, Sam thought.

The taxi driver pulled up round the corner. If Sam was thinking correctly the two men would be off reasonably soon to catch their 'ten thirty' appointment. She would need to keep an eye on the house to watch for them leaving. The street was narrow, so the good news was the Terrano would need to drive past her junction; it couldn't turn round where it was.

She took out her phone and looked at the photos she had taken of inside the Terrano. She played with them a bit and zoomed in. The emblem on the corner of the document that she had taken a photo of was half of a white headed bird, with gold wings. From what she could make out the bird was enclosed in a circular frieze, which was white with blue lettering. She made out '*RTMENT OF DEFENS*' in capitals.

A penny dropped. She would need to get on the internet to confirm, but she was pretty sure the emblem was the badge of the US Department of Defense. *Oh my God,* she thought. *What have I got myself into?*

Tubmanburg Main Police Station, Liberia

Henry was on his feet as soon as he heard American voices coming down the corridor. They were led by the Deputy Chief. Two men, a white man and a black man, both casually dressed in tan and khaki. He glanced at his watch. It was ten thirty.

The white man spoke. 'Mr Middleton.' It wasn't a question. 'I'm Mr Lightman and this is my colleague, Mr Shultz.' They were stood on the other side of the barred door. 'Please gather yourself together, you're coming with us.' He was smiling. Henry thought it a forced smile. But it was effective.

'That's, eh, great.' Henry replied picking up his jacket from the only chair in the cell. 'Where you guys from?' They sounded Texan to Henry.

'We're friends, Mr Middleton. Close friends of your Government.' Lightman nodded to the metal gate and the Deputy Chief quickly pulled a set of keys from his pocket and opened it. It was clumsy. *The man's in a bit of a panic,* Henry thought. That seemed odd.

'We need to move quickly Mr Middleton, so let's not hang around.'

Henry was out of the cell in a shot almost pushing the Deputy out of his way. There was a lightness to his feet. Freedom was already smelling good. In his elation he didn't bother to ask any more questions, but the gentlemen in him did make him stop and turn to his warden. He reached out for his hand. The warden half stood and took Henry's hand, still smiling.

'Keep making the coffee.' Henry said. He found himself smiling now.

Outside Tubmanburg Main Police Station, Liberia

The taxi was about thirty metres from the police station parked among about twenty other cars. Sam had seen the two men go in and had clocked the time: ten twenty-five. The taxi driver was more relaxed since they had left Petersville Street and the guarded and gated houses. Rap played on the radio and he was tapping away at the steering wheel.

At ten forty (Sam clocked that as well, all safely tucked away in her brain) the two men came out of the police station with a third man. The new man was early thirties, white, well dressed but scruffily so. He had no possessions with him apart from a jacket. Wayfarer had the man by the arm. He was being escorted, almost pulled to the Nissan. The three of them looked an unlikely trio. Two composed Americans and the third, looking like he had been plucked straight from the cells after a hard night on the tiles.

They quickly got into the Terrano, with the new white man and Wayfarer in the back seat - *that's interesting* - and the vehicle moved off.

'Follow that car.'

She was getting good at this.

Chapter Eleven

A taxi, outskirts of Tubmanburg, Liberia

Sam was reasonably confident that the occupants of the black Nissan hadn't realised they were following them. The taxi driver was good, Sam thought. He was always four or five cars back and switched lanes often, hiding behind the odd large truck, but always popped out in time to see if the Nissan had changed direction. When it turned left at one point the taxi driver stopped just shy of the junction and let the Nissan get ahead for a bit before making the turn. Sam was in the front passenger seat and helped the driver spot which way the car was moving. It was all very professional, she thought. And frightening - but fun?

They had been driving for about fifteen minutes. Sam had remembered the route. She could follow it again if she needed to.

'Indicating right now.' Sam told the driver. 'No cars are following.'

The taxi driver nudged forward to the end of a street that was defined by two ramshackle double storey buildings, a metal fenced area and a farmstead of sorts with a perimeter wall consisting of handmade red clay bricks. A huge pile of litter was dumped on one corner of the junction. Nearby was a shell of an old car, ripped clean of any useful accoutrements. The sun was high now, there wasn't a cloud in the sky and, as far as Sam could tell, there was no wind. It was a hot, sultry day.

The Nissan had turned right down between the farmstead and the end of the brick made housing. It was on its own, moving slowly, weaving from left to right avoiding large potholes. Sam motioned for the taxi driver to stay still. She slid out of the car, crouched at the corner of the junction and stared down the road. The black Terrano was approaching what looked like a disused warehouse on the left of the track, its metal frame browned with rust, a corrugated iron roof and some plastic sheeting for walls. There was a sign proclaiming the name of the compound but the sun had all but made the letters fade away.

The Terrano pulled in beside the gate and the driver (it was Binos man) got out and seemed to be opening the gate. It took him some time. It must be locked well, Sam thought.

Sam jogged back to the taxi driver. His window was open.

'Stay here please. If I'm not back in an hour please go to the police and let them know what happened.' She fumbled for her waist belt and took out another fifty dollars. 'Just for safekeeping!' She smiled at the man, and he returned the smile but didn't say anything.

Sam opened the back passenger door and took out her daysack. She then carefully headed down towards the warehouse.

A black Nissan Terrano, outskirts of Tubmanburg, Liberia

Henry's mood had shifted. Twenty minutes ago it had been one of elation. He was a free man. The Americans, he noted - not the UN nor the Brits - had come to his rescue. It was understandable. To all intents and purposes he was in a jail of an American protectorate. So to be released from somewhere he didn't deserve to incarcerated in, by Americans from their Embassy was cool. Cool. That's how he had felt. He had survived a Liberian jail for two nights and was now a free man. What a story that would be to tell his mates. Actually to tell anyone who would be prepared to listen. Yes, it was a good story.

He also felt safe with them. In their hands he was no longer at the mercy of the man who had killed Solzman and then probably killed his contact in Spud's Bar. No, they couldn't get him when he had the might of the US diplomatic corps at his side. No sirree. Cool.

And, noting the steadily rising temperature, warm at the same time.

But since his release he had felt more and more uncomfortable. The two men had not spoken a word of explanation since they had got in the black car (Henry thought it was probably another Toyota, but he couldn't be sure). He'd continuously pressed them about his release, who they were and what was going to happen now. Nothing in return. The best he could get was 'Don't worry about a thing Mr Middleton. You're in safe hands now. All will become clear in a while.'

After he gone through a long list of questions again, the black man who sat next door to him on the back seat (Henry did find that a bit odd, but strangely comforting at the same time), turned to him and said, quite sharply, 'No more questions.' So Henry had shut up at that point and stared out of the window.

Perhaps they were Secret Service? He looked around the car for any sign of officialdom and spotted nothing. Oh well, he thought. At least I'm safe now.

Disused Warehouse, Tubmanburg, Liberia

Sam edged her way forward along the metal fence that surrounded the warehouse. The metal looked almost new, thick and strong, held in place by concrete posts. She reckoned the wall was about eight feet tall. Tall enough to stop the casual observer looking in, but not tall enough to prevent somebody trying to scale it. Except, she now noticed, the top of the fence had spikes on it, about six inches apart. *Ouch*, she thought.

The Terrano had gone into the compound and she heard in the distance the sound of chains being clanked. *Probably locking the gate* Sam thought. To her left further along the fence she spotted a thin gap between two metal sheets. It was just wide enough to peek through.

She stopped and looked in, checking out what she saw. Warehouse, about forty metres long. Held together with metal columns, but the sides now covered with opaque plastic sheeting. To the right side were two ISO containers. They both looked newish. Olive green, with a couple of small windows. Each had a door; both were closed. The Nissan had pulled up outside one of them. On the top of the left-hand container was a satellite dish and a couple of other antennas. Not quite the same setup as the house in Petersville Street, but she did notice a small microwave dish pointing back towards the town centre. That could be linking the two together.

From what she could see the metal fence seemed to completely surround the enclosure. And, hang on, there was another disused building towards the back of the compound. She had no idea what was the other side of the warehouse as the plastic sheeting shielded her view. That's all she could make out.

The three men had got out of the Terrano. The two Americans appeared to be walking the third man to the building at the back of the compound, not into one of the ISO containers. They looked locked, or empty. Or both. There didn't seem to be any other vehicles in the compound. What caught her attention, and made her flinch, was Binos man. He was walking a couple of paces behind the other two men. He seemed to have taken something out from his gilet. She knew for certain that it was a hand gun.

Rather than drag the man to the building at the back of the compound (dragging was an apposite description, he was no longer walking freely), they were taking him somewhere else. Somewhere she couldn't see. Then they were out of view.

She immediately ran back in the direction of the taxi. She had no intention of getting back in her vehicle; she was going to try and find another gap in the fence and see if she could establish what was happening.

'Hey, that hurts. What the bloody hell are you playing at? Let go of me you idiot!' Words that were lost on the heavily-built black man who was now pulling Henry by his right arm across the broken concrete paving. In between protestations Henry noticed that there was a large building with some plastic on the bottom floor walls, a couple of other sheds and they were heading for a garage type affair. He was sweating now. The air conditioning of the black car lost as soon as they had got out.

'Where are you taking me? What the bloody hell's happening?' Not a word in response.

Henry looked behind him to see if the white man was following on. He was. He looked to his front again to make sure he wasn't going to fall over any of the rubbish that was lying about the place, and then looked back again.

Christ! Henry thought, *the guy has a gun. He has a gun! What the flipping hell have I got myself into now?*

He needed a pee again.

He stumbled over a big rock that was in his path, but the man who was dragging him forward, steadied him with the hand that was holding his arm, squeezing his bicep tight; his nails digging into his flesh.

He didn't fall. But all of a sudden he didn't have much energy to walk.

Outside the Warehouse Compound, Tubmanburg, Liberia

Sam was sprinting now. She reckoned the compound was square, about a hundred and fifty metres in length. She was running for the far outside corner, or at least until she had cleared where she thought the inner warehouse would finish and then hopefully she could find another gap in the metal fence and get a view of the three men. As she ran she took in her surroundings outside of the compound. Scrub farmland to her left. A makeshift shack in the far distance. The road was potholed, but in good order. It ran on for about another four hundred metres where there was a small hamlet of shacks either side of the road. Trees were behind them. Thick jungle type. Somewhere perhaps to hide the taxi if she needed?

There was no one else around. It was all pretty deserted. She could make out nothing beyond the compound to her right. The metal fence was too high.

At last another gap in the fence. She skidded to a halt, breathing deeply, but steadying herself quickly. She wiped the sweat from her eyes and peered through. There were five or six decrepit buildings behind the warehouse. Most were clay brick built. No roofs. Rubbish lay everywhere. Just to one side were a group of large oil containers. Behind the clay buildings a more modern (but not as new as the ISO containers) single storey building but with an apex roof. A garage of sorts, it was difficult to tell at this angle, but probably wide enough for four cars and at its tallest point, bus-sized. Corrugated iron again. Slightly rusty, but probably waterproof. Sam could just make out from this oblique angle the garage was open; sliding metal doors. But little else, the angle was too narrow.

The three men came into view. The new white man was not happy. He was twisting and turning. Barking at Binos and Wayfarer. They were nonchalant, staring ahead, ignoring the man. She decided to call him James. He looked well-dressed enough to be a James. A sort of Englishman on tour who hadn't really appreciated the climate. Hot, bothered and now in some trouble. Yes, James would do.

The garage was close to the back wall, Sam reckoned almost opposite the front entrance but with the warehouse between it and the main gate. The men went in together. Into the thin slither of blackness that she could see. She had to know more.

She took off to her left again and ran as fast as she could continue round the perimeter of the compound. She aimed to get to the far bit of fence directly behind the garage. And then reassess.

Inside the Warehouse Compound, Tubmanburg, Liberia

Henry was thrust onto the floor. He required no instructions. His knees gave way and he fell with a thud and checked himself with his hands. *Bugger, that hurt.* He lifted his right hand. In the half-darkness he could see something oozing from his hand. Blood. He must have put his hand down on glass or some other sharp object. *From freedom to slavery*, he thought.

He wanted to say something to these two thugs, but couldn't think of anything which might help the situation, especially as he knew there'd be no response. He looked left and then right, but couldn't take any of it in.

There didn't seem to be much in the garage. He thought he saw a wooden crate or something in the distance and there may have been a window on one side, but it seemed to have been blackened with something. Sweat was dripping into his eyes.

He stared at the floor. Except it wasn't a floor. He suddenly realised there was a dark hole in front of him. A big black hole. It wasn't dug, like a grave - *blimey, did he really just have that thought?* - but more like a pit. Yes, he got it now. It was an inspection pit like his Uncle had in his workshop at home. You drove your car over it, got in the hole and with a torch checked underneath. Henry had always admired his uncle for managing to drive his cars over the pit without falling in.

He took a breath. It felt like his first breath of the day. *Bloody hell!* The stench. It wasn't sick or faeces. It was something else. Something rotten, evil almost. He held back his stomach.

'So Middleton. What do you know?' It was a black man's voice. Slow and strong.

'What? What do you mean? About what?' He turned to look at the man, but a boot caught him on the side of the head. It wasn't a kick, more of a nudge. 'Ow, bugger, that hurt!' An instinctive retort.

'Don't look up Middleton. Just answer my questions. Who were you meeting at Spud's?' That deep voice again. Quiet, but threatening.

'I don't know. I don't know. He asked to see me.' His voice was a shriek. Pleading almost. Henry now knew where this might be going. He felt sick again.

'Come on Middleton. We need to know everything. Every little detail.' There was the sound of a chair being pulled up and, he supposed, the black man sitting down. 'I want you to tell me everything from the beginning and don't leave out a thing. I have all day.'

Back Wall of the Warehouse Compound, Tubmanburg, Liberia

Sam positioned herself behind the warehouse. There was no gap in the metal fence anywhere near. She listened as hard as she could. She held her breath and listened some more. Nothing. Nothing at all. Whatever was happening in the garage was staying in the garage.

She had no choice. She had to get closer. She looked up at the metal fence and then to her surroundings. Just over the road was a wooden pallet. She looked left and right - no sign of anyone. Dropping her daysack she dashed over to the pallet, picked it up and then placed it at an angle against the metal fence. Balancing on top of the upturned pallet she put her daysack on top of the spikes. In a double bound, grasping two spikes either side of her daysack, she had her stomach on the pack. She flipped her legs over and then hung by her arms from the two spikes.

She looked below. Sand and a few rocks, then the back of the garage. It was all in shade. She let herself fall, turning immediately and crouching down - all in one movement. Ouch - her stomach hurt. She ignored it and held her breath. She listened again. Nothing apart from some incomprehensible talking in the garage. She glanced behind, looking upwards. Her daysack was still on the spikes, the plastic canvas sticking up, but the metal hadn't penetrated. Good. She only had clothes in the daysack. It would stay where it was.

She looked for an equivalent to the pallet that she could place against the back wall as an escape route. Over to her right was a rusty metal barrel a couple of metres away, just in the open beyond the back of the garage. She looked around: no one. She moved quickly and quietly. The barrel was closed on the top. She made an effort to move it. It felt half full. She pulled the top towards her and rolled the barrel back to the bit of the fence that had her daysack impaled on it. She constantly checked to her right to see if anyone moved out of the garage and came round to see what was happening. Nothing. Nobody.

She listened again, holding her breath. Just muted sounds. She dismissed the niggling pain in her stomach. She put her ear to the back wall of the metal garage. Nothing coherent. She had no choice, she had to get closer still. As quietly as she could she walked carefully along the edge of the garage. She had gone round the side furthest from the Nissan so if the men came out she would still not be in view. She picked her feet up over some old metal detritus, and had to navigate round another couple of barrels. She stopped just short of the end of the garage. She listened again. Some words now, slightly clearer. It was the bleating sound of the new white man.

'....so I arrived in Monrovia a couple of days ago...why are you doing this to me?' A shriek from the man. Followed by a thud and a scream. She thought she heard crying. She didn't like hearing men cry.

'Listen Middleton...' (She noted the name.) It was Wayfarer's voice. 'Just keep talking. Everything. I need to know everything.'

Middleton spoke some more between sobs. But Sam had tuned out. She was angry. Angry that these men, possibly working for the US government, had made her cry and were now making some other seemingly innocent man cry. She clenched her teeth. She felt the red mist descending, just gently, but enough for her to shake her head and clear her thoughts. She had to remain in control. She looked around at her feet - she needed a weapon. A thick piece of wood, possibly a metre long, lay a short distance away to her right. She crept on all fours to pick it up. It was heavy, but not too unwieldy. With strength she didn't know she had, she dragged it back to the garage wall as if it were balsa. She inched forward.

Reaching the corner of the garage she peeked round and immediately drew back. Binos had left the garage and was walking towards the corner of the warehouse. Her first thought was he was heading to the Nissan, or maybe to one of the ISO containers. She watched him until he had turned the corner and was out of view.

With the piece of wood in her right hand she shuffled to the garage opening and looked in. It was dark, but her eyes quickly adjusted to the scene. About ten metres in was the silhouette of a man sat on a chair, his back to her. In front of him she thought she could make out another man on all fours. 'James' Middleton. He was talking and sobbing at the same time. Then she smelt the awful smell of rotting meat. It was overpowering.

Middleton bleated some more. It was pitiful. Wayfarer was rocking back on his chair. She couldn't see his face, but she thought he was probably smiling. Red mist again. Not good. She looked over her right shoulder and checked for Binos man. Nothing. She looked back into the garage and caught what she thought was the sight of a gun in Wayfarer's hand. Did they both have guns? That would make sense.

There was movement. Wayfarer had stood up and kicked Middleton in the stomach. He fell awkwardly onto his side and curled up in a ball.

'You don't get to ask questions Middleton, I thought we had that by now?' The words were menacing, but touched with a degree of boredom. Wayfarer was losing patience. He sat down on the chair again, pushing immediately backwards, rocking.

Sam had had enough. The red mist was back, but she somehow took control of it. After a glance over her shoulder she picked up the club and walked into the garage. She tried to be as quiet as she could, but also mimicked a male pace so that if Wayfarer heard he might think it was Binos returning. Sounds now filled her ears. Middleton's words, her breathing, her feet being placed carefully on the floor, one foot after another. There was pressure there too, between her ears as if they had been screwed on too tight. Everything in her head started to congeal into a single focus. She lost all sense of peripheral vision.

She was now a few paces from Wayfarer. She had instinctively placed the club on her right shoulder. She was ready to strike, her focus sharp; her body on edge. She pushed her shoulders back and lifted the club. Just then Wayfarer turned his head and spoke at the same time.

'Kurt, you're back so....what the fuck?!' He started to stand, but it was too late. Sam had unleashed two months, no two years of frustration and anger. The club was already in motion and Wayfarer's attempt to stand only meant the blow was delivered to his neck and chin rather than the top of his head. The *crunch* sounded so satisfying to Sam. She was amazed at how quickly the club had moved through the air and by how much her arms and shoulders hurt immediately after contact.

Wayfarer didn't have time to say anything else. The force of the blow to his lower head caught him off balance, the smashing of bones and the shock of the impact on his skull sent his brain into shutdown. He collapsed onto the floor unconscious, landing just clear of Middleton, his gun flung across the concrete floor.

Sam dropped the club and put her hands on her knees. She was just about to take one or two deep breaths when Middleton turned round and mouthed *bugger me*. Sam immediately came to. She put both hands up and said quietly, between breaths, 'Shut up. Don't say a word. I've come to get you out of here.'

Sam saw Henry blinking a couple of times as he gingerly stood up; he swayed a bit but got a grip of himself. He opened his mouth to say something, but Sam stuck out both hands again and said, 'Not a word. We must act quickly.' She was silhouetted against the light from the garage doors. Almost like an angel.

Sam leant down and felt for Wayfarer's pulse. Yes, there was one and he was breathing. *I haven't killed him then.* Sam didn't know if that was a good thing or a bad thing. She wouldn't have been bothered if she had.

She then spotted the hand gun. She turned to Middleton.

'We're going out over the back fence. I need to see if the coast is clear. When I signal, you follow me at a run. But be as quiet as you can. Understand?'

Middleton nodded.

Sam dashed over and picked up the gun. It looked like a 9mm, but not a make she recognised. She cocked it, found the safety catch and turned it off. She then went to the edge of the garage, looking out but staying in the shadows. It was still clear. Binos man was not yet on his way back.

'Now!' A harsh whisper. She ran round the side of the garage and then hid behind the back in the shade. There was a noise, as if somebody had fallen, followed by a grunt. She looked back round the corner. The man Middleton had fallen over something, but he had picked himself up and was almost with her.

Stage one complete, Sam thought.

'We are going over that fence. She pointed at the barrel. Use my daysack to protect you from the spikes. There's a pallet on the other side to help get down. Come on, get up on the drum.' Sharp, crisp orders.

Middleton needed a bit of a shove on his backside to get on the drum, but once up managed to get his torso onto Sam's daysack. She was now immediately behind him on the barrel and pushed his legs over, even though he was tentative.

'Hey, don't do…' Thud. More sound effects.

Quickly putting the gun in her waist belt Sam followed him removing her daysack from the spikes on the way over. Middleton was on his feet by now, brushing himself down. He had blood coming out of one ear and the makings of a black eye. Dried tears were evident across his red cheeks. His hair was a mess. Actually, *he* was a mess.

What have I got myself into? Sam thought.

'Follow me. Don't fall over unless you can't help it.' A bit of Army humour coming through.

They quickly made it to the corner. Sam saw her taxi parked where she had left it. She didn't know if this would work, but she gave it a shot: she waved at the taxi, beckoning it to come to them. Save them from being seen from the front gate if the assailants had made it that far.

The taxi took off almost immediately and was with them in a couple of seconds.

What a team Sam thought.

'Get in Mr Middleton.' She had remembered his name. She knew she would. Binos man's first name was Kurt. She'd remembered that as well.

Henry stopped just for a second. He looked at her fearfully.

'Get in. I'm on your side and we have a lot of catching up to do.'

Henry got into the back seat. Sam got into the front, immediately engaging the taxi driver.

'Somewhere in the thick of Tubmanburg where we cannot be found. We'll take it from there.' She emphasised her order to the taxi driver by repeatedly pushing both hands forward in a flick, indicating movement.

She then sat back in the seat holding her daysack close to her middle. She closed her eyes hoping that that might lessen the pain in her stomach which was now flooding back. *Breathe deeply,* she thought to herself.

Chapter Twelve

Taxi Driver's House, Tubmanburg, Liberia

Henry was exhausted. But at least now he was out of immediate danger. What a day: the frightening, humiliating and painful hour in the garage followed by the 'escape'. Then the last two hours of intense discussion - an overall sensation of incredulity, disbelief and still that nagging sensation of fear, and of what to do next. Especially when it appeared that he, or should he say, *they* were on their own. Who could they trust?

He looked across at his rescuer, Miss Sam Green. She hadn't wanted to talk on the drive to their current location. She was on edge, constantly looking over her shoulder. She had answered his questions but in a perfunctory manner. She was Sam Green. She had followed them to the compound. She was trying to make sense of something that had happened to her back in the UK. One of the men that had been with Henry was involved in some way. His release just seemed like the most humane thing to do. She had constantly put her hand up to quieten him. She had engaged the taxi driver as though he was working for her. Calm and clear instructions. He had followed her words to the letter.

Now, some three hours later, she was sat in a tattered old red chair fast asleep. Her mouth was slightly open. She held her small backpack to her stomach like it was an infant of hers. And she was gently whistling whilst she slept. A young woman's snore. They were in the taxi driver's front room. Just the pair of them. He lived in not much more than a shack. Four clay brick walls with two doors and a couple of windows, one of which was broken. The floor was makeshift, pieces of old wooden pallets stripped and made into floorboards. In the corner was a simple kitchen, there was a small table and two chairs and a big tub that Henry thought was probably a bath. They had entered from a busy street having squeezed past a number of other dwellings (Henry couldn't call them houses) through one of the two doors. The other door was just a frame and beyond it was blackness lit by a couple of sheaths of light. Henry couldn't make much of the detail, but he assumed that this was some form of bedroom. It seemed small, but comfortable from a West African perspective.

The taxi driver had dropped them off, boiled some water using a small primus stove and showed them the scant provisions that he had in his one kitchen cupboard. 'Help yourself' he had generously said. He then explained he had to go back out to work, but they were to make themselves at home. His rescuer had seemed uncomfortable at first, not sure about letting the taxi driver leave for fear, he guessed, of him going to tell someone where they were. Although she didn't say anything. And she didn't stop him.

She was very cautious, Henry thought. But soon after the taxi driver had left she seemed to calm down a bit. She had sat him down and with a bowl of hot water had tended to the blood and mess on his face, asking about his other bruises. There was a tenderness about her, but a thoroughness as well. At that point he still hadn't established who she really was, or what was going on. But, unlike the other two hoods who had taken him from the jail this morning, he knew instinctively that he could trust her. He didn't know why, but there was a combination of vulnerability and kindness, mixed with this streak of iron-clad efficiency, that made her seem human. She was on his side. He had wanted answers to many more questions that buzzed around his brain, but in the first half-an-hour it just seemed right to let her take the lead; to settle things until they were ready to talk in detail.

Then they started, her in the big red chair, and him on one of the two wooden stools. They weren't far apart; but they filled the whole room. It was not somewhere Henry would have wanted to live for more than a couple of days.

Sam Green was looking for some answers. Who was he? He had been tentative at first; actually they had both been tentative, neither sure how much information to give away. When she knew who he was and the vaguest details of why he had come to Liberia, she started to open up. Her story began on the island of Mull and she explained about Doctor Tebie, his wallet and the burning of her campervan by two villains, one of which Henry had started to get to know quite well.

She had waited for him then. He spoke about Report 1415, but didn't divulge any of the details. He went onto Solzman's death and his reasons for coming to Tubmanburg. It was her turn. She had talked about her contact with MI6, her lack of trust for everyone and then this independent drive to connect Tebie with his roots in Sierra Leone; hence her finding herself in Liberia.

Henry had filled her in about his involvement with MI6 (he didn't mention David's name, he wasn't sure why but he thought that was a big secret), the murder of his contact and then being arrested. Their stories had come together at that point, with Sam bringing in her recognition of Binos man and following them first to the jail and then to the warehouse.

So that was that. Except he still didn't know anything about her. Not really - and she wasn't in any hurry to tell him. Maybe she never would?

She had taken control of things at that point. Henry could see that she was terribly analytical, institutionally so.

'There's something we're missing.' She had said. 'What's in that Report? It must be the connection.'

Henry explained that the Report was secret and he couldn't tell her. She had stiffened at that point and then become indignant.

'Look, Henry, we've both been let down by our governments. You were close to being murdered and who knows what they would have done to me if I had been with the van in Mull. Come on, let's try and piece this together. It might save our lives.'

Reluctantly after a couple of minutes of thought, mostly going back over his short time in jail and the seeming lack of support from his government and the UN, Henry had let Sam know about the dreaded report.

'The report was written by Solzman, the UN member of staff who was murdered here about a month ago. It seems that having made some contacts in Tubmanburg whilst on UN business, one of them had taken him to see the burnt-out wreck of what looked like a modern building. The building was 'in the jungle' north of here and was, according to the contact, a biological clinic. The contact said he had worked at the clinic; it was all very hush-hush and to get a job there he had to go through a special process. Solzman surmised that it was some form of security vetting. They were paid very well.'

Sam had been leaning forward at this point, head in both hands. Henry continued.

'The building was American run, but there was nothing official, or governmental about it. But Solzman reported that the contact had seen enough clues to establish the place as US government funded.'

'What were they doing?' Sam had pressed.

'Making and studying contagious diseases: Ebola, HIV, meningitis, even measles. The place was apparently very well run, state-of-the-art and incredibly secure. When Solzman had been taken to the site, most of the fences had been removed but he had snapped a couple of photos of what looked like the remnants of high security fences.'

'And what happened to the clinic?' Sam had asked.

'Solzman was told there was a fire one night. Nobody could be sure what had happened. The staff were scared. Scared that the diseases might have leaked, blown away in the wind. They were sworn to secrecy, and the message that was disseminated among them was that if there were any dangers of biological contamination the agents would have all been engulfed and destroyed in the fire. There was, apparently, no risk of wider contamination.'

'Wow.' Sam had said. She sat back in her chair. 'When did this all happen?'

'About a month before the outbreak of Ebola across West Africa.' Henry replied.

'But I thought the Ebola outbreak was meant to have stemmed from a small village in Guinea - that's hundreds of miles away. Something to do with bats?'

'I can tell you that nobody knows where it started. And if you were the American government, wouldn't it be convenient if the outbreak was attributed to a country as far away from your Liberian clinic as possible - a country which itself has semi-closed borders and is run by a tyrannical family? Many Guinean officials do not believe the bat story.' Henry responded.

That had brought both of their disclosures to an end. They both agreed that there was nothing else that could be added to their sum of knowledge. They spent some more time talking around the margins of the where they found themselves now. Sam had been forensic with Henry, asking him for more detail about the last couple of days than he could remember. But they both knew that the outstanding question was: what should they do now?

A groan from Sam broke his train of thought. He looked across at her. She was waking up, but he could see pain etched across her face.

'Are you OK Sam?' Henry asked.

She shook her head violently, as if to expel the remnants of a good sleep.

'I'm fine, thanks. How long have I been asleep?'

'About half an hour.' Henry replied. 'Now you're rested a bit can we discuss what we should be doing next?'

Sam was already on her feet stretching, her daysack now down by her feet. 'Sure,' she said. She sat down again, yawning putting her hand in front of her mouth. She blinked the sleep from her eyes, yawned again and then, all of a sudden fresh as a daisy, she started.

'The thing I don't get is why the contact wanted to get in touch with you having already spoken to Solzman? Unless he had found out something new? And, whilst I think I understand why the US government, or someone working for the US, would want to stop the story dead, surely these people don't kill innocents? Do they?' There was disbelief in Sam's voice. 'And how does Tebie fit into all this? What's he got to do with the clinic?'

'Solzman didn't have any names.' Henry said flatly. 'The thing is when we first read the report we assumed that it was either fabricated, or that Solzman had been led astray by some local Liberians wanting to either undermine the US or just get some notoriety. It wasn't until he was murdered that we all sat up and paid attention.'

Henry stopped. He could see that Sam was in deep thought. He had no idea what this woman did for a living, but part of him suspected that it was important. He had asked her once what her line of work was and she had declined to answer. He didn't feel it was right to press. There was something in the background, Henry felt, that was too deep for her to talk about.

'Ok, Henry. It seems to me we have two choices.' Sam had both index fingers raised; there was a finality about the gesture.

'Hang on, Sam, what do you mean we? I'm tempted to phone my driver and get him to take me back to Monrovia.' The words came out of Henry's mouth without any conviction. He knew that if he stepped out there, back into the arms of officialdom, he might well be picked up by the hoods, or the Liberian police. Before he knew it he'd be either back in jail, or in the ground somewhere, covered in earth.

Sam ignored him. 'We can either stay here in Tubmanburg and surreptitiously ask around and see if we can find the remnants of the clinic.' She waited for a second, still gathering her thoughts. 'The problem with that is they will be looking for us here.' She dropped one finger. 'Or we can get into Sierra Leone, go to Kenema and see if there are some answers there. Tebie is the key here. Binos man wanted to cull you - and he sure as hell wanted to kill a story that might put Tebie out of Sierra Leone at a time when he was supposedly being buried.' There was a lightness to her round face, her curly hair the perfect frame for her enthusiasm. 'Yes, go to Sierra Leone. Chase the Tebie story. They won't be expecting that.' She was looking directly at him.

'But how are we going to get across a closed border?' Henry's voice was a little high-pitched. He coughed to show that his tone wasn't necessarily based on anxiety.

'I know someone who can get us across.'

Henry looked at his resourceful rescuer. His options were limited. He knew that. In his current state, assuming Sam Green was alive and kicking, he would probably follow her anywhere. They were now a team, albeit he was definitely the foot soldier in the organisation. He had no problem with that.

Headquarters MI6, Vauxhall, London

David was musing over the latest reports from his agents and GCHQ. There wasn't a great deal that was new. GCHQ had intercepted a single call from an attributable mobile in London to an, as yet unknown, number in West Africa. The call did not make a lot of sense, but the three words that caught their and his eyes were: *target* and *St Paul's*. The rest was nonsense, some sort of pre-agreed simple coding which, if you didn't have anything to go on, you could never really unravel. The simplest codes were often the most difficult to break. If you pre-agree with someone that blue means red, even the most powerful supercomputer would struggle with breaking the code unless there is repetition, or some form of associated action that you could attribute to the code.

What was interesting about the intercept was its timing. In light of the current threat they had found a coded message between a number in London and a number in West Africa. And there were plenty of terrorist cells in Nigeria and even Cote D'Ivoire. St Paul's was an interesting inclusion. Quite a target. High profile religious centre, full of tourists. *Sorry, Christian religious centre.* If there was a biological attack in the Cathedral and you could infect everyone inside, all of the tourists, then the disease would travel the world before you could stop it. It would be an extraordinary coup for ISIS, or Al Qaeda.

There had been nothing new from Langley. But with this single intercept they might be onto something. He would get a team together ASAP to look at options.

Of course that team wouldn't include Jane, David thought. He looked at his watch. She should be at the embassy in Monrovia by now. He was expecting a call from her at any moment.

He stood up and walked across to the window. The Thames as always was alive with activity. His job definitely had one of the best views in town. And that was a good thing because, although he loved his job, it came with enormous stresses. The latest from the Liberia that poor old Henry Middleton had been arrested and was playing merry hell had added to the strain. There was little he could do that the Embassy weren't already doing. Jane would be able to add some weight, calm Middleton down, when she got there. It may all take some time. And he might have to go over the Ambassador's head, but they would have the man out of the jail and on a plane to the UK soon enough. *He'll probably lose his job with the UN, though,* David mused. Oh well. The bigger picture and all that.

His phone rang - he looked back at his desk. It was one of the secure lines. He walked over and picked up the handset.

'Jennings.'

There was a crackle, so often the case on the secure lines. Then a slight delay.

'It's Jane sir, I'm at the embassy.'

'Go on Jane.' David walked round the desk still holding the handset to his ear and sat down.

'Henry Middleton has been sprung from jail. Nobody has any idea where he's gone.' A further crackle.

David used his spare thumb and index fingers to rub his eyes. 'How does this happen?'

A further pause. 'No one knows. The Embassy's man Tweedle went to see him this morning and he was gone. The whole police station was shtum. Nobody could help. It appears that the Deputy there has also disappeared. I'm not putting the two together, but when Tweedle asked to see the man in charge, the sergeant there said that the Deputy who was on duty wasn't there anymore. He gave Tweedle the impression that this was very unusual.'

Crackle. 'Anything else to add? Any sign of Green?' David felt his throat was dry. He needed a drink.

Pause. Crackle. 'No, nothing. I can't push the Liberians, you know - put out a blanket search across hotel networks - not without letting my oppo in Langley know that I'm on his patch and why I'm here. Do you want me to do that?'

David waited for a second. 'No, not yet. Get up to Tubmanburg and stick your nose in. See what you can come up with. Keep our Embassy informed and ask them to shake all the contacts they have. Are there any press there yet?'

'According to the Embassy just a Reuters agent who is providing the other outlets with the news. It seems there isn't much ambition to fly into Monrovia at the moment. The Embassy isn't going to release this latest information about Middleton's escape unless asked, although that's likely to be soon as the Reuters man is coming in this evening for a briefing. Middleton as a suspect in a West African murder is noteworthy. But him absconding from jail adds a much more interesting dimension. I reckon the British press will want to send some hard hitters over soon.'

David waited for the pause.

'OK. Let the Embassy deal with that. You get up country and try and put some flesh on the bones. If we have nothing by close of play tomorrow, then we might have to engage the Americans. Keep in touch.'

David put the phone down. He rested his chin on his hand and stared out of the window again. He then took out a piece of A4 from his desk drawer and jotted down a few thoughts:

Chronology: US sponsored secret lab in Liberia destroyed by fire. Ebola crisis starts. Solzman makes connection. US informs UK of biological threat to high profile countries in Europe. No independent corroboration. Green finds Ebola expert's wallet in Scotland. Two men try and seize wallet. Green goes runabout. Middleton agrees to meet further Solzman contact. Contact murdered. Middleton arrested (not important). Middleton absconds from jail (important). Unlikely a solo act. Deputy chief of police also disappears. Potential narrowing of threat to St Paul's.

David thought that connecting the current biological threat and the pantomime in Liberia had no intellectual rigour behind it. It was solely a coincidence. Surely? The lab, which they had known nothing about until the UN report, was allegedly being used to look at a number of diseases that could be used as biological agents. If you were a terrorist, which one would you choose? Whilst current and media-friendly Ebola was difficult to transmit. It can be passed between animals and humans, and humans to humans, but that can only happen when bodily fluids or blood are exchanged. How do you do that on a mass scale in the form of a weapon? You can't terrorise people into kissing each other?

Unless, of course, the clinic had perfected a way to transmit it orally or respiratorily. It didn't bear thinking about. He needed to get a team together. He felt they were running out of time.

Taxi Driver's House, Tubmanburg, Liberia

Sam and Henry had spent some time reviewing the options. Sam had assumed that Henry was now part of 'her team'. It was a natural military assumption. If he were rational he didn't have any other options. He now needed to understand what was happening, to work out who were the good guys and who were the crooks. Only then would he know who to trust. They both had to work that out for themselves. And now they had to do it together. And currently Sam didn't trust anyone. Except Linda.

She had told Linda she would let her know every couple of days that she was OK. She and Henry had agreed that, before they do anything else, they needed to let someone in the UK know that they were alive - Linda was the obvious choice. But they also felt they needed to somehow feed in what had happened, hoping that Linda might be able to get the information to one of the good guys. Sam had decided to use the SIM she had picked up in Monrovia to text Linda. Then she'd throw it away.

Sam had drafted a SMS which Henry had looked over and agreed. Sam read it one more time before she pressed 'send'.

Hi L. Sam here. Am ok but have picked up UN Middleton. He was kidnapped by 2 US men, poss DoD or sim. They might have killed him. One was man who torched van. We don't know who to trust. Let Col Tim know this word for word. He will know what to do. Will use different SIM next time. If no contact within 7 days presume worst. Ack within an hour pse. xx

It all seemed very Secret Squirrel, but at the same time she had neither elaborated nor embellished what they had been through. Linda would do what she was being asked.

Then she had phoned the bus man's uncle using the number he had given her in Monrovia. The uncle seemed kind and genuine. They had agreed to meet at a particular crossroads off the main square at ten this evening. He had made the point that what they were asking him to do was dangerous. They should travel light, no more than one small bag apiece. The cost was one hundred dollars each.

'Well as I have no bags at all, you can take as much as you like,' Henry had commented.

Sam didn't know whether that was meant to be humorously sexist or not. She smiled at him as if he were a child.

The taxi driver had turned up at that point. Sam couldn't stop herself looking over his shoulder to see if he had brought any cavalry with him. No, he was on his own.

Sam checked her watch. It was six thirty. They really didn't want to hang about on the street corners of Tubmanburg for three hours, but she sensed the longer they stayed here the more chance there was that they would be discovered. They were also both famished. The throbbing from her stomach which ebbed and flowed was being overtaken by the gnawing sensation of hunger.

'How about we take you out for something to eat? We owe you that.' Sam said. Henry looked across at her, puzzled.

'Dat's good.' The taxi driver was a man of few words.

'We need to go somewhere out of the centre where nobody will recognise us. But we also need to be in the town centre for about ten o'clock. Do you know somewhere?'

'Sure. Go now?'

'Why not?' Sam looked across at Henry and raised her shoulders, asking for agreement.

Henry nodded.

Good, she thought. He gets it.

Just as they walked out Sam's phone pinged. She looked at it. There was a single line reply from Linda: *Ack xx.*

Chapter Thirteen

British Embassy, Tubmanburg

Jane had found a small corner of the Embassy main office with a chair parked next to a desk. She'd been met at the main entrance by one of the admin staff and offered a cup of tea. They hadn't sent anyone to the airport - she's wasn't expecting them to, but it would have been a nice gesture.

She knew it was going to be a difficult visit. The staff member she had spoken to at the Embassy when she was organising her trip had been curt, but efficient. He'd made it clear that Henry Middleton's plight had caused upset, added to the staff's workload and look set to continue to make life difficult for the Embassy. Her arrival was, among other things, supposed to reduce the friction and provide some added horsepower to the Embassy. But the initial reaction she'd got from the staff in the office was frosty.

'The Ambassador will see you now.' The call was from a woman she had not seen before. She'd arrived unnoticed beside Jane's chair whilst she had been rereading her notes.

Jane looked up and flashed a smile, gathering her papers together quickly. She glanced up at the clock on the wall; it was seven fifteen. The hour put paid to the belief that Embassy staff live royally, a colonial lifestyle of pink gins and waiter service. Nobody looked set to leave the Embassy any time soon. She was surprised.

She followed the woman down the corridor passing formal photo after photo of Embassy staff throughout the years. The pair of them stopped briefly at a desk, which was set in a recess outside of a big well-polished wooden door. The woman, who Jane had now clocked as the Ambassador's PA, motioned for Jane to go in.

'Thanks.' It was a muted acknowledgement. Jane stood outside the door briefly, took a deep breath, opened the door and walked in.

She had done a little research on Ambassador Clive Mason on the flight over. Career Civil Servant, in his mid-forties (which was very young for a Head of Mission), married, no children, degree in PPE from Oxford and a Masters in International Relations. This was his first Ambassador post and almost certainly a springboard for a bigger position provided he kept his nose clean. She'd asked around her office before she'd left that morning - no one had a bad word to say about the Embassy in Monrovia.

Those in the know had said that they thought they'd handled the Ebola crisis really well so far.

'Hello Jane, it's good to meet you.' The Ambassador offered his hand. He looked younger than she thought he would. He wore a light linen suit and a big smile. *Very casual,* Jane thought.

'Hello Ambassador. It's good of you and your people to accommodate me at such short notice.' Their handshake lasted longer than Jane expected. Tactile, but not uncomfortably so. He offered her a seat in a big red leather sofa. She sat at one end, he the other.

'No problem. It's good to have someone from MI6 here to take control of this affair. We are a little out of our depth and, frankly, with not a great deal of understanding as to why this has developed as it has. It's good to have someone here who can answer those questions for us and take responsibility for where this goes from here.' He was still smiling, but there was steel behind the gentle facade.

Jane was nodding. She was also thinking that she might have less answers than the Ambassador wanted. And there were some things she couldn't divulge. But he should know where those boundaries were.

There was a pregnant pause.

'Sure, sir. I'll fill you in on everything I know, but there are plenty of unanswered questions. That's one of the reasons I am here.' Jane moved in the soft red leather sofa a little, getting more comfortable.

'Well we have another press conference in an hour. There are some local press, there's the Reuters man and we believe there may be a couple of UK broadsheet press coming having left Ghana. They were following the Defence Secretary's visit, but all of a sudden this has got much more interesting.' He paused. Smiled again (it was disarming). 'Have we any idea what Middleton is up to?

'No, sir. Sorry. We really don't.' She emphasised really hopefully making the point that she wasn't holding anything back. 'I know David Jennings has talked to you and I don't think I can add much more. His whereabouts is a complete mystery to us. However I'd like to brief you on two other parallel developments which may or may not be relevant to the Middleton case.' She paused giving the Ambassador time to comment. There was nothing in return. He just showed the palms of his hands in a 'come on then, I'm ready' motion.

'I have to ask that what I am about to tell you does not leave this room and certainly should not be divulged to the press. I think we keep the press line vague. I am happy to lead, if you like, and on behalf of the FCO appear pretty witless, so I take the flak on behalf of London so to speak. I

can deflect and stall easily enough. Unless your staff want to head it up?'
Again Jane waited for a response.

'No, that's fine. My Deputy is ready to stand with you on the dais,
but I'll brief him to let you take the questions. Now, please, let me know
what's really going on.' He leant forward, the smile not so evident now.

Jane described in as much detail as she thought necessary MI6's
involvement with Henry Middleton. Looking to the Ambassador's face this
was clearly not new news. David had briefed him well. She then went on
to talk through her involvement with Sam Green. The Ambassador
seemed to take it all in, although he must have been surprised that there
was a second Brit on the loose potentially causing trouble on his patch.
His expression hardened further.

'And we have yet to let the Americans know of our involvement
with Middleton and they certainly haven't been told about Sam Green.
David thinks we ought to try and get a better handle on what's happening
before we piece together this part of the jigsaw for them.' Jane waited for
a reaction.

The Ambassador sat back in his chair, brought his hands together
as if about to pray and raised them to this lips. He stared beyond her.

'That's a mistake.   We have very good relations with the
Americans.' It was his turn to emphasise 'very'. 'They have contacts
everywhere as you'd expect and they obviously know about Middleton. I
have avoided a couple of calls from their Embassy this afternoon as I was
waiting for you to brief me on what you know, so I wouldn't come across as
a complete fool. I'm having lunch with their Ambassador tomorrow and
should, out of politeness, phone her in the next hour or so. Are you telling
me that I have to feign ignorance of Middleton and Green?'

'I'm sorry sir, but those are the orders I have. The thing is, and I
am speaking a little out of turn here, I get the impression from my boss that
he's worried about the American's position and even their involvement with
the whole episode. I'm not sure why, but it's as though he doesn't wholly
trust them at this point.' She was leaning forward now, hoping to win over
the man opposite her.

'It's still a mistake. David is wrong about the Americans and he's
wrong not to have involved them from the beginning. They almost certainly
know more than we do about Middleton's escape - they run the bloody
police force for Christ's sake.' The gentle facade was now broken. The
Ambassador was angry, almost indignant.

Jane flinched inwardly at the language. But, she thought, when you mess about on someone else's turf you shouldn't expect an easy time. It didn't help that she agreed with the Ambassador.

'I'll phone David Jennings now,' the Ambassador said, 'and let him know what I think. I'll then phone my opposite number. You'd better get ready for the press conference.' He stood up, the meeting clearly over. 'Is there anything else I can do for you?'

'Ehh, yes please. I need to get up to Tubmanburg tomorrow first thing. Can someone take me there?' She had no choice but to ask.

'Yes, that'll be fine. Speak to Sue, my PA. She'll sort it. And ask her for my mobile number. Please also make sure we have your telephone number and that I hear of any developments - that is *any* developments,' he was looking directly at her, 'as soon as you hear of any.' Point made, Jane thought.

He held open the door. Smiles again now. 'Where are you staying?'

'The Hilton, it was a quick and easy choice.' She was almost apologetic.

'Good. The food's ok there. Keep in touch.' He looked beyond her to the desk outside his door. 'Sue, could you help Miss Baker please. She needs, among other things, a car and a driver for tomorrow.'

Central Tubmanburg, just off the main square

The food had been average but edible. Neither Sam nor Henry's minds were up for much small talk with the taxi driver. In between mouthfuls they had discussed life in Tubmanburg, the Ebola crisis and the problems with just getting by in a third world country. Sam had let Henry lead the conversation. Even though tired and distracted he couldn't contain his fascination for people and cultures. She learnt as much about life in a third world country by listening to his questions as she did from the taxi driver's responses. He had a kind manner, but he didn't flinch from difficult questions and managed to get their guest to offer more than she felt the taxi driver was comfortable with divulging.

Henry had cleverly got onto the possibility of a clinic in the jungle. She had rather hoped that the taxi driver might know something about it, but he obviously didn't. If it had been common knowledge in the area, surely he would know something in his position, driving people about all day? So whilst Henry's murdered contact was in the know, the Americans had certainly kept the collateral as narrow as possible if the local taxi

118

drivers were unaware. Sam thought that killing one or two of the workers would be one way to reduce the opportunity of rumour, and certainly keep those in the know quiet.

Oh well, their decision to travel to Kenema now seemed a much more sensible tack than kicking around Tubmanburg trying to find out about the clinic which was clearly a well-kept secret - whilst avoiding both the police and some dangerous American hoods.

The taxi driver had left them at about nine-thirty and Sam was insistent with Henry that the pair of them stay away from the agreed pick up point until just before ten. They would only arrive at the place after they had given the area the broadest possible once over. With half an hour spare they popped into a small bar about a hundred metres from the junction that the 'uncle' had described as their rendezvous point.

Sam went in first to check it out - Henry's face was news, hers was still an irrelevance. The bar, which was just a shack with a couple of tables and red plastic garden chairs, was almost empty. The barman glanced across at Sam and then back to the TV that hung on the wall. It was showing some indiscriminate football game. She stuck her head back outside and called Henry in.

They both had a cold coke; clear heads were essential. Neither of them said much. Henry seemed content on watching the football whilst she took in their disposition. They were both wearing reasonable sensible clothing. Henry's gear may have been in the 'Englishman abroad' style, but they were sturdy and still reasonably clean. He had not been back to his hotel, but thankfully had his wallet and passport with him. He had nothing else, not even a toothbrush. They would need to sort that out at the first opportunity. She had her waistband with money, cards and passport. She also had her daysack, which had ripped at one point on the spikes at the warehouse, but it was usable. She had enough anti-malaria medication for the pair of them for about two weeks, some toiletries and a change of clothes.

Oh, and she had a hand gun. She had dismantled it, cleaned it and put it back together whilst she and Henry had been talking in the taxi driver's house. The magazine had twelve rounds. On inspection it was Sauer P229, not a weapon she recognised, but its mechanism seemed simple enough. She had stuck it among her clothes in her pack and had surprised Henry later in the afternoon by practising removing the gun cleanly. She'd done that three or four times until she was comfortable that she could get at it as quickly as possible.

So between them they had one change of clothes, one toothbrush, some malaria tablets and one 9mm pistol. *Better to travel light than be overburdened.*

'So, Sam, what do we do when we get to Kenema?' Henry had stopped watching the match and broke her train of thought.

She looked at him. He looked tired, but somehow relaxed, almost resigned to where they were. 'I'm not sure. Find somewhere discreet to stay and then try and track down Tebie's family. I checked before we came out here. There are 120,000 people in Kenema, about the size of Cambridge, assuming Wikipedia is right. But Tebie's a big name and I'm sure, eventually, we'll find someone who will lead us to some conclusion. His funeral was recent enough for it to still be in people's minds. We'll unearth something. I know we will.' She glanced at her watch. 'Drink up. Time to meet the *Man from Uncle.*' She smiled at her own joke. Henry looked at her as though she were mad.

She walked the empty glasses to the bar, said 'thanks' and led Henry out onto the street.

'You wait here. Remember, stay in the shadows. You'd be surprised how little people see into the shadows. I'll be back in a minute.'

Sam walked slowly towards the junction. It was a simple crossroads, brick buildings on all four corners. The road was part tarmac, part red clay. There were a number of mostly men wandering about, a few sat on the corners of the junction drinking beer. There were no streetlights, but there was enough ambient light from the buildings for her to take in the scene without too much effort. There were cars parked along all four roads, with just a few gaps. They were all driverless, one or two seemed abandoned. She turned the corner, walked about ten metres, turned back and looked again. Nothing seemed untoward. None of the cars were modern, they were all old and battered. Across the street about three cars back was a yellow taxi. Again it was driverless.

From the opposite direction a car pulled up at the crossroads. It hesitated and then turned towards where she had left Henry and pulled in, double parking. The lights remained on. She studied it for a while and clocked its number. It was a blue Mercedes 190. Probably late eighties. None of the wheel trims matched and the boot was a lighter blue to the rest of the car. She waited for a few seconds and looked around. Nothing suspicious that she could tell.

Sam took off and crossed the road away from the blue car. She stopped again, checking. Nothing.

'Hey white girl. How's doing?' The words startled her. Sam glanced round. They came from a young black man who was sat on a stool just round the corner of the street. He's not sinister she thought.

'Fine thanks.' She raised her hand in acknowledgment. 'Got to go.'

She crossed the road again, this time not stopping but still looking for the absence of the normal. The blue Mercedes stayed where it was. She checked her watch. It was ten thirty.

She was just about to cross the street to the car when another car drove past in front of her. It didn't stop. Not theirs. She approached the driver in the Mercedes. The side window was open.

She lowered her head and peered through the window. The driver was a middle aged man, his face turned to her.

'Are you the Uncle?' She was direct, looking in and around the car for clues, anything that she should be aware of.

'Yes. There are two of you?' A dead pan face and a very American accent.

'My friend is just down the road. You can get us across the border into Sierra Leone tonight?' Sam had to stand up briefly as another car drove by. An old black Ford pickup. Nothing suspicious.

'Yes, we should go now.' The man was getting a little nervous now. His hands gripped the wheel tightly.

'Follow me down the street please, and I will get my friend. It's only a short distance down there.' Sam pointed in the general direction of the bar.

'Ok. Please go now. I will pull over when I see both of you. Then get in the car as quickly as possible.'

Sam stood up, and physically checking she still had her daysack on her back by touching it, strode off to find Henry.

Headquarters MI6, Vauxhall

It was late again. David was just about to leave the office when his phone rang. It was one of his staff, probably one of just a couple still in the office.

'Jennings.'

'Sir. I've just had GCHQ on the line. They've picked up an SMS onto Linda Ross' phone from, we expect, Green's mobile in Liberia.' There was a pause.

'Go on.' David was tired, but this news made him perk up a little. He reached for his notebook and removed the top off his biro with his teeth.

'I'll read out the text word for word: *Sam here. Am ok but have picked up UN Middleton. He was kidnapped by 2 US men, poss DoD or sim. They might have killed him. One was man who torched van. We don't know who to trust. Let Col Tim know this word for word. He will know what to do. Will use different SIM next time. If no contact within 7 days presume worst. Ack within an hour please.'* He left off the double kiss that was at the end of the text. 'It's worth noting that Ross acknowledged the message about forty minutes later. So far she has not used her phone to contact her commanding officer as Green asked her to do. It's possible that she might do that face-to-face.'

David stared into space. His mind raced trying to piece together possible scenarios. In his recent conversation with the Ambassador in Monrovia he had been emphatic about not sharing their info with the Americans. The man couldn't get it, but he pulled rank. And now he knew he was right. He wasn't in any way sure what the US' involvement in this whole affair was, but his hunch had been correct. There was now a clear link between Green, Middleton and the Americans. It was all about Report 1415 and the Ebola outbreak. He didn't know any more than that. He could understand why they'd want to keep the knowledge of a secret clinic on close hold, but why were they worried about Tebie and his wallet - and to spring Middleton from jail and then try to kill him? And how did Green and Middleton end up together?

There were too many questions. His only hope was that one of his staff would uncover something somewhere which could throw further light on the case. Or that Jane Baker would unearth something in country.

'Get this word for word to Jane Baker. Remind her that the US are not to be given access to any of this yet. Tell her I want an update by midday tomorrow. And, Mike, have you got any further on how to spread Ebola in droplet form?'

'I'm waiting for Porton Down to come back to me sir. Their main expert was in conference this afternoon.'

David thought for a second. 'If necessary go down there tonight. Tell the scientist that we think the Americans have succeeded in non-contact transmission. We have no idea whether they have or not, but put him under pressure. I want a committed response by five o'clock tomorrow afternoon on the art of the possible.'

'Ok, sir. Will do.'

The line went dead. David sat back down at his desk and let out a sigh. This was getting very complicated indeed.

Approaching the Sierra Leone/Liberian Border

It was difficult to keep track on where they were or where they were going. Sam had sat in the front of the car and Henry had sat in the back. The road was atrocious, a snaking muddy path through hilly jungle. At one point the car had stopped, its back wheels spinning. The driver, still known as just 'Uncle', had expertly turned the front wheels from left to right, reversing and then driving forward and the car had lurched and rumbled on.

They had all remained fairly quiet. It was pitch black, with the only lights the one headlight that worked. Even the dashboard lights didn't illuminate. Sam had reaffirmed the cost and Uncle had agreed that he would drive them all the way to Kenema. Sam had asked if getting across the border would be easy. Uncle had said they were driving on a little used road, known only to diamond smugglers and other traffickers. It seemed the border post was unmanned, a sort of undisclosed trade agreement between the two countries. The danger, Uncle had said, wasn't from the police or military, but from the traffickers. *Great* Henry thought.

'Pay attention now.' An order from Uncle. 'The border is just coming up.'

Henry thought he saw Sam reach inside her daysack. *Bugger*. He had that feeling that he needed a pee again.

The headlight caught a sign in the distance, the only shape in a sea of black and dark green. Henry made out *Border Crossing Closed*. Uncle drove past the sign, slower now. The muddy track broke into reasonable tarmac, the car weaving from right to left missing potholes.

In the distance, illuminated by their headlight, Henry picked out a small hut beside the road and he was sure he caught sight of a vehicle of some kind. Their car slowed further.

And then it all started. Mayhem and madness.

God, he needed a pee.

Chapter Fourteen

Illegal Border Crossing Point - Liberian/Sierra Leonean International Border

The moment Sam picked out the truck in the single headlight from Uncle's Mercedes 190 she had the Sauer out of her daysack, cocked and lying on her lap - her finger on the trigger. It was dark everywhere, except in the beam of the single light from the front of the Mercedes. She'd spent six weeks training in the jungle of Belize with an infantry battalion on a short secondment. She knew what the jungle was like. Dense, thick, spiky, unwelcoming, unforgiving, full of biting insects and, at night, black as if you were blind. She could have been naked in the passenger seat of the car and Uncle wouldn't have noticed.

But a light, a single bright headlight from their car, that was a beacon. A target. And, all of a sudden, that's what they were.

Uncle had spotted the truck as well. It seemed to Sam that in a split second he had two choices: slow down and have a conversation with anyone who might be at the crossing; or put his foot down and run the gauntlet. It was well past midnight and it was possible that anyone at the crossing might be asleep, although the main beam of the Merc and their noisy engine would soon wake the most dedicated sleeper. Both were risky. And neither were her decision. Uncle was the expert. He would know what to do. She hoped.

Uncle flattened the accelerator to the floor and shouted out, 'Get down. Traffickers!' Sam knew just then that he had made up his mind.

The Merc shot forward, bouncing hard over potholes, throwing them all from side to side. He was good, Sam thought. He was soon keeping the car as steady as possible, having now dropped the revs slightly lowering the noise from the two litre engine. She guessed they were travelling at thirty, maybe thirty-five.

Then it was clear that they were not alone. The truck's headlights came on, some forty metres ahead of them, spreading a beam of light across the road, stopping abruptly on the far side by a wall of impenetrable jungle. The gap between the truck's light and the trees was about fifteen metres Sam thought. It was difficult to see much else. As the light from the Merc swayed about Sam picked out maybe a couple of huts and perhaps another vehicle. Then two, maybe three men moving out of the buildings and one possibly from the cab of the truck. The one closest to the road, more silhouette than man, was now waving his arms frantically, trying to make the Merc stop. Sam spotted the outline of a rifle in the man's left hand. *Shit*, she thought.

Uncle floored the pedal again; the revs rose. The truck was now twenty metres away.

Above the noise of the revving engine there was a loud crack and then a heavy thump as Sam recognised the familiar signature of a high velocity round as it flew over the roof of the car. They had travelled another couple of metres and Sam felt that time was slowing down, everything was coming into focus. Her, the Merc, the truck's lights and the men. She knew both her and Uncle's side windows were open. She tensed, her eyes working angles, distances and opportunities.

Crack - smash - thud. Another shot at them, this time hitting the target. No pain. A glance left, Uncle still alive. The second round must have hit the car somewhere, but no sign of any damage. The man closest to them was now on the road, bringing his rifle down from the air to beside his hip. *Not the best place to take aim from. Could go anywhere.*

In one motion she lifted herself off of her seat, pushed her head and torso out of her side window and took aim with her Sauer. The Merc jerked, then steadied briefly. She fired. Bang, bang. A double tap. Ten rounds left. She must conserve her ammunition. The man with the rifle fell to the floor. She caught him moving in the illumination of their single headlight and the lights from the truck. *Still alive. That's ok.*

'Cut your lights!' She yelled at Uncle who, after a quick glance, she now realised had the look of a man terrified beyond recognition. His eyes were out on stalks, his hands clasping the wheel as if to release his grip would mean to fall to a certain death. But he immediately obeyed Sam's order and, without taking his eyes off of the road, reached forward and flicked off the Mercs lights. They were now a fast moving black object, surrounded by blackness a few metres from the beam of the truck. She fell back into her seat.

Crack - thump - ping. Another shot fired at them. This time the round had hit the car just behind her. She felt no pain and with the Merc on a straight path, she assumed Uncle was ok.

She steadied herself again, arms out of the window ready for another shot. They were coming up opposite the truck. Bang, bang. Another double tap. This time Sam fired between the two lights of the truck. Ping, ping. She hit it. She hoped enough damage would be done to stop the traffickers following them.

Then they were past the truck. Blackness in front of them. Uncle was driving blind.

'Lights on now.' Sam yelled. The taxi driver instantly lunged for the dashboard. The single headlight lit up again. *Shit* Sam thought as the black and green of the jungle sprung up in front of them, the road veering off to the left. Immediately the Merc slewed left hitting a small muddy bank before righting itself back onto the potholed road. Uncle was ahead of her now. He braked, compensated again with his right hand and they were then back on the track, slowing down.

Sam let out an audible sigh. *Good work, Uncle*. Then she was back on guard. She looked over her right shoulder to see if there were any lights following them. Nothing. Not yet anyway. And then she thought *Henry - where are you*?

'Henry!' Her voice was a shriek.

Nothing, then, 'What? What? What the bloody hell is going on?' Henry's voice was a shadow, a quiet, frightened and muffled bleat from a man who was obviously very uncomfortable with the recent experience.

'Where are you?' Sam was frantically looking for Henry in the dark; there was no silhouette of him against the back window.

'I'm down here.' The reply came from the footwell behind her seat.

'Are you alright?' Sam's tone had softened a little, but it was still a voice of alarm.

'I think so. I'll know in a bit when I can stop myself shaking.'

'Thank goodness.' She felt a wave of relief pass through her. She sat back in her chair and put both her hands back on the Sauer.

They weren't through it quite yet, she thought. But hopefully the worst was over.

She stared out into the inky darkness, wildly illuminated by the spotlight effect of the single headlamp as the Merc lurched from right to left to miss the holes in the tarmac. All of a sudden, above the noise of the engine, the tension was broken by the sound of laughter. She turned to her right.

Uncle was laughing and laughing, the belly laugh of a man who had heard the funniest joke in the world. In the light from reflected trees Sam was sure she saw a tear rolling down his face.

'What's so funny, Uncle?'

But he couldn't seem to reply. In the darkness his head was nodding up and down, his words lost between snorts.

Could be hysterics, Sam thought. She had seen men react in a number of different ways under fire, but this was the first time she'd ever experienced raw laughter. Oh well, she thought. If it works for you...

Headquarters MI6, Vauxhall, London

It was an eight o'clock start for David's complete team. On a Saturday morning. He presumed many weekend plans would have had to have been changed due to the current threat. But that was the nature of the job.

The chief of staff of COBR (Cabinet Office Briefing Room - the Prime Ministerial level security committee) had asked for a threat briefing by mid-afternoon. He wanted to know whether there was a need to call the committee together concerning the potential biological threat that MI6 had raised. He needed David's recommendation, and supporting report in writing to make a decision.

The brief would take one of David's team an hour and a half to write, and he would need a further hour to put his stamp on it. The problem was he didn't have much to say, other than conjecture from a small number of leads. He certainly wouldn't be able to add much from Porton Down as that report wouldn't be with him until later in the day.

They were all sat round a small circular table in one corner of his office. Six of them (it would be eight if Jane were present and Mike Hazlewood were not at Porton Down) and him. He went round the table for updates. Nothing from the Americans at staff level. He had spoken to Deputy Director of the CIA late last night. The Deputy couldn't add anything new - which was in itself odd; they had issued the threat warning in the first place so they must be able to press their sources, surely? Other than the fact that Muslim extremists continued to show clear intent to attack a European capital in the next ten days or so. Pressed on the likely biological threat the Deputy was noncommittal. David had asked about whether their people had any idea if Ebola could now be transmitted respiratorily, and the Deputy had paused on the line for a second; it was though he were thinking of an appropriate response - to choose between the truth and something else. He'd eventually replied that as far as he knew it was not possible, but he'd get his team to look into it. And that was that.

GCHQ could only provide one further intercept and that was a basically coded SMS from a different mobile number in the UK to the one used last time. Changing SIMs was old hat now to terrorists of all persuasions. The text was sent to a mobile number in Liberia. GCHQ were pursuing this number, but, as David had directed, without recourse to US assistance. The SMS had a couple of interpretations, but using sophisticated computer algorithms the most likely included the numbers one and twelve split by a forward slash, and the abbreviation SP. The latter could be read as shorthand for St Paul's - corroboration of the last intercept. Without any imagination at all David had checked his calendar. December the first was a week away.

David was trying to draw together the conclusion of this afternoon's COBR report. Bringing all these threads into a single sentence and coming up with: *'a biological threat, probably airborne Ebola, is likely to occur on 1 December in St Paul's Cathedral'* seemed so farfetched that he couldn't contemplate writing it. But that's what he had at the moment.

He briefed his team on Jane's report which had just come in. She had added nothing that his team weren't already aware of. She was insistent that they should involve the US in their investigations, even after he had briefed her on the SMS they had intercepted from Green to Ross.

It was true to say that without letting the Americans know about all of their independent leads, and particularly the latest on Green and Middleton, they were dealing with a major terrorist threat with both hands tied behind their backs. But if his hunch was right, involving the US at this point might give their neighbours the chance to spoil what few leads they had. He knew this made no sense whatsoever - historically they had absolutely no reason to doubt the Americans' integrity, but these were complicated times. He had told Jane and now he told his whole team, that if they had no further leads by close of play the day after tomorrow then they would swamp their opposite numbers with inquiries. That gave them about forty hours to make some significant progress. And central to their success was Jane's ability to uncover something in Liberia. In an ideal world she should grab Green and Middleton and give them a good talking to.

His parting words to his team were along the lines of a 'leave no stone unturned' pep talk. He cancelled all leave passes and he didn't need to tell them that they were to spend as much time in the office as they needed to make progress.

He had just gestured for them to leave when Justin Twell, the youngest of his staff, stuck up his hand.

'Sir, this may be an irrelevance, but I picked up something from the Scottish Police.' Justin was hesitant, but clearly wanted to make a final point. He had declined first time round.

The two or three of the staff who had stood up, sat again. They all turned to look at Justin. David said 'Go on'.

'It's odd, but the Strathclyde Police found the body ten days ago of a late middle-aged black man who was washed up near Oban. They've not been able to identify him, but from the photos I have seen, even after maybe a day or two in the water, he looks a little like the images we have of Doctor Tebie. Oban, of course, is on the opposite side of the Firth of Lorn to Mull where Green found Tebie's wallet.' He didn't need to add anything else; that was enough to whet David's appetite.

'Stop.' A direct command from David to Justin. There was a pause. His team waiting for David to speak. 'If Tebie died in West Scotland what does that mean for the investigation?' David comment was put out to the whole team. Silence followed. His staff deep in thought.

Justin spoke again. 'What if Tebie brought his Ebola expertise over here? Moreover, what if he brought Ebola over here? Is he the terrorist?' It was a wild, mad statement, but exactly what David was thinking.

There was a further pause. Everyone taking in Justin's comment.

'Brilliant, but completely implausible; there is nothing to suggest that this is anywhere near to being a possibility.' David words didn't match the tone of his voice. It was considered, not desultory. 'Justin - and Susan - one or both of you get to Scotland and see if you can positively identify the body. Fifty percent probability will do. At the same time put together three possible threat scenarios with believable modus operandi using everything we have. Everyone else, don't be distracted by this avenue - keep a completely open mind and see what else we can come up with. We'll meet again same time tomorrow unless we get anything new.' David took a deep breath. 'And Justin...well done.'

HQ IMATT Leicester Square, Freetown, Sierra Leone

Bomber was sat on his usual chair round the rectangular conference table in the IMATT headquarters. The boss, Colonel Simon Peacock, was running through the day's business. All the main staff officers were present.

'G2 - what do we have on the intelligence front?' The colonel looked across at the captain responsible for intelligence updates in country and the state of the intelligence effort from the Sierra Leonean National Army.

'Pretty quiet, Sir.' The captain offered. 'I'm running through the IPB process for their UN deployment to Sudan with my opposite number in the Army Headquarters this afternoon. They seem to have a grip of the ground and the likely terrorist threats. Actually I'm really impressed with how the Major there has grasped the process.'

'Anything else?' Colonel Simon was obviously keen to move on, Bomber thought.

'Yes, something a little odd. There are reports from G2 in the Brigade in Kenema that there was a firefight at Border Crossing Delta Five last night. There was no police nor Army presence as usual, but they picked it up from a source they have, probably linked to someone who was at the crossing. It seems a car charged the crossing point which was being occupied by local hoods.' The captain, always keen to impress, Bomber noticed, was happy with that bit of the report but he wasn't finished.

Colonel Simon had begun to speak, but was stopped by the ambition of the young man.

'The odd thing was, the source reported that the passenger of the car, a battered blue Merc, was a young white female. The driver was a black man. The report has the woman firing a handgun, wounding one of the hoods at the checkpoint and disabling a lorry. Apparently the rest of the men took cover for fear of being shot. The source reckons she was a pro.' The captain was beaming now. Some real intelligence to report.

The Colonel deliberated for a few seconds, obviously unsure as to how his peaceful nation building post had developed overnight into the Wild West.

'Thanks for that. Erm, get a full report from the Brigade Commander and let me know if there is any action that needs to be taken.' Yeah, keep it at arms' length, Bomber thought.

But he also connected to a conversation he'd had with the local Brigade Commander about Sergeant Green. *Young woman, good shot, capable of looking after herself entering from Liberia. Could be a match.*

He needed to make a phone call. Fast.

Hotel Washington, Tubmanburg, Liberia

Jane had got to Tubmanburg as quickly as she could. The Embassy driver had turned up at her hotel at six o'clock as agreed and they had made it up country in a couple of hours. She had no idea what she was hoping to achieve and she was uncomfortable that her boss had put her under pressure to find some lead in the next twenty-four hours.

Her job was to run agents, to develop and use known local sources to follow leads, and to mix in communications and email intercept from agencies like GCHQ. She did all that so that she could piece together threats and make recommendations.

She was starting from nothing in Liberia. This was an American ex-colony with agents and contacts being either US citizens or locals run by the Americans. The CIA would have a handle on most things. By comparison, whilst she didn't know the scale of the UK's influence in Sierra Leone, she imagined she felt like a CIA field agent would feel if dropped off in Freetown and told to establish a network of contacts within twenty-four hours. They wouldn't be happy.

She had zip. And the Embassy had nothing. They relied totally on their American neighbours for all intelligence, not that they needed anything in particular. From that base and with no US involvement she had absolutely no chance of identifying any contacts in the next couple of days. She had made this clear to David Jennings when they had spoken this morning.

It was worse than that. She didn't want to admit it, but she hadn't a clue as to what to do next, other than perhaps follow in Middleton's footsteps calling at the bar and then the police station. What she had tried to impress upon David was that if she popped round to the US Embassy she would probably unearth a good number of leads which she could then prioritise and ask for further help on. Whilst she got his point about potential involvement of US staff with Middleton and Green, they had to trust each other. *Surely*? There would be good reasons why Middleton may have been targeted and they could only establish what those were if they spoke to the Americans.

It didn't make much sense to her. None at all. But she would do as she was told. For now.

She threw her suitcase on her bed, checked her day bag to make sure she had everything, and headed down to the hotel lobby.

As she took her last step off the staircase she looked down and attempted to brush at a mark on her light green slacks. A few steps later she was caught totally unawares by a welcome from the area to the left in the lobby.

'Hi, Jane. It's good to see you here at The Washington.'

She stopped in her tracks looking up and left whilst the cogs in her brain span out of control. The greeting was slow, white, Southern American; probably Texan. As she processed the words she took in the scene. Two men, one of whom she recognised instantly; white, crew cut, sharply dressed but casually so. It was Kurt Manning. Her opposite number at Langley. The second, stood next to Kurt, was a stocky black man. Equally well dressed, but suitably so for the climate. He was sporting a small bandage across his left ear. There was bruising around his eye, but it was difficult to see against his dark skin.

If she saw them across a crowded room she would assume they were high ranking businessmen, or a pair running a top-rate security company - or a couple of spies. They were, she knew, the latter.

'Kurt. Well, fancy seeing you here?' Jane was thinking fast. 'How did you manage to escape your desk?' They were shaking hands now. Kurt was completely at ease, she thought. *He's not surprised to see me at all. Is this a set up?*

'Just here tidying a few things up. Liberia, as you know, is one of mine.' Kurt checked himself and half turned to his colleague. 'Sorry, how rude of me. Can I please introduce one of our Embassy staff - Ralph Bell.'

Having already shaken Bell's hand Jane nodded and smiled. 'Hello, Ralph. Jane. London.' When among folk of her kind she always added the final word. It required no amplification.

'I heard you were on your way up here, so I thought I'd look you up.' More confident smiles from Kurt.

Jane felt completely on the back foot now. *How did he know she was here?* She'd only arrived yesterday afternoon on a trip pulled together at the eleventh hour. How did the CIA have any idea she was on her way? And how did they know she was coming up to Tubmanburg? Anyway, what was Kurt doing in Liberia? Ok, Liberia was part of his portfolio at Langley, but like her, he rarely travelled to the countries he was responsible for. *Unless there was a crisis.*

'Well, that's, ehh, surprising.' *Think quickly Jane.* 'But really nice. It's good to see you. And good to meet you too, Ralph.'

'Sure. Kurt has told me a lot about you,' was Ralph's response.

God. I'm under scrutiny; they have a file on me. Both of them are so cool. Measured. It's two against one. What now?

'Well, how reassuring.' Jane was trying to regain her composure. These two were, that is, *should be,* her friends. Her allies. But instead she felt quietly threatened. She had to grab the conversation back onto ground of her choosing. She had to appear strong. She turned directly to Kurt. 'There must be some big draw to bring you to Tubmanburg, Kurt. Is it 1415?'

Kurt laughed. 'Well, straight to the point. You Limeys are always the same. No, not exactly. There are a number of things on my desk that are West African based, so I thought I'd start here. What about you? I guess you're here on business? Is it the Middleton affair? Messy that, don't you think?' The American was smiling obsequiously.

Jane was ahead of Kurt now. 'Yes. We weren't concerned when he was originally arrested - we were confident the UN or the Embassy would clear him and get him out.' she quickly looked left and right to ensure they didn't have unwelcome company. 'But as soon as he was sprung from jail and disappeared my boss thought it might be sensible to get first hand intelligence. I was on the next plane out of London'. It was a story that could be easily unpicked. Henry Middleton only disappeared yesterday morning. No matter who you were, getting on a flight hours later was a neat trick. Even for MI6.

But that didn't seem to bother the two Americans. They either knew it was a lie, or hadn't yet done the maths. Kurt moved on. 'Yes, good choice. We'd have probably done the same.' Jane was unsure If the Kurt was humouring her. 'It's a mystery. The whole affair. We should probably go somewhere more discreet to talk all this through. Gather our resources. Are you free now?'

Jane's mind raced over everything she had on the case. *Hang on. Are these the two American operatives mentioned in Green's SMS? Surely not. Not these two.* What should she do? There was potentially huge mileage having a meeting with the in-country CIA, but it would be against her boss' strict instructions. That is if she shared anything sensitive with them. And what was Kurt doing in Tubmanburg? She had to find out. The alternative was chasing shadows for the next twenty-four hours.

'Yes, of course. Why not?'

'That's great; bless you Jane.' Kurt was nodding. 'We have an office a couple of blocks away. Can we give you a lift?' Kurt smiled, and it made Jane's stomach tighten, but against the feeling of uncertainty growing in her belly, she nodded and responded.

'Lead the way.'

Chapter Fifteen

David's phone rang. He looked at the screen. It was Mike Hazlewood's mobile who, hopefully, had something from Porton Down.

'Hi, Mike, what have you got - do you need to get to a secure line?' David was hungry for something tangible to add to the paltry information he had so far on the biological threat.

'Hi, Sir. No, I should be able to paraphrase this and have a full report to you by secure email within a couple of hours.' There was an audible breath from Mike. 'The people here believe that it is possible to disseminate E,' he used an abbreviated form of Ebola which he knew David would recognise, 'in some type of aerosol form, although they haven't and wouldn't aim to replicate that at Porton. They reckon if you spent some time and effort biologically engineering it, it should be possible to suspend it in a very fine vapour and for it to survive in that form for up to twenty minutes.'

David interrupted. 'But as far as they are aware it's never been achieved?'

'Not that they know of, no - it's a dangerous science. They did add that to actually infect people you would either need a huge amount of the suspension, maybe forty or fifty litres of the stuff, or put it out in a small confined space. A small office, say, with air conditioning would be a suitable target.'

Not St Paul's Cathedral then, David thought. Although just saying that you've infected the area would be enough to send everyone into a frenzy. 'How much do the scientists think you'll need for a small space, let's say my office?'

'They gave me an example of the office they worked in, which is more like the size of our conference room. They reckoned ten litres of the suspension into the air conditioning or heating vents would be enough to contaminate the whole space for just under half an hour. They reckoned that everyone in the room would be contaminated. Provided they decided to keep breathing in that time.' A touch of humour from Mike, David acknowledged to himself, with a difficult subject.

David thought out loud, 'So I guess if you fill the space up with more people, then more people would get contaminated.' It was a statement not a question.

Mike came back, 'Yes sir, that's correct.'

'Did you talk to them about the likely target?' David was keen to try and establish the plausibility of attacking St Paul's.

'Not in so many words, sir, no. But they thought that if you wanted to contaminate as many people as possible you'd go for a small space with lots of folk. Although they acknowledge that an attack on a large public space would have the same significant terror effect, albeit with only a few casualties. Maybe none if the space were big enough.'

'Thanks Mike.' David was keen to move on. 'I look forward to your report. Make sure it includes what the boffins believe the equipment might look like to make this happen. We need to know what we're looking for. And, well done.'

The line went dead. His report to the COBR Chief of Staff had been dispatched, but he'd now update it with this info. He reminded himself of his earlier conversation with his opposite number in the States. It was odd that he didn't know at first hand if it was possible to effectively vaporise Ebola. Well at least he had something on him now.

The St Paul's connection didn't make a great deal of sense if you were after spreading the disease to as many people as possible, although from an Islamic Extremist perspective it was a fabulous target.

He was now waiting for his team to report back from Strathclyde with information on whether or not the body the police had found was Doctor Tebie's. And then it was a question of how much Jane could find out by digging around in Tubmanburg.

He glanced down at his desk calendar. It was the Twenty-Third of November. The scant intelligence pointed to an attack on the First of December. Just one week therefore before an almighty terror hits the streets of London and sends the whole nation into a xenophobic whirl. After the attack on the Charlie Hebdo offices and the resultant banner of *Je Suis Charlie* he wondered what the aftermath of an attack on the main Christian icon in London would deliver by way of a catchphrase.

Whatever, they were running out of time to prevent it from happening.

CIA Operations House, St Petersville Street, Tubmanburg, Liberia

It had taken them ten minutes to drive from the hotel to the CIA house in downtown Tubmanburg. They'd not discussed business at all in the car, but exchanged pleasantries about the equatorial weather and the state of the Liberian economy. Jane had spent the time working out all of the possible permutations as to how and why Kurt had known about her arrival in Liberia. She surmised that things in the American camp were not all under control if they were watching their borders closely and keen to meet up with her and compare notes.

As she sat in the back of the car she also had the chance to look at the mess on Ralph's face. She noticed that under a six o'clock shadow he appeared to have some black stitches around his cheek bone which had quite a bruise on it. When he spoke she now recognised a slight slur as though his tongue was too big. He'd obviously been in the wars, but she knew not to ask him. If she did, he'd give some stock, almost humorous answer like 'slipped on the soap in the shower.'

In the house Kurt showed them to a small but comfortable lounging area with a coffee table and four leather office chairs. Jane quickly took in her surroundings. It looked as though the house had a fairly narrow frontage, but was quite deep. She only saw the front end of the first floor. There was a security area with CCTV cameras being pored over by, what looked like, a youngish black local lad. There was a couple of smart offices and then a corridor leading to a set of stairs. The lounge was halfway along on the left. There were no windows.

Kurt poured them all coffee without asking if they wanted one.

'So Jane, what else do you have for us?' Kurt was reaching inside his gilet for a notebook.

She knew her boundaries. Middleton was fair game. Green was off the agenda.

'Nothing that I haven't already told you. He's a UN man, not one of ours. We did ask him to keep us updated on what he found out about 1415 and any other developments.' She took a sip of her coffee. What she was about to say was a slight disclosure, but it might lead to something. 'We knew that he was due to meet a Liberian who had contacted him once he arrived in Monrovia. He found the contact dead in a bar, we asked him to press the local police for the name of the man and the next thing we know he's been arrested.' She stopped at that point. She forced her lips together, opened her eyes wide and looked directly at Kurt hoping for a response.

'So why didn't you let us know you had a man in country? We might have been able to help.' Kurt's tone was non-threatening.

'It all happened so quickly. He was here on UN business, we managed to make contact with him and before you know it it was all a bit out of control.' She gave an honest answer. 'But what do you know? Any idea who Middleton's contact was?'

Kurt laughed now and sat back in his chair. Jane noticed that Ralph was ignoring his coffee and drinking some Diet Pepsi. *God,* she thought, *His face is a real mess.*

'We knew about Middleton and his trip to Tubmanburg. We are still waiting for an answer from the local police as to who the now dead contact was. Apparently the Deputy, who was running the station in the absence of the Chief, has disappeared. Did you know that?'

'No, wow. I didn't.' Jane put on her best surprised face, raising her hand to her mouth. *Come on fellas, give me something I don't know.*

'We have no idea how Middleton managed to get out of jail, nor where he is now. He's clearly a resourceful character, which is a bit of a surprise from a UN staff officer. Are you sure you haven't got an SAS team in country who have whisked him away from under everyone's noses?' Kurt was smiling now, but it was a hard, edgy smile of someone who was under a bit of pressure.

'Not that anyone's telling me, I'm afraid. In any case, if we had I'm sure the CIA would have been aware of it. After all you managed to clock me coming into Liberian airspace. And as a member of MI6 I am almost invisible.' Jane was mocking them now. They clearly had no idea where Middleton was, which gave her some sense of relief. But it also worried the hell out of her for his and Sam Green's safety.

She looked at Kurt and then briefly across at battered Ralph; *could these two be the pair that had taken Middleton from jail and that Green had managed to rescue him from? Did Sam Green make a mess of Ralph's face? If so, good girl...*

She took a risk. 'I did hear that Middleton may have been released from jail by a couple of Americans. Did you hear that?'

The was a momentary silence, but discernible enough for Jane to know that Kurt was thinking on his feet.

'Really? I'm sure we'd have known about that. Where did you get that from?'

'Just something I picked up at the Embassy. We're not completely reliant on the US for all our Intel.' She had the upper hand now and was enjoying it. She looked across at Ralph who was very gently touching his bruised chin, possibly picking at a scab.

'Well that's *very* interesting. We'll get that checked out right away.' Kurt reached for his cup, but just before he took a sip, 'Can we give you a lift back to the hotel?'

My presence here is no longer welcome, Jane thought.

'Yes please Kurt, that would be nice.'

After the incident at the border crossing point the remainder of the journey to Kenema had been uneventful. Uncle had driven carefully and it didn't take long for them to emerge from the jungle and find a half decent road. As the sun started to show signs of rising they had stopped on the side of the road in a clearing where it looked like someone had started to prepare the secondary jungle for felling. Uncle had pulled the Merc some distance off the road so passing traffic would not see them unless they were looking really hard. And they had all slept.

Henry had woken first. He looked at his watch. It was ten thirty. The sun was partially covered by menacing rain clouds. He got out of the car and wandered around for a bit. Last night's events had come back to him vividly and he found himself looking around the outside of the blue car for signs of gunshot. Sure enough there was a bullet-sized hole in the rear off-side door, the one he had just got out of. He looked inside and there was an ugly slice of brown plastic ripped from the inside of the door and another hole, with burn marks round its edge, in the back seat. Henry stood up and put both of his hands on his head. *Bugger* he thought. That bullet went right through where I had been sitting before bravery got the better of me and I dove into the footwell. His brain continued the evaluation. If I had stayed in the seat it would have passed straight through my groin.

He let out a long sigh and felt himself squeezing his knees together and bending at the hips slightly. It had been quite an experience and, he guessed, without Sam he would probably have been at the mercy of the traffickers just now.

The other two woke a short while later and in broad daylight they drove to Kenema, passing through small hamlets of wooden shacks with straw roofs, children playing in the sun with a half blown up football or a couple of sticks. Some men were working on the side of the road breaking rocks for aggregate and the women were washing clothes in rusty tubs, or cooking over an open fire.

Kenema was much like Tubmanburg. Ramshackle on the outskirts, old and broken in a colonial style at its centre. Sam told Uncle to take them to the fifth best hotel in town, an approach, Henry thought, to make any pursuers work harder to find them. Traffic in the town was busy, but not overwhelming, and smartly dressed policemen tried to direct traffic with shiny whistles and white gloves. Not that anyone paid much attention to their efforts.

Henry had been to Kenema before when he had worked for the UN Mission and it seemed that little had changed. The people certainly seemed happy from a distance - most people were all smiles. The colours and sounds providing a backdrop of liveliness and joy in spite of such poverty and the threat of disease. It was, in that regard, different to Liberia.

What had changed and what did surprise him were the number of men dressed in Army fatigues wandering about the town. One or two carried rifles. A couple gave them a long hard stare.

The hotel was basic, but comfortable. They had both said farewell to Uncle after he had dropped them off and Henry had slipped him another twenty dollars, which warranted a big smile. They took two single rooms signing in as Mr Jones and Mrs Smith (Sam had been insistent on changing names) and still without much conversation had made their way to their rooms. Henry was finishing washing his face when there was a knock at the door.

'Who is it?'

'It's Sam. Can I come in?'

'Yes of course.' Henry finished drying his face and reached for his shirt.

Sam came in, still carrying her daysack. Henry's first thought was *where's the gun*?

He followed that theme. 'You know that one of the bullets that hit the car last night flew very close to my groin. If I hadn't moved I'd be missing some important parts of my anatomy right now.'

Sam smiled, a broad smile that lit up her face. She had a very open and welcoming face, Henry thought.

'You did a clever thing ducking down like that. That's what you're trained to do. The terrorists aim at the glass, not at the doors. So you're less likely to get shot if you do that.' She smiled again. 'They're rounds by the way.'

'What?' Sam was always crystal clear. This is the first time she'd said something that didn't make sense.

'They're rounds, not bullets. We don't use the word bullet. That's for cowboys and Miami Vice.' She was still smiling and moved across to the window, pulled back the curtain and looked up and down the street. 'What do we do now?'

Henry knew that Sam wasn't expecting a coherent answer from him, but he guessed was asking him so that he felt involved.

'I don't know. How do you think we should find what happened to Tebie? How his body and wallet became divorced by almost three thousand miles?'

Sam turned away from the window.

'In a second, Henry.' Sam paused, her hand reaching up and fiddling with her ear. 'Let's talk first about routine from here on in. Then we'll talk about what to do next.'

Right, Henry thought. I'm now waiting for my orders.

'First we only stay in the hotel for a night. We move on every day. And whenever we leave the hotel we take everything with us.' Sam stopped. Henry looked at her. She appeared to want acknowledgement.

'Yes, I get that.' Henry replied.

'For brevity, say *Ack*. It's short for acknowledge. It can be a question and an answer. You never know we might need to use it sometime.' Sam looked for somewhere to sit and found a small wooden chair beside the main door.

'Ack.' Henry replied. It seemed an unnecessary lesson, but she had been right about everything so far.

'We do not speak to police nor to anyone in uniform. We use different names in hotels and in conversation. And if we're in a crowded space call me anything obviously British, but don't use my real name. I shall call you James as that's what I thought you probably were when we first met. Well, when I saw you being dragged across the compound by those American thugs.'

'James? Where did you get that from?' Henry didn't know if it was a compliment or not.

'It just seemed appropriate. You did look like an Englishman, what with your linen and cotton clothes and the foppish hair.' She was smiling again. Unnerving smile, Henry thought.

'Typical,' he said.

'And, back onto people in uniform. We run scared of all of them. I'm not sure if Liberia and Sierra Leone talk to each other between police forces but I'm certain the little gunfight last night has made it round the houses down here.' Sam's smile had gone; she was still holding her daysack to her stomach. When she was like that, Henry thought, she looked forlorn and vulnerable. If only people knew.

'Is your stomach all right?' Henry felt the first tinge of masculine responsibility for Sam. Up until now he had been hiding it well away from danger. It was a mixed emotion, something that confused him. He felt tender towards her, but at the same time in awe of her abilities.

'Yes it's fine, just a bit sore. Old war wound.' Patting her daysack, Sam smiled again.

She continued. 'So we should go to the local press, the odd bar and maybe a taxi rank and ask about Tebie. We must try and work out if the funeral was for real and see if he lived round here. Whether he has got any relatives. His picture showed a wife and a teenage child. If they're still alive they're likely to be around here somewhere.'

'But wasn't the funeral held in Freetown?' Henry sensed they may be looking in the wrong place.

'Yes, but this was his home town and he worked in the local hospital. We will check there if we get nothing from our casual conversations - people in hospitals wear uniform. Not good. If nothing comes of any of this in say a couple of days then we'll head for Freetown, but I do think the trail will have gone cold down there. Here's where the action is.'

Henry visibly flinched at that word. 'Let's hope not.' He said almost under his breath.

HQ IMATT, Leicester Square, Freetown, Sierra Leone

'Brigadier Lester?' Bomber asked into the handset of his office phone.

'Yes, is that you, Major Brown?' Brigadier Sembe replied.

'Yes, sir. I've just heard the report from your G2 about the border incident last night. I guess you are aware?'

'Yes, of course. We often get skirmishes on the illegal crossing points, but last night was different in that one of those involved appears to have been a white girl.' The Brigadier reaffirmed what Bomber had heard at the central briefing about an hour ago.

'Is there any intelligence to suggest that the girl in question was Sergeant Green?' Bomber asked.

'As you know, Major Brown, we have a number of white women working in and around Kenema. NGOs, running orphanages and similar. But I have never come across a white woman involved in any illegal cross border activity. From where I'm sitting it appears too much of a coincidence to be a coincidence. I would say that Sergeant Green was in the car last night and from what I've heard, she's a very good shot indeed. It seems one of the traffickers needed a slug taken out of his pelvis at the

141

local hospital this morning. He was lucky to survive with his manhood.' Bomber could sense the enjoyment in the Brigadier's tone.

'Can your boys pick her up. I don't mean actually grab her, but identify where she is staying, get some idea of her movements and report back?'

'They're onto that. You'll understand that they're just soldiers, not policemen nor CID. As such they are a blunt weapon, but they will do their best.' The Brigadier had his matter-of-fact tone back now.

'That's great, sir. Is there any chance that the traffickers will be after revenge?'

'It seems unlikely. They're local boys, a couple of whom we know. We'll get the word out that they're to leave well alone. They've certainly learnt a lesson.' The Brigadier laughed out loud now. He obviously found amusement in a little white girl giving some local boys a lesson in tactics and weapon handling. Bomber had real sympathy with that.

'That's great Brigadier. Thanks very much. I look forward to hearing from you.'

Bomber put down the phone. Well, how about that. A medically discharged ex-Intelligence Corps sergeant giving the local hoods the run around. Well done her.

He had to do something with this. He'd call Colonel Tim in Aldershot and brief him with what they had. Tim could have something to add to the whole business. And that might further help the Brigadier's boys in Kenema. Yes, he'd do that as soon as possible.

Chapter Sixteen

David looked at his watch. It was three thirty. He was expecting a surprisingly short-notice meeting called by his old friend Colonel Tim Brand in half an hour. They'd not met since the start of the Sam Green affair. Tim had information on Green that he wanted to pass across. David already knew that Green and Middleton were together in Liberia and he wondered if he should let Tim know that they were monitoring Linda Ross' phone. It was currently their only lead as to what was going on in West Africa. However, he'd see how the meeting went. It could be in everyone's interest to share their current sources.

His phone rang. It was Justin Twell. Hopefully something helpful from Scotland.

'David here, Justin. How's it going?' He noted that the line was not secure.

'Good sir. I need to talk securely. I'm still in Strathclyde police station. We can chat using the web link; I'm at a police computer now if you're ready.'

David rested the receiver between his ear and shoulder before reaching for his laptop's mouse to open up the application. 'Go ahead. I'm on.' He put the phone down and watched the cursor blink across the screen.

Body is definitely Tebie's. I spoke to British High Commission in Freetown. No secrets passed, but one of the staff had known Tebie. We were able to get basic height and weight. Importantly BHC told me Tebie broke his left arm last year in a fall. Checked body here. Left arm definitely broken in the same place. Pathologist confirms break is recent.

Well that's something, David thought. Justin had stopped typing, waiting for a prompt from him.

David typed: *Anything else?*

The cursor moved again.

BHC chap knew Tebie reasonably well. Apparently he converted to Islam about the same time as his fall. No banging of drums, but a very clear statement which made the press in Freetown. I pushed on anything else we might need to know. It may or may not be significant but his son needed major surgery. He's got liver or kidney failure (the chap couldn't be specific) and Tebie had been round the houses asking for donations to send his kid to America for the operation. The chap thinks the son went about a couple of months ago. But, again, couldn't be sure.

The cursor hovered. David typed: *And?*

It moved again. *Nothing sir, will both be back in London this evening.*

Good. Get everything you have on Tebie and his son's operation. See you tomorrow. David pressed the 'return' button and sat back in his chair.

'Mmmm,' David voiced out loud. There were all sorts of possible scenarios which arose from Tebie's conversion, his son's illness and not to mention how, why and where Tebie died. He reached for his summary sheet of A4 but his train of thought was broken by a knock on his door. It was Deborah, his PA.

'Hi, sir. I've got Colonel Tim Brand for you now. He's a little early. Are you happy to see him?'

'Yes, please. Could you get us some tea?' David stood up and walked across to the door as Deborah beckoned Tim into the office.

They shook hands and exchanged hellos. David graciously pointed to the corner of his conference table and motioned for Tim to take a seat.

'It's good to see you Tim. I don't normally take visitors into the office - it's such a kerfuffle getting people through the vetting and security. But I'm glad you could make it.'

'Thanks David. I was in a bit of a rush and I thought we'd be better doing this face-to-face. You only had this slot available so I took it. Actually the security was straight forward, but I guess they make it look that way?' Tim took a notebook from his jacket pocket. He didn't have anything else with him. His briefcase and phone would have been taken from him on arrival.

'I think for you military types it's simple enough, although to be frank I had to put a special case forward to make this happen quickly. You've not visited before and there are a number of background checks we have to do, even for you Pongos.'

They both laughed at David's slang description of members of the Army.

'What do you have?' David was keen to press on - he needed to think through the latest on the erstwhile Doctor Tebie.

Tim cleared his throat with a slight cough, hiding his slight embarrassment.

144

'I am sorry that I haven't passed on this information up until now but I can tell you that Sergeant Green has made her way to Liberia...'

David stopped Tim by putting up his right hand.

'I think I'm ahead of you. We have been able to follow Green.' David decided not to share his source. 'We know she's in Liberia.'

Just then Deborah came into the office with a tray of tea. Both men went silent. She placed it on the conference table. Tim offered a polite 'thank you' and she left as efficiently as she had entered.

There was a further pause as David reached for the teapot and raised it, the motion asking Tim if he wanted a cup. Tim nodded.

'We have been able to keep tabs on her from a distance. Not as closely as we would have liked, but we do have a reliable but not a real time source.' He was pouring milk now.

Tim reached for his cup. 'But has your source told you that she's now in Sierra Leone?' He took a sip, looking at David and judging his reaction. David had stopped in mid-motion. A spoonful of sugar poised over his cup. He finished the job and stirred his tea.

'No we didn't know that. Not yet anyway.' He put his spoon down on his saucer. 'How do you know this?' David was all focus now.

'Well, I'm afraid to say that I've known about Green's trip to Liberia for a while. She confided in an Army colleague who shared that confidence with me.'

'Linda Ross?' David wanted to move things along and at this point was prepared to share his source. Tim might have other avenues which he could exploit.

Tim sat back in his chair. He initially looked surprised but then smiled. 'I should have known you were onto Green via any method possible. I guess your people picked up the SMS between Ross and Green referring to the UN man Middleton? Which, I have to say, went right over my head.'

'Yes we did. We intercepted that yesterday I think. The days are all a bit of a blur at the moment. I had hoped that if Ross passed that onto you as Green asked, you'd have phoned me straight away?' David's tone was slightly chiding. He didn't enjoy the idea that other government professionals might be withholding important intelligence from him unnecessarily.

'Yes, I was going to. But...'

'But what?' David was pushing now.

'Well the reason I didn't share any of this in the first instance was because I was trying to protect Green. She was one of mine, as you know,

145

and after the Mull incident I didn't know who to trust.' Tim gave a small shrug with his shoulders.

David was straight in. 'Why come to me now?' A pause for effect. 'If you don't trust me...'

'Oh come on David, it's not a question of trusting you. It's just...never mind. I'm here now. And there's more.' It was Tim's turn to sound inpatient. 'I contacted an old pal in IMATT, the British Army's Sierra Leonean training team. The long and the short of it is he's had pretty clear intelligence that Green crossed the border last night. There is no indication if the UN man is with her or not.'

'How certain is your pal?'

'The source is the SLA, the Sierra Leonean Army. There was an incident on an illegal border crossing point involving a young white woman in a car. The direction was Liberia to Sierra Leone. The SLA think that the woman was almost certainly Green.' Tim paused.

'There are a lot of white women in Sierra Leone, Tim. And if the sources are SLA, we'd have to question their reliability.' David was much more conciliatory now, but still fascinated by where this might be going.

'There was a firefight. The girl shot a trafficker whilst driving through the checkpoint at speed. That doesn't sound like your everyday nun or orphanage worker.' Tim reached to finish his tea, looking over his cup as he did.

David sat back in his chair and thought for a second. 'And do they have 'eyes on' at the moment?'

'They're trying to, according to my friend in Freetown. He phoned me within minutes of a conversation he'd had with the local Brigade Commander. As soon as he has any more he'll come straight back to me.'

David's mind was now in a spin. *Firefight?* Bloody hell. He stood up and walked across to the window. His usual stance for when he needed a bit of space to think. *What should he get Jane to do now? Tubmanburg or Kenema?* He made up his mind.

'That's great Tim and really helpful. I have one of my staff in Liberia at the moment. I will share this with her and get her across the border. Somehow. We should arrange for her to meet up with the SLA top man, the Brigadier? And they can work together. Green, and let's assume she has Middleton with her, is onto something, something which might help us with an emerging but pretty imminent threat here in the UK. Pooling and directing resources seems key.' He looked across at Tim who was following every word.

David continued. 'Can you speak to your contact in IMATT and let him know what we're up to. In many ways it would be ideal if I could deal with your man directly. Are you happy with that?' David stepped back towards the conference table. He was taking things forward now; he could see an opportunity and he needed to act

'One thing.' Tim said. 'Green could have lost her life in Mull. And she could have lost her life last night. I've already made the point that she's one of mine.' Tim let that sink in. 'I want to be involved in this too, and if necessary, veto anything that might endanger Green. Can we do that?'

David was sat down again. He lent forward. He needed to be as blunt as possible. 'Green might be on the cusp of helping us cull a threat that could be catastrophic, both for those who would be immediately at risk, but also for the repercussions of the event. She is, I'm afraid, one life against hundreds, maybe even thousands.'

David stopped briefly, thinking again. 'Why don't you take a space in my office for a couple of days, no more than about a week. You can run your pal in IMATT from here and attend all of the threat briefings. I'd need to clear this and we'd have to make security arrangements, but would that work for you?' David was speaking before he actually thought through the consequences of his words. But he would make it happen.

'That would work for me David, thanks. I'll have to let my boss know and get my deputy to step up, but the next ten days or so look fairly quiet in my calendar.'

'That might not be the case here...' was David's response.

Ericson Lodge Hotel, Kenema, Sierra Leone

Sam and Henry shared a pot of tea in the simple lounge of the hotel. They were both shattered. Having settled into the Lodge they had decided that they'd spend the day doing some admin round town. They both needed a new set of clothes, Henry had no toiletries to his name, but what they both required more than anything was a good rest - an afternoon free of drama.

The heat of the day, the aftermath of the rescue and then the shock of the firefight at the crossing point had reduced Henry to the point of exhaustion. Sam had wanted to press on during the afternoon and start asking around after Doctor Tebie. Henry had put his foot down. After some discussion they agreed that they needed to regroup - to rest. An afternoon of 'admin' (he was getting accustomed to the vernacular) and then back to the hotel for a cup of tea.

'We'll start in earnest tomorrow Sam. I'll be full of beans by then.' Henry was struggling to keep his eyes open.

'That's fine Henry. I understand.' Sam was still holding her daysack to her stomach. 'What shall we do about dinner?'

'I'm ok thanks. I'll eat the fruit we bought at the market and some of those crackers. What about you?'

Sam smiled, her head on one side. 'I'll be fine.' She sipped her tea. 'Remember we book out tomorrow. We'll book into that hotel on the corner by the mobile phone hut, do you remember the one?'

Henry nodded, but didn't really register the question. Tiredness was a big bear on his shoulder who was about to take a swipe at his senses. He needed to sleep. If it had been left up to him they would stay put at the Lodge, but if he really thought about it, constantly moving made sense. He was so glad that he wasn't leading this particular mission.

'I'm sorry Sam, but I've got to go up to my room and get my head down. See you tomorrow?'

Sam was on her feet. She offered Henry her hand and he took it. Between them he managed to stand and tentatively he walked off towards the stairs, feebly waving at her as he did so.

Hotel Washington, Tubmanburg, Liberia

Jane came out of the rusty, reasonably ineffective hotel shower and reached for her towel. She knew as soon as she was dry she would be wet again with perspiration. This was down to a combination of the evening heat in Tubmanburg, but also because of her recent instructions from David Jennings.

He'd told her that Green and probably Middleton were now in Sierra Leone possibly heading for Kenema. She was to arrange with the Embassy to get to a border crossing point which was deemed the safest to cross and to let London know when and where that would happen. Through their contacts they would instruct the SLA to meet her at the border and take her onto Kenema. She would then work with the SLA to track down Green and Middleton and find out what they were up to. Her job was now to try and establish why Tebie's body was in Scotland when he was apparently buried in Freetown. She was briefed on Tebie's conversion to Islam and his son's illness. This, according to David, might be key to what was going on.

David had taken the fact that she had met with Kurt and Ralph reasonably well. The phone had only gone silent for a short while. She had repeatedly assured him that she gave nothing untoward away, but was reasonably confident that Kurt and Ralph were the two Americans who had taken Middleton from jail.

David had been silent for a good while longer at that point and Jane had to check that he was still on the other end of the phone.

'No further contact with them. Understood?' His direction was, as always, clear. This time though, his tone was uncompromising. And that was that.

Having spoken to the Embassy she was now waiting for a call back from the Ambassador to arrange for a trip to the apparently closed border. His staff had told her he was not available for about an hour but would call back at eight o'clock. It was now a couple of minutes to eight. This, she thought, was going to be a very interesting conversation.

Chapter Seventeen

Approaching Illegal Crossing Point, Liberian/Sierra Leonean Border

Well this is something else, Jane thought. Here I am in the dead of night, sat in the back seat of the Ambassador's Range Rover with the Ambassador beside me, his driver at the wheel, being driven to a closed border crossing point to be handed over to the Sierra Leonean Army. She felt like a prisoner in a Cold War exchange.

She had to hand it to David Jennings. When he wanted something to happen, no matter how off-the-wall, it happened. The Ambassador had phoned her exactly at eight o'clock and told her that he had already spoken to 'Jennings' - *no love lost there then* - and was preparing to drive her to the border himself. He said he first had to clear his lines with the Foreign Secretary (*Foreign Secretary - wow, we're not messing about here*) as what he was about to do was unconventional and a risk to 'the Service' as he called it. But as such if there was going to be an issue at the crossing he wanted to be there himself. If any diplomatic weight needed to be thrown about, it couldn't get much bigger. *Well, not in Liberia anyway.* She had added the final thought herself.

He said it would take them about three hours to get to Tubmanburg. According to the Ambassador, David had used his contacts in Sierra Leone to get the SLA to meet them at the border where Jane would be handed over safely. 'I'm expecting a cash reward in exchange!' was his final remark before he put the phone down. *Very droll.*

Jane had used the three hours to sort out her life and think through where they were with this case. She had access via an encoded link to much of the briefing material that was being passed around the team back home, albeit on a small Samsung screen. What she couldn't fathom was why Kurt and his pal might want to hijack Middleton from jail and apparently, deal with him in such a way that he needed rescuing by Green? Moreover why was Kurt involved in torching Green's camper in Mull?

And what on earth was Green doing in having recent contact with Kurt anyway? If she were Green there wouldn't be a barge pole big enough to keep them apart.

It was all linked to Report 1415 and according to David also linked to the emerging but now very present threat to London. The key to this was Tebie. Perhaps Green knew that? Perhaps she was well ahead of them all? She'd really like to meet this girl.

It was pitch black outside. She'd never been to West Africa before, but had served in some remote places and wasn't surprised at the darkness of the jungle. The driver was doing well with the big heap of Range Rover and she and the Ambassador sat in supreme air conditioned comfort, enveloped by the soft leather seats. This was the way to travel.

A pair of headlights flashed ahead of them.

'It's the agreed sign,' the Ambassador said. 'Flashing headlights. They also said they'd phone me if there was an issue, but there's no coverage here. So let's keep our fingers crossed.' The Ambassador's a cool dude, Jane thought. 'Slow down and flash your lights please Smith.' Direct instructions to his driver.

Smith did exactly as he was told. The lights ahead of them kept flashing.

'Drive on.'

The Range Rover drove gently on until, in their headlights, Jane could make out an olive green Army Land Rover with three soldiers stood around it. The Range Rover pulled up. Smith dropped the lights.

'Let's go.' The Ambassador said as he opened up his own door and got out into the still of the night.

Jane checked her bag and did the same. She made her way round to the front of the vehicle and was met by a tall man in Army fatigues. She noticed he was wearing the rank of Major. The two other soldiers remained by the side of the vehicle. They both had slung rifles. The officer looked like he was sporting a pistol belt.

The Ambassador greeted the Major by extending his hand. 'Good evening, I'm Clive Mason.'

Jane was impressed that he didn't use his own position and status. The car, of course, made its own statement.

'Good evening Sir. I am Major Donald Emphettie. Brigadier Sembe sends his regards. I am his representative here tonight.' He looked across to Jane and offered his hand. 'Good evening Ma'am. You must be Miss Baker?'

Major Emphettie, whose smile filled his face, had the whitest teeth Jane had ever seen. Even in the dark they shone like a lighthouse. 'Yes Major, I am. I'm very pleased to meet you and delighted that you are here.'

'Good. Well we shouldn't spend too long here. Our Police know that we are in the vicinity, but I do not know what the Liberians would make

151

of such an exchange.' Major Emphettie turned back to the Ambassador. 'Thank you for bringing Miss Baker to Sierra Leone Sir.'

The two men shook hands again. Jane lifted hers and waved at the Ambassador which, she thought, probably wasn't the right protocol for saying cheerio to Her Majesty's Representative. But, hey, this was the middle of the jungle. In the pitch black.

Jane followed the Major who took the driver's seat of the Land Rover whilst one of his men opened the passenger door and let her in. The two soldiers then got into the back, an open space covered in a green tarpaulin, by jumping over the tailgate. Jane saw the Range Rover's lights twist left, then swung right as it disappeared back into Liberia. They did the same, but headed off into her second new country in three days.

Sierra Leone. Blood diamond country.

MI6 Headquarters, Vauxhall, London

David had his team gathered again for the eight o'clock briefing. He had stepped the briefings up a gear. The focus of the meeting wasn't to share new information, all staff had to file a report by six o'clock in the morning which everyone had to read and digest before they met at eight o'clock. The aim was to issue direction for the forthcoming twenty-four hours. In times of a major threat this was the way he ran the show.

David looked up from his tablet and across at his team. In a day or so they may have to meet every twelve hours, he thought. Assuming that his hunch was right. If it wasn't, he had them chasing shadows when they were possibly missing other threats.

They had all been briefed why Colonel Tim had joined the group and this morning, for the first time, he had the Metropolitan Police Liaison Officer at the meeting. He was an extremely experienced Sergeant from the counter terrorism branch, SO15. With the threat now solely focused on London (David really hoped he was right with that assumption) having him along at this point was a no-brainer.

'Morning everyone. I hope some of you have had some sleep?' David knew that many were surviving on very little. Getting that balance right, especially among the younger members of his team, was always tricky. Work required effort. Effort needed feeding, both in terms of food, but also sleep and exercise. He was ruthless with those who spent every moment of every day in the office. Indeed he had recently sacked a member of his staff for not being able to get that right.

'You all know about Colonel Tim's role in the current scenario.' David pointed across the table to Tim, who nodded and put up his hand by way of saying 'hi'. 'And welcome back to Trevor from the Met. We always know when things are getting complicated because Trevor turns up. Welcome Trevor.' Trevor made a half gesture of standing and bowing to the team. Everyone smiled.

'So, you've all read Justin's Scottish report. And Mike's from Porton Down. What's that you've got there Mike?' David pointed at, what looked like, a garden weed killer spray that Mike had placed rather proudly on the table in front of him.

'I got this from B&Q on the way back from Porton yesterday. It's a garden spray thingamajig. You put your liquid in here,' Mike was standing now and pointing to various bits of the apparatus, 'and pump on this pump here,' which he was now doing by way of demonstration, 'and press this lever here on the spraying arm...'

Vapour in a fine spray came out of the nozzle at the end of the long arm and, because Mike was pointing away from the conference table, it shot out across David's office floor and onto his rather nice leather sofa.

'Enough!' David protested. Mike stopped spraying and smiled. 'We get the point, I think. And this is how a terrorist might atomise and distribute Ebola in droplet form?'

'That's right Sir, yes. It seems primitive, but the boffins at Porton reckon that this would work if you could develop Ebola that survived in a suspension. But you'd have to keep it in refrigerated conditions whilst you carried it to the target. They were clear that out of refrigeration Ebola would last no more than twenty minutes, half an hour tops. And once in the air a maximum of twenty minutes more.' Mike was looking very pleased with himself. One member of the team was brushing vapour from their shoulders which had managed to drift gently across the room.

'So we're looking for a man with one or two of those contraptions which are either cooled themselves, which would be quite a big pack, or leaving a vehicle with a decent cooler on board? It would have to be a short distance away' David asked.

'That's about right Sir.'

Trevor from the Met was making notes.

'Can I take a photo of that please?' Trevor's accent a thick London drawl.

'Yes of course,' said Mike offering the contraption down the table.

'Later Trevor,' said David moving things along. 'Justin. Good work in Glasgow. Anything else to add to your report?'

'No sir. I've got a call arranged with my Freetown contact in about an hour. I will press him for more on Tebie. There's nothing from any source we have exploited on why Tebie should have converted to Islam last year. And without contacting the Americans I can get nothing on his son's illness nor operation, assuming that he has travelled there. Our Embassy in Washington is looking into it, but don't hold out much hope' Justin looked across at Susan, who had accompanied him to Scotland, for reassurance. She nodded.

'Well we remain shtum with our US colleagues at the moment. Anything on the web?'

Susan took over at this point. 'No sir. Nothing. Tebie was a very respectable Doctor, a leader in the field against West African diseases. There isn't anything anywhere that seems to suggest otherwise. His conversion to Islam gets a small paragraph in the 'Awareness Times', the main Freetown broadsheet, but nothing else. He seems to have been of exemplary character.'

'Thanks Susan.' Before I sum up, anything else from around the table?'

'Sir.' It was Jonathan Clements their GCHQ rep. 'We have another intercept between two cells, one here in London, one now in Sierra Leone. It came through just now. The doughnut has traced the receiving call to the northwest of Sierra Leone, possibly Kenema.'

The doughnut was the colloquial title for GCHQ, named because the relatively new build was circular in shape with a round open space in the middle. 'Go on Jonathan' David encouraged him.

'The call in London was from Trafalgar Square, so we are discounting its location as relevant. There's nothing really to pick out of the text that we could add as intelligence with regard to target or delivery method, just two men asking how each other are doing. But the boys think the exchange of the expression 'are you ready' and the reply 'yes, set as asked' amongst banter seemed to be odd and out of place in the general run of the conversation.' Throughout Jonathan used his hands to amplify his words.

'Thanks Jonathan. Interesting that the intercept is now Sierra Leone based, not Liberia?' David asked. Although his brain was racing around the prospect that the terrorist cell in London was ready for operation now.

'That's right, sir, yes.' Jonathan placed his hands on the table. He was finished now.

There was silence for a while. David looked round his team and then spoke.

'Jane is now in Sierra Leone. Her aim is to track down and question Middleton and Green. You've seen my report.' He stopped for a second.

'Justin and Susan press on with Tebie and get what you can. Let's work on two West African men, both Muslims or recent Islamic converts, in the UK to effect the biological threat. One is now dead. One is alive and well and operating in London. Trevor. Get your usual team together, use Sophie as well. Let's see if we can trace Tebie and A N Other entering the UK by air. We know they can't have come in direct from Freetown as there are no flights, so check all flights from Charleroi. But extend that to all flights from Washington and New York.' David waited again.

'Why the States, David?' Trevor was a police sergeant; he rarely called people sir.

'Because I remain convinced that our colleagues across the Pond have something to do with this and routing Tebie via the States would make both administrative and security sense. We have less than a week, and if Jonathan's people are right they are set now. Mike, I want you to get back onto Porton and work together on at least two terrorist options for transporting and vaporising Ebola into a large space. Let's assume the cell is based in, say, Wimbledon. What would their MO be? Equipment, transport, timings, use of air ducts. I'll release Steve and Ginny from the Afghan cell to help out. Let's get a complete rundown on how St Paul's heats and cools itself and then I want to see how the three of you would make it happen. Let's bring this to life.' He paused again, looking down on the notes on his tablet.

He looked up. 'Come on. What are you waiting for?'

Kenema High Street, Sierra Leone

It had been another frustrating day. Sam and Henry had now visited every bar, cafe and taxi rank (not that there were that many) and, apart from a number of locals who had known of and respected Doctor Tebie, they had no new leads. Kenema was busy, despite the continuing Ebola crisis, although new cases, according to the people they had spoken to, were down to a handful a week.

Henry had taken the lead on interviewing. He had a natural way with people. He didn't approach them like a journalist, searching for a story or a lead. He was much more gentle, genuinely interested in them and their lives. Sam first thought it was a cynical ploy by Henry to make those he spoke open up and reveal the information they needed. But it soon became clear to her that he had a natural love of people, for their lives, their troubles and their joys. Initially Sam was impatient as he seemed to take forever to get to the nub of the questions they have agreed to ask. But the beauty of Henry's approach was that when they'd finished chatting, each person didn't feel as though they had been robbed of information and so they seemed to give more. Many wanted to carry on chatting and those that could afford it often offered them a drink.

She looked at Henry now. He was talking to the latest bartender. They were both laughing about something and then the bartender put his hand on Henry's shoulder. Henry was in full flow. Sam was beside him, disengaged from the conversation, but she but could feel the warmth generated by the two men.

She had a lot of time for Henry. He was easy company; easy to open up to. He wasn't Chris, nor was he like any of the Army types she was used to. Her previous experience was of competitive men, men who would face down a problem rather than run away from it. They certainly wouldn't have cowered in the footwell of a speeding Mercedes when the only woman on the team was taking in gunfire and returning it. Her men were alpha males; metaphorically fighting dragons and dropping their cloaks on puddles to protect their maiden's new shoes. She had grown to love and admire these men, and many of the women too.

Sam was staring into space. She found herself thinking about the one man she'd really loved - Chris. God, how she missed him. He was an action man, but a quiet one. Strong, but not gregarious. He was often clumsy in company, especially with small talk. But she had seen him give instructions to a group of soldiers, many like herself, and his words were clear, lucid and inspirational. When they had been out together they had kept themselves to themselves, him preferring to have time alone rather than share their precious free time with others. She missed all of that. And it hurt to know she'd never get him back.

Henry was laughing out loud. A genuine guffaw of a man who had heard the funniest joke ever told. The barman was sniggering, one hand on his mouth the other on a bottle of beer. Henry turned to her, smiled and winked. It was a knowing wink of a man who had unlocked the crown jewels. The conversation calmed a little. She tuned in.

'So Danny, you're an old friend of the good Doctor Tebie?' Henry raised his bottle of beer to his mouth. Sam noticed he hadn't drank any of it; the bottle was still three-quarters full. *You sly old fox, Henry!*

156

'Yes, James, man. I know de family. Mrs Doctor live here in Kenema. She very upset.' The barman was more sober now and used Henry's pseudonym which Henry'd slipped into easily. A natural actor, Sam thought.

'And you tell me you know where they live? I'd love to meet the lady. I have the greatest respect for Doctor Tebie's work and would like to pay my compliments to her if I could.' Henry took another un-swig of beer.

'Dat no problem. We could go and see her 'morrow?' The bartender was Henry's best friend now.

'Perfect Danny. Just perfect.' Henry was touching the bartender's shoulder. They were both being tactile Sam noticed. 'Where shall we meet you?'

'Come here 'morrow James. We'll go and see her 'morrow.'

'And you will have spoken to her by then?' Henry was just checking they weren't on a wild goose chase.

'Sure t'ing James. Sure t'ing.' The barman offered his hand for Henry to shake. They completed the deal with a Caribbean handshake and Henry turned to Sam and gave the broadest of smiles.

'Before we go Danny, could I have your mobile number in case we need to change our plans?'

Danny reached for a beer mat and scribbled down a long number and handed it to Henry. They shook hands again.

Henry turned to Sam and smiled. Sam stayed on her barstool taking in the warmth of Henry's smile, returning it with affection.

'Time to go you smoothie...' Taking hold of her daysack she reached for the bartender's hand and shook it.

Maybe it hadn't been such a bad day after all.

But that thought evaporated as soon as they walked out of the bar. The light was fading, but it wasn't so dark that Sam missed the Army Land Rover parked across the street. The two soldiers in the vehicle were paying particular interest in the pair of them.

Sam steered Henry left down the street heading back to the centre of town. After a few paces she dropped to one knee, pretending to retie a shoelace. Henry carried on walking for a bit, but stopped when he realised he was on his own.

Sam glanced back over her knee, the two soldiers were getting out of the car. Both had rifles slung over their shoulders. They were moving in their direction. One, surprisingly, seemed to be carrying a camera.

Shit she thought.

She stood up and walked briskly towards Henry and put her arm through his.

'Don't look back; we're being followed. Two Sierra Leonean soldiers.' she whispered.

Henry started to turn his head, but Sam barked at him under her breath, 'Stop it. I said don't look back.' His head shot forward and he pulled her arm to his. 'Do exactly as I do and do as I say. We can lose these two goons.'

She picked up the pace and without looking back turned sharply left between two shacks, one had an old woman out front selling vegetables.

She ran now, dropping her arm from Henry's but taking his hand. They wove left and right through mud streets and narrow alleys pushing past laundry, chickens and some small children. After a couple of minutes they were out onto another road, this one less populated but still bordered with shacks and houses.

Sam immediately turned right down the street. She ran for about twenty metres and then turned back into the area of housing they had just left, dragging Henry behind her. She was sure she heard him wheezing. After a couple of minutes of zigzagging and without looking back to see if they were being followed, they split out onto the same road they had started from but about fifty metres down from the bar, Sam stopped briefly, picked out the Land Rover and, still with Henry's hand, headed away from it. After another a minute she pulled Henry into another alleyway and held him still. He was huffing and puffing.

'I must get into training....' he managed to say.

'Stay there.' Again, another direct order.

She poked her head around the corner of the building and looked back to where the Land Rover was parked. There were maybe ten or twelve people idling up and down the pavement, a couple of cars in the street and in the distance she could just pick out the Land Rover. She watched it for a couple of minutes.

Eventually the two soldiers returned to their vehicle. She couldn't make out any details, but she was certain that they both got in. A few seconds later it drove off away from where she stood.

Chapter Eighteen

In a taxi, Outskirts of Kenema, Sierra Leone

Henry had had trouble sleeping. It was another warm night and the replay of their chase through the tight packed alleys of Kenema regurgitated through his mind. When he met Sam first thing she was as bright as a daisy. *Typical* he thought.

They ate a slow breakfast, packed and booked out of the hotel.

Under instructions from Sam, Henry had phoned Ralph the bartender and changed their rendezvous. If the Army had followed them to the bar last night they might be there waiting for them again. Sam had ummed and ahhed about whether to stay in their original hotel the previous evening. It had taken a lot of checking out of the window for them to feel reasonably certain that they had given the soldiers the slip. They had, however, booked out of the Ericson Lodge and would find somewhere else to put their head down for tonight. It was all Sam's lead - she made it all seem so straightforward.

Ralph had hailed one of the few taxis in Kenema and he had taken the front seat and given the address to the driver. He turned round with his arm on top of the seat, smiling.

'A good day today. Mrs Tebie nice lady. She wasn't in when I phoned last night, but she will be so pleased to see you. I know!' His voice was full of excitement. He was obviously happy to be of service to the pair of them.

The taxi didn't take long to reach the outskirts of the town. Just as the town ran out, they took a left into a side street. A short drive later they stopped outside of a low walled compound with rusting metal gates. Behind the gates Henry could make out a single storey house against a backdrop of secondary jungle.

Ralph insisted on paying the taxi driver the few Leones it had cost to make the journey and without any ceremony he pushed the latch on the metal gates and let them in.

Henry wasn't great at observing detail, he was much more of an atmosphere man, and just inside the metal gate he immediately became uncomfortable. He couldn't put his finger on why, it just didn't feel right. The house was a bungalow with a roof that needed some repair. Round the outside was a covered terrace that had seen better days. The whole place felt dark, almost unloved. The neighbouring high trees hung heavy branches over the property as though they and the building were one. If there was someone at home, they didn't seem to want visitors.

All three of them stood in the yard, not quite knowing who would make the next move. He could see Sam taking it all in, he guessed working distances and escape routes, looking for, as he had learnt from her, 'the absence of the normal'. It didn't feel very normal. Henry thought they were about to invade someone's very private place, a dark space signposted 'leave me alone'. Even Ralph, who, up until a moment ago, was all smiles, now looked tentative, almost shy.

'Come on,' Sam said. 'Let's do this.'

She led the way. Henry followed. Ralph now a couple of paces back. She made light work of the four steps up onto the terrace and approached the front door. Henry stood slightly behind her. She hesitated.

'This doesn't feel right,' Sam said, almost in hushed tones as if she were talking to herself. 'The place is dark. There's no light or life from the windows. The curtains are either closed or partly closed. Everything is shut. It's like no one's at home.'

She knocked at the door. It opened slowly until it was half ajar. Henry sensed Sam take a metaphorical step back.

'Mrs Tebie? Are you at home Mrs Tebie?' Sam had raised her voice. The noise of birds and insects from the trees wasn't so loud that Sam's voice wouldn't be heard inside.

There was no answer. Sam knocked again, using the door frame this time to generate more noise. A dull but loud knock. 'Mrs Tebie! Are you in?' Sam again, this time louder still.

Nothing. The darkness, and now Henry felt the dampness too, exaggerated the quiet. He thought he heard the buzzing of insects inside.

Sam pushed open the door fully. As she did some paper caught on the bottom. They both looked in. There were papers and files all over the entrance hall floor and one or two books too.

'I don't like this Sam. We shouldn't be here.' Henry had felt his heart rate pick up when he saw the mess on the floor. He was no longer looking for the absence of normal. He felt he was being engulfed by the presence of the abnormal. 'We should go.'

Sam didn't answer. Instead she tentatively stepped into the house, on tiptoes avoiding the paper where she could. Henry hesitated and followed gingerly. He sensed Ralph a couple of steps behind him. Sam had turned immediately left into what Henry thought might be the sitting room.

160

There was mess everywhere. Henry had never been burgled, but he had watched enough TV to know when someone has been through your stuff looking for valuables. The furniture was tipped over, its contents strewn everywhere. Pictures were smashed and glass lay all over the floor. A sofa was upturned, its innards spewing out through rips in the fabric.

'What a mess.' Henry whispered. His unease was overtaken by the scale of the devastation. He tried to make his way across the room but to do so meant he would have to stand on something that ordinarily would be off the floor.

Sam was already ahead of him into the next room. He glanced over his shoulder and saw Ralph stood in the doorway shaking his head. He thought he saw tears welling up in his eyes.

'Ralph?' It was Sam from the next room. Hollow, lifeless.

'Yes, Miss Sissie.' A quiet reply, using Sam's alias.

'When was the last time you spoke to Mrs Tebie?' Henry could hear Sam rustling through paper next door. He had stood still whilst she had moved on, out of sight.

'Maybe week ago? I came here for tea. She teaches piano and I have lessons with her. She very good teacher.'

'And she gave no indication she was leaving anytime soon?' Sam asked.

'No, Miss.'

There was further rustling from next door, but it seemed to be more distant. Sam had obviously moved into another room.

Henry walked and talked at the same time, 'Come on Sam. We're in enough trouble as it is. We don't want to get caught here with this mess. Who knows what crime may be pinned on us.' In his head he was quickly recounting the bar in Tubmanburg, the dead contact and then the oppressive jail.

Again there was no response. He was in, what he assumed was, the dining room. The mess was the same everywhere. In the corner an upright piano lay on its side.

'Oh my God….' Sam's words from the next room. Her voice quiet, but raised a couple of tones. 'Henry, I need you here.'

Henry immediately sensed the distress in Sam's voice and ignoring the detritus he moved quickly into the next room which turned out to be the kitchen. Sam was in the far corner stood by a stove. She was looking down. Henry couldn't see what she was looking at because of the packets of food and other kitchen equipment which were strewn about the floor. But he guessed what to expect.

He moved to her side in a couple of strides and held her shoulders tight; she gave no response. In the corner, partially hidden by an upturned cupboard was the body of an elderly black woman. She was sat, slumped down, her head on one side with a stain of dark red blood on the side of her cheek. Her eyes were open staring into space. Henry let go of Sam and instinctively bent down so that he was level with the woman's face. It was then he saw the deep purple wound running horizontally across her neck, a ribbon of old blood dripped dry against her skin. Her throat cut from one side to the other.

Henry couldn't stop himself. He retched. Thankfully he turned at the same time, the vomit spewing onto the floor next to the woman. His eyes flickered as he looked at the contents of his stomach. He had missed her legs. *Thank God for small mercies* he thought.

He was just beginning to take stock when he heard a piercing cry from behind him. It wasn't Sam; he felt her standing motionless beside him. Henry turned at the same time as Sam dropped down, bumping into each other as they did. He was trying to stand up and work out where the noise had come from. She was bending down at the same time reaching for something about her waist. Neither of them toppled, but it was a faintly comic moment when the tension couldn't be higher.

The screaming continued.

Henry was first to register that the noise came from Ralph who, unexpectedly, had caught up with them in the kitchen. He had one hand to his mouth; the other was pointing in the direction of the corpse. He was still screaming, his body shaking, tears streaming down his cheeks.

Sam spoke first. Henry looked down to where the words were coming from. Sam was expertly crouched with the gun in both hands pointing at Ralph. 'Shut up Ralph, shut up!' Her voice hardly heard over Ralph's screams. The noise was intolerable.

Henry stepped forward and with reasonable force and a flat hand slapped Ralph across the face. There was immediate silence. The shock on Ralph's face was the same intensity as the fear and grief he had shown just before. He tried to say something but nothing came out. He turned and ran.

Henry shook his head. He hadn't struck anyone since he was involved in a stupid teenage fight back in the playground of his public school. He raised the weapon to eye level and stared at his hand.

'Look at this, Henry.' Sam interrupted his train of thought.

Still looking incredulously at his hand he turned to her.

'Look. Look at the scratchings on the wall.' Sam was cool as a cucumber, Henry thought. I am as agitated as a bright red pepper.

'What? What!' He was struggling to take it all in.

'Look at the scratching on the wall. Mrs Tebie has written something into the plaster, scratched with her fingernails.' She was inspecting the woman's left hand.

'What? Come on Sam. We need to go. Now!' He was insistent. Frightened *and* insistent.

'Wait. She has scribed A W as clear as anything. I wonder what that means?'

'Who cares what it means? We need, no, no, we *must* get out of here. Ralph will have gone to the police. They could be here in minutes.' At that point he was tempted to leave even if she wouldn't come.

Where would he go?

'Go back into the living room. See if you can find anything among the breakages that gives us a clue to the letters AW.' She looked across at him. 'Do it now. I'll take the dining room and then the rest of the house.' She smiled, that smile again. 'We don't have long.'

You don't say Henry thought. He was close to losing his temper, but did exactly what he was told to do. And very soon, just perhaps seconds later, he was on task moving quickly from pile to pile. He had to find something. Now. Otherwise he knew he'd experience another jail.

After what seemed like a lifetime, but was probably now more than a couple of minutes, he came across a relatively new photograph. It was one of those staff photos. A group of men and women posing in a line, commemorating an end of year or similar. The photo had names underneath. Seven of them. He spotted Doctor Tebie's name straight away and registered him on the photo. Standing to Tebie's right was a woman. Standing to his left was a shorter man. The corresponding name was Doctor Arthur Wesley. AW. That had got to be it. He could make out both men clearly from the photo. That *was* it. He had found the connection, or at least a connection.

'Sam!' He shouted and looked up at the same time.

'What?' The reply was quiet. She was stood in the doorway they had come in through previously.

'Here.' He passed her the photo without explanation. There was a little bit of a test in his decision not to elucidate his thoughts about the connection.

Sam took it and within a second said 'Let's get out of here.' She flashed him an efficient smile. He started to move towards the front door. She darted back to the kitchen.

'What the f...' Henry stopped himself from swearing.

He was immediately lost for direction when he heard Sam shout, 'This way Henry. The police will use the front door.'

She was right. As soon as he changed direction he heard the sharp 'nee-naw' of police sirens getting louder from the direction of the street.

She was waiting at the open kitchen door.

'Come on fella.' Sam said. And as he passed her heading for the back wall he heard spoken quietly, 'And well done, Henry. Good work!' Then she was running after him.

With that compliment ringing in his ears he almost vaulted the brick wall in front of him with a single bound. He led the way into the trees with the sound of police sirens ringing in their ears behind them.

Outskirts of Kenema, Sierra Leone

Jane managed to get a couple of hours sleep in one of the barrack rooms of the SLA Brigade Headquarters. She'd ask Major Emphettie if someone could make sure she was awake at eight. Sure enough a young soldier popped his head around the door of the small room whilst she was getting dressed. Thankfully she was nearly fully clothed. The young man gave a casual salute, smiled and disappeared. She thought she had probably made his day.

The Major met her for breakfast in a small mess building where a couple of other officers were making the best of some cereal and strong coffee. They ate more slowly than Jane would have wanted and then made their way to the main headquarters. The Major's office sported a wooden plaque with gold letters spelling the words 'Chief of Staff'. Jane thought she understood the role and appreciated that the Brigade had sent one of their top men to look after her.

The first part of the morning was spent looking over possible sightings of Green and Middleton. It was a slow process. It started with the Major interviewing each of his soldiers individually. They were all lined up outside the office, with the Major asking them into his office one at a time. They came in, saluted and all of them reported that they had nothing to report. It seemed that after the sighting from outside the bar the previous night there was little else to go on. She took a break to give and get an update from London, but nothing that David Jennings had told her added much to where she found herself. After another coffee she pressed the Major on what he knew of Doctor Tebie. The Major was considered in his responses; not avoiding, just slow. Nothing of importance was forthcoming and so she asked if she could wander around the headquarters and quiz others. The Major nodded his agreement and off she went.

Her second interviewee was a much sharper young Captain who knew Tebie and most of his whole family. The Captain told Jane that Tebie's wife was still in Kenema (he knew her address) and he was certain that the son had travelled to the States over a month ago. He didn't know what the illness was, nor if there had been any treatment; and if there had been, whether it had been successful. Jane pressed him on Tebie's conversion to Islam. The Captain knew nothing of it but seemed mildly surprised that the Doctor had changed religions. 'I always saw him as a truly Christian man,' the Captain had remarked. Jane didn't press on whether or not the word was spelt with a capital C.

Jane thanked the Captain and was about to find her next victim when she stopped and thought for a second.

We should go and see Mrs Tebie now. And if I were Green that's where I'd be. She turned about and found the Captain still at his desk.

'Can you take me to see Mrs Tebie?' Jane asked.

The Captain thought for a second. 'Yes, of course. I will need to get clearance from the Chief of Staff.' He was already standing up.

A couple of minutes later they were all in the Chief of Staff's Land Rover. The Chief of Staff was driving, she was in the front passenger seat, and the very eager Captain (who Jane was warming to) was in the back with his head poking through between the front seats. He was giving very clear directions.

It took about fifteen minutes to drive to Mrs Tebie's house. It seemed the Brigade Headquarters was south of Kenema and the Tebie's lived to the north. It was the first chance Jane had to see Kenema in daylight. It felt different from Tubmanburg. Jane couldn't put her finger on it, but the place felt lighter, more welcoming.

But that feeling ended abruptly when they turned off the main drag and into the street where the Captain said Doctor Tebie's house was. They all knew immediately something wasn't right. Towards the end of the road three police cars with their lights flashing were parked haphazardly on one side of the road. There was an ambulance and around ten uniformed people stood around the cars. There was yellow and black 'Police Line Do Not Cross' tape everywhere.

All three of them remained silent. The Major pulled the Land Rover off to one side of the road just behind the first police car they came to. 'Stay here, please,' he ordered gently.

All Jane could do was watch. There were at least two scenarios she could think of: Tebie's wife was dead or injured; or the same fate had come to Green and Middleton. Neither of them bore thinking about in respect to taking the case forward.

The Major was talking earnestly with one of the policemen. Jane couldn't see his rank. Eventually the Major saluted the policeman, a compliment which wasn't returned, and got back in the Land Rover placing both hands on the wheel.

'Well?' Jane wanted answers. And she wanted them now.

'Mrs Tebie has been brutally murdered.' He paused gathering his thoughts. 'It seems that your two countrymen visited the house about two hours ago, maybe less. Apparently they came to the house to see Mrs Tebie and found her dead. The police know this because they were accompanied by a Keneman who brought them to the house. He left them in the house and went to find the police. When they returned your countrymen had gone. The place has been burgled but, according to the police, this had been done before the three arrived. What they are concerned about is why your people disappeared?' The Major had turned to look at Jane.

Jane shrugged. 'Beats me,' she said. She was thinking the same thing, and trying to work out what she was going to do now that one of the major leads had been murdered. And they still hadn't managed to track down Green and Middleton. Although at least now they knew that they were in Kenema. And were just behind them.

The Major was still staring at her. Jane thought he was probably waiting for further instructions. She was thinking fast.

'Are the police looking for the two English people?' Jane asked.

The Major was looking forward again. 'This isn't New York, Miss Baker. Most of the Kenema police are here at the scene. This is a high profile murder; they are rare here. The Chief will want to take things slowly, do things properly.' The Major used his hands pedantically to make the point.

'Was he the man you were speaking to?' Jane asked.

'Yes, Miss Baker. It was.'

166

'Do you think he'd let me have a look in the house?' Jane knew it was too much to ask, but she gave it a go.

'I think that's very unlikely Miss Baker, certainly for the moment. He wasn't keen on spending too much time talking to me. Our relations with the police have improved over the past few years, but there is still suspicion between both forces that originate from the civil war. I think you will need to work on another approach for today? We'll ask tomorrow and see if you can get access.' The Major looked dead pan, resolute.

I'm pretty confident that my Embassy can get me in there sooner than that Jane thought. She would speak to David, update him and get him to brief the High Commissioner. In the meantime they had to find Green and Middleton.

She thought for a second and then decided to try some honesty. She was taking a risk, but she needed to do something and do it fast. She took a deep breath.

'Major Emphettie. The UK faces a major terrorist threat that could impact upon the lives of thousands in and around London. However farfetched it seems there is a strong possibility that Doctor Tebie and maybe another man from Sierra Leone was involved in developing that threat.' She paused watching the Major's face. It had become sterner, even more intense. 'I will speak to my Embassy and see if I can get access to the house. I won't involve the SLA so there's no potential embarrassment of one force getting one over on another. In the meantime we need as many of your boys as possible out on the ground trying to find Green and Middleton. This time they should arrest them. But, under no circumstances, are they to be harmed.'

The Major took it all in. Slowly. He was solidly built, Jane thought; and dependable. But obviously didn't move quickly, both on his feet and intellectually. She needed him to sharpen up - move things along.

She nodded her head at him, hoping that it would expedite his decision making.

'Let's get back to the Headquarters. You call your Embassy, and me and Captain Sobeme,' he flicked his head gently backwards indicating that he meant the young officer in the back, 'will get as many troops on the ground as is possible and find your two countrymen.'

Jane was nodding furiously. Major Emphettie looked back at her, still a face of concentration and seriousness. 'Well, come on then, Major. The British and their best allies, the Sierra Leoneans, have a terrorist plot to thwart. It's in our hands.'

That gave the Major something to smile about. He turned the engine over and did a careful three point turn in the Land Rover. Jane looked over her shoulders at the young Captain. He grinned and raised his eyes to the canvas roof.

Somewhere on the outskirts of northern Kenema, Sierra Leone

'What do we do now?' Henry's question was more by way of conversation than inquiry.

They had run and walked what Sam thought was probably two kilometres. After Henry's initial lead into the forest Sam had asked him if he knew where he was heading. To which the answer was 'no'. So she had taken the lead, but she kept the pace steady. Henry was not fit. And her stomach was giving her some stick. They both needed to pace themselves.

She had a good sense of direction and knew they needed to head back into town, but not before they had put some distance between themselves and the police.

The jungle was thick, but passable, and only once did they meet impenetrable undergrowth which made them turn back and take a different route. Sam had spotted the odd spider's web and pointed it out to Henry so that he missed it. She could sense him flinching behind her. Her jungle training was short, but effective, and she understood what might hurt and what might not. The important thing was to avoid being scratched by thorns or anything else that might open a wound to infection.

They had reached a clearing beside a dirt track. In the distance across a field they could see dwellings. Further away she could pick out the centre of town.

'Let's stand here in the sun and dry our clothes.' She looked at Henry. They had had the sense yesterday in Kenema to get some lightweight clothes from the market; they were part European, part African style. His clothes were holding up well but from the waist downwards he was drenched, and he had sweat stains around his armpits; a combination of heat, wet undergrowth and working hard. She gave herself a look over as best she could. She was in a similar state.

'No, better still, there was a stream back in the jungle about thirty or forty metres? Let's go and rinse our clothes. Then we'll come back here into the sun and dry ourselves. We can't wander round town looking like this.' She was already moving.

'Wait, Sam, come on. What do you think we should do next? Surely we're no longer welcome in Kenema?' It wasn't an exasperated statement, it was more resigned, more a speed bump on the road of following Sam Green.

'Henry...' She stopped herself. That sounded patronising she thought. 'Look, I reckon our final destination is the British High Commission in Freetown where we give ourselves up. But before that we need a story to tell them that has an ending. I want to find out more about Doctor Arthur Wesley. Mrs Tebie was telling us something.'

She stopped and looked at Henry. He had his hands on his hips, his head to one side with a withered look on his face. 'I need to follow this through Henry, I really do. And I think you do too. There's something really unhealthy going on here and I am determined to get to the bottom of it.'

Henry was still looking directly at her, meeting her eye to eye. 'Even if it costs you your life?'

Sam dropped her head, avoiding his stare. She kicked at the dirt with her shoes.

'I have nearly died once and the man I intended to marry was killed at the same time. My mum is dead and my dad can't remember who I am. I have diagnosed Post Traumatic Stress Syndrome. When I can be bothered I have thought about ending it all. But just now, here with you, in this mad place being pursued by the CIA, the Liberian and Sierra Leonean police, I have found a really worthwhile distraction.' She was looking at him now. 'I can understand if you want to give it all up, I really can. But I can't. Not yet. Not now.' She smiled a half smile at him.

Henry thought for a moment. He smiled back.

'Well I don't know about you but I'm going to rinse my clothes.'

Chapter Nineteen

Headquarters MI6, Vauxhall, London

'David Jennings.' He didn't even look at the number on the display on his mobile. He was still trying to wade his way through the update to his COBR report. He had been summoned to attend a face-to-face briefing with the Chief-of-Staff later this afternoon.

A crackle and a short pause. A secure line.

'Hi David, it's Jane.'

'Hi Jane, what have you got?' He didn't look up from his keyboard and kept tapping away.

'Tebie's wife has been murdered. The SLP, sorry the Sierra Leone Police, are at the scene. Her house has been ransacked.'

A further crackle.

David stopped typing. 'Somebody is covering as much of the Tebie trail as possible, aren't they? Have you got access to the house?'

'No, not yet. We need to talk about that. But key here is that Green and Middleton were at the house before the SLP arrived.' The crackling continued.

'Any chance that they were involved with the murder?'

'No. Apparently the SLP were called by a local who had taken the two of them to the house. My view is that they're doing exactly what I'm trying to do, and that's establish why Tebie was reported to have been buried in Freetown whilst his body was discovered in Scotland.'

A pause.

'If Mrs Tebie can't speak then her house might. You need to get in there ASAP.' David was already thinking of ways he could help. 'Look, I'll get in touch with the High Commissioner now and tell him what I can. I'll ask him to get you into the house this afternoon. You need to find Green and Middleton.' David had already buzzed Deborah who came into the office. He put the handset onto his shoulder.

'Get me the High Commissioner in Freetown now, Deborah. No, make it a three-way conversation with the African lead in the FCO. Thanks.'

Deborah nodded and walked out.

'Sorry, Jane. Can you find Green and Middleton?'

Crackle. 'I have the whole of the local Brigade here in Kenema working for me now. I'll do my best.'

'And Jane...'

'Yes.'

'If Mrs Tebie is dead then you understand that you've got company?' David's tone was fatherly.

'Yes sir, got that. I need to find Green and Middleton before they do.'

'Indeed.' David agreed. 'I'll call you as soon as I've spoken to the Commissioner.'

Heading south into Kenema, Sierra Leone

Henry's mind couldn't work as fast as Sam's. His legs also struggled to keep up with hers. They were working their way through Kenema, using, where they could, side streets and alleyways, heading for the Kenema Government Hospital. They were following the only lead they had: Doctor Arthur Wesley worked there.

They had established that fact using Henry's mobile. Earlier, as they were stood in the clearing drying their damp clothes Sam had asked, 'Do you have your mobile with you?'

'Yes, of course.'

'Does it still work?' Henry could feel that Sam was coming up with a plan.

'Yes, I think so.' He reached into the side pocket of his trousers. He took it out of the plastic bag that Sam had given to him when they were in the taxi driver's house in Tubmanburg. 'To keep it dry,' she had said. She also told him to turn it off. 'They can track you...'

'Before I switch it on, are you sure you want me to do this? We might need it later and it won't have much battery left.' He was fastidious about battery life and always switched Apps off and turned down the screen brightness whenever he could.

'Yes. Search for Doctor Arthur Wesley and see what you come up with.'

They had spent about five minutes peering at the small screen on Henry's phone. 'This is going to cost the UN a fortune,' he'd said at one point.

The outcome was that there were plenty of good photos of Doctor Wesley and a recent paper on dealing effectively with Lassa Fever patients. The paper was signed off from Kenema Government Hospital. They had googled the hospital and found its location, about five kilometres away on the east side of the town. Sam had stared at the small electronic

171

map for about ten seconds, handed the phone back to Henry and said 'Let's go.'

Henry had no idea how far they had got. All he knew was that he was tired and so far they hadn't encountered any policemen or soldiers. Sam, who had constantly checked behind her to see if he was ok, put her hand up at one street corner. They both stopped. She peered round and gave a thumbs down to Henry. Another signal which he was beginning to understand.

She moved back beside him, looked slightly up so that their eyes met (at least I'm taller than you are, Henry thought) and then she flicked her head in the direction which they had just come from and said quietly, 'Follow me'.

They continued their weaving until, after what seemed like an hour, and now in the terrific heat of midday, Sam stopped at another corner and again put her hand up.

She beckoned Henry forward. They both looked. Just down the road was a blue and white signpost notifying everyone that this was Kenema Government Hospital. The hospital was bigger than the photos they had seen. What they hadn't shown were the large number of prefabricated buildings and tents that appear to have materialised since the photos were taken. *Must be catering for the Ebola epidemic* Henry thought.

'You ready?' Sam said.

Henry nodded. Without further encouragement they made their way across the road and walked into the main entrance of the hospital.

Henry knew what to expect when it came to third-world hospitals. Although he'd never been to this one, he had visited a couple in Sierra Leone and also in Bangladesh. There was a simple front desk manned by two nurses and corridors with peeling paint leading off left and right. Patients in all manner of dispositions stood, sat or lay about the place. The very sick mingling with family and carers. Gurneys laden with patients being fed by drips were haphazardly placed on any spare bit of floor. Wards here were a luxury; space clearly in great demand.

He saw Sam stop and take it all in. She didn't move. Henry decided to take the lead. He walked up to the front desk, the nurse on the left having become free after she'd directed someone down into the bowels of the hospital.

'Hello,' Henry said.

The nurse was a big woman, dressed smartly although a bit tightly into her light blue and white uniform.

'Yessir, how may I help you?' No smile from the lady. I'm going to have to use all of my charm here, Henry said to himself.

'I'm looking for Doctor Arthur Wesley. I understand that he works at the hospital?' Henry tried his best smile.

'No. Not no more. He left a couple of months ago. Sorry.' The nurse was already looking over Henry's shoulder for her next customer.

'I'm sorry too,' replied Henry. 'Is there someone here I can talk to about him? I work for the UN,' Henry was reaching into jacket pocket for his wallet to find his ID card out, 'and I really need to speak to someone about him.'

The nurse was just about to dismiss him again when a tall white man turned up beside her. 'Is there a problem?' His accent was northern European. Henry looked up at him. Late middle-aged, blond hair. Probably Scandinavian.

Henry didn't let the nurse start her explanation. He stood up.

'Hi. I'm Henry Middleton from the UN,' he had his ID card out now and was surprised he'd been clever enough to use his real name. Anything else and his ID would have been useless. 'I need to talk to someone about Doctor Arthur Wesley. It's very important. Oh, and this is my colleague Susan Price.' Henry introduced Sam.

The man offered his hand having visually taken them both in. With his free hand he took Henry's ID and gave it a quick glance.

'I'm Doctor Klas Urgsmund. I knew Wesley.' His face scrunched a little as though talking of Wesley was uncomfortable. 'I have a ten-minute break. Perhaps we could go to my office?'

Henry almost blurted out 'Yes, please,' and a few seconds later they were crammed into Doctor Urgsmund's very small office. Every spare piece of wall was bookshelves. In one corner of a desk covered in papers was a small upright flag: a yellow cross on a blue background.

As they sat down Henry said 'Swedish?'

The Doctor nodded. 'And missing it like nothing else. I fly home next week.'

Sam interrupted the congeniality. 'Sir, you've told us you don't have much time. We need to know about Doctor Wesley and, if you know of Doctor Tebie, that would be really helpful.'

Henry anticipated the Doctor's likely question and added, 'The UN are investigating the death of one of our staff in Liberia. We think there may be an Ebola linkage and as Doctor's Tebie and Wesley were so involved in the disease,' (he made the last bit up), 'here in Kenema, we thought we'd explore every avenue.' He glanced across to Sam. She gave a small nod as if to say 'I couldn't have put it better myself.'

There was no reply. The Doctor rose, turned and went to the small dirty window behind his desk. He spoke with his back to them.

'Wesley and Tebie were best of pals. I think they probably graduated together from a hospital in the UK. Tebie was the real Ebola expert; Wesley focused on less of the moment diseases like Lassa and latterly malaria. But it was Tebie who was the driving force; the real expert. He was invaluable to the hospital and with him gone our ability to fight the disease has dropped markedly. Although...' He paused for a second. 'The pair of them were often not here.' He turned back to face them. He looked at both of them in turn. He was tall, but just now, Henry thought, he looked shorter; hunched. Things were playing on his mind.

They waited for him to continue,

'Look. There was something untoward going on; something unethical. None of us could quite understand what was happening. Tebie and Wesley were often unaccounted for. They'd disappear for days at a time, sometimes on their own, sometimes together. Tebie was a God round here, so nobody pressed him on where he had gone to. Wesley less so, but he lived in Tebie's shadow and was untouchable.' He sat down. And continued.

'My understanding is that they were working in Liberia. There was rumour of a secret clinic somewhere over the border that was looking into pandemic African diseases. It made sense. Tebie would make huge leaps in countering the disease overnight. Infected blood would disappear, unaccounted for. A new pill or drip would suddenly materialise. There was no explanation.' He paused for a second, seemingly gathering his thoughts. 'And Wesley lived well, flashed money about a bit. He was that sort of man. Tebie didn't. It was common knowledge that he was saving up for his son to be flown to the States to receive a new kidney.' He stopped then, looking at them impassively.

Henry pressed him. 'And Tebie's death?'

The doctor leaned back in his chair and put his hands behind his head. He thought for a while. 'What the hell,' he said, 'I'm leaving in ten days. Tebie's death was mysterious. He was here one moment and dead the next. His wife reported that he succumbed suddenly to Ebola over one weekend.' He lifted his hands in the air to signify disbelief. 'The next thing we know his body was taken to Freetown for a national level funeral.'

'Why is that surprising?' It was Sam's turn now.

'Because I was with him on the Friday. And he looked well. You don't develop Ebola symptoms and die in forty-eight hours. It's not possible.' He looked over his shoulder back to the window as if looking for an escape. 'Anyway we were so busy we didn't have much time to discuss it. But it will always be a mystery to me.' The Doctor was facing forward now, both his hands back in front of him.

'And Wesley?' Henry's question.

Doctor Urgsmund scrunched his face up again. 'I'm sorry but I didn't like the man. He was an adequate doctor but there was something of a preacher about him. He was a Muslim. Not that I have anything against people who follow Islam.' The doctor quickly added. 'He preached in the local mosque and was always quietly bitter about those of us who were Christians. Sometimes it was a bit uncomfortable.' The doctor looked at his watch. He stood to leave.

'One last thing sir, if you don't mind. Where is Wesley now?' It was Sam again.

'It's funny that. He disappeared at about the same time that Tebie died. The hospital chief said he had been 'reassigned', but gave no details. I was delighted, but it has to be said that we lost two doctors in a short space of time when we could least afford to.' He had opened his door and was showing them out.

'And Tebie's conversion to Islam?' Henry asked.

The Doctor stopped and smiled, nodding his head. 'Doctor Tebie was a deeply religious man. I should say a deeply Christian man. His conversion to Islam was a sham. I tried to press him on it, but he wouldn't talk to me about it. It all occurred at about the same time that his son flew to the States.' He ushered them out. 'I can tell you that Doctor Tebie was a Christian till the last. No matter what they said about his conversion in the papers.'

Henry and Sam thanked him and walked back to Reception. Neither of them spoke. It seemed to Henry that they had a lot more information, but were no closer to solving the riddle.

Instinctively they exited the hospital together, side by side. It was getting dark. Henry turned to Sam to ask the obvious question 'what shall we do now' when a blur of action and movement saw Sam fall to the floor as if her legs had collapsed. Instinctively he started to drop down to her side, when out of the corner of his eye he saw a black and yellow object held in a man's fist. The sharp prick of the Taser's two metal spikes piercing his side was instantaneously overtaken by the surge of electricity that shot through the whole of his body. He didn't know if his brain gave way before his muscles collapsed on him. Either way he joined Sam on the floor unconscious.

Chapter Twenty

David needed some good news. He'd had a tough time with the Chief of Staff of COBR. He was there with the Deputy Commissioner of the Met and the Permanent Under Secretary to the Home Office. All he had for them was a strong hunch. He'd had nothing new from Jane other than the murder of Doctor Tebie's wife, which was interesting but hardly sharpened the intelligence he had. He'd phoned his oppo in Langley, the Deputy Director, and there was nothing new from him. There was some good news. Trevor from the Met had probably found Tebie disembarking a plane into Heathrow from Dulles, Washington in early November. But the film was grainy and the angle oblique so they couldn't be sure. There was no one on that flight named Tebie, nor anything about the manifest which might have given them a clue to the fact that it was him. In any case Tebie was dead. They needed to find the person who was in London communicating with someone in Sierra Leone. And, to cap an afternoon when nothing much happened, GCHQ had had no further intercepts that could help.

That wasn't altogether fair. Mike, with support from the boffins at Porton, had knocked up two computer generated 3-D models of gear that might be used to disseminate Ebola, including the necessary refrigeration. One could be carried by the assailant to the target from anywhere, the second required cooling in the boot of a car. The latter seemed to give the terrorist a smaller package to carry, but he would need to be driven to the target, or abandon the car somewhere close. Mike reckoned fifty metres (he was looking at likely car parks and dropping off points now close to St Paul's. If you knew what you were looking for, and they now presumed they did, you could probably spot a terrorist carrying the weapon no matter how hard they tried to disguise it. That was a positive.

The problem for the meeting was he didn't have anything concrete to give them. His line was that there was a 50-60% chance that a man, probably of West African origin, would try to disseminate Ebola in vapour form within the next four days (although the latest intelligence they had was that the cell or terrorist was ready now). The target was St Paul's Cathedral. His three colleagues had quizzed him, searching for more detail. But he had none. He had strung together a series of what could be unrelated leads, including, implausibly, some suspicion of US state level involvement. And he had come up with a clear and present danger that only seemed to make sense in his head. He had coerced a British UN staff member to spy for his country whilst on UN business, and into this was mixing the wanderings of a psychiatrically ill ex-Sergeant of the Intelligence Corps. Neither of whom they could track down.

The outcome of the meeting, which didn't surprise him, was the intelligence wasn't strong enough to close St Paul's to the public. The Met had twenty-four hour surveillance on the entrances to the building. They now had the blueprints of the possible weapon and had experts inside the Cathedral looking at air ducting and heating to see if they could spot anything untoward and try to establish an MO for polluting the building if they were the terrorist.

It was also agreed that there would be no public threat warning, nor would the COBR committee be called formally. Both of these, and the closure of St Paul's, would be under constant review in case either David or the Met came up with anything more substantial. David knew it was only his reputation and good relationship with the Deputy Commissioner that had enabled him to get the Met to sweep St Paul's and have the Cathedral under surveillance.

On his way out of the Cabinet Office he received a call from Deborah.

'Hi sir, I've just sent you a Reuters' newsflash. It'll be on your phone now. I took the liberty of asking around the office if anyone knew anything about it. The answer was no. I hope I caught you before you left the meeting?'

'Eh, no, Deborah. Not quite. I'll look at it now.'

With the dexterity of a teenager David closed the call and swept open his Inbox. He pressed on Deborah's email and read the text:

Reuters, 25 November, 18.15 GMT. A reliable intelligence source in the US has told our reporter that they are expecting an imminent Islamic based terror attack on a European capital in the next two or three days. The nature and scale of the threat was not specified, although the source did say that the likely weapon was new to the terrorist's arsenal and could deliver mass casualties.

'What the fuck are they playing at?' David swore through gritted teeth. He immediately pressed 'Forward' and found his Met and Home Office contacts' addresses who had left the meeting before him. He typed at the bottom. *Be aware. I will speak to Langley. Unsure as to what they're up to, or what this means.*

He pressed 'Send'.

He rode his bicycle hard over the Thames and by the time he got back into the office he was sweating a little. *Too much time sat on my soft backside, and not enough time in the gym*, he thought. He needed to sort that.

As he strode past Deborah he said, 'Get me the Deputy Director of the CIA on the phone now!'

He was almost past her when she replied, 'Will do. I have Jonathan Clements waiting. He needs to see you urgently.'

As he reached his desk he shouted back over his shoulder, 'Get him in now!'

He needn't have said anything as Jonathan had seen him coming into the building and was right on his heels. David turned round and was surprised to be faced by Jonathan. David looked him up and down. He looked a bit flustered.

'Go on Jonathan. What have you got?'

'The latest intercept from GCHQ. Same coding format, but they're still no clearer deciphering the whole lot.' He was talking quickly, almost tripping over his words.

'And?' David needed to move things along. He needed to know what Langley was up to.

'In among the stuff they couldn't, or more accurately, haven't yet been able to decipher, they picked up the key phrase *act tomorrow; expect results by evening.*' David stared at Jonathan not saying anything. He continued. 'What was significant is that the caller in Sierra Leone used the same mobile number they used two days ago. But they spoke to a different number in London. My interpretation of that is the lead from Sierra Leone is not within his usual environment. He would have dialled from a different number, use a different SIM to disguise his call. Up until now he has had access to multiple SIMs. The operator in London clearly has that.' Jonathan had slowed by the time he got to his analysis.

'So, let's get this straight', David was thinking, 'The lead in Sierra Leone isn't in the country by choice. He's had to move and has left his home base. He has few resources with him.' A further pause. 'It could be Kurt and Ralph, our two US men.' He couldn't call them CIA. He had no idea whether they worked for the US government or were rogue. 'They're in Sierra Leone, controlling the operation when they'd rather be in, say, Liberia?'

Jonathan was nodding. 'That's my view sir, yes.'

'Any idea where in Sierra Leone the call was made from.'

Jonathan, for some reason sheepishly, replied, 'We managed to narrow it down to four potential towers in, you won't be surprised, Kenema. It was a voice call only and the transcript was less than a minute long. The team didn't have much to go on but have produced a map. It's a fairly big area, maybe five blocks by five. I'm just about to email the map round the team.'

'Good work Jonathan. Make sure Jane gets a copy and she knows it's coming. Get all of this to the team with any further analysis ASAP. And press GCHQ harder.' He put a hand up to dismiss Jonathan.

'Deborah!' He bellowed. 'Get me the Deputy Director now. And arrange a meeting for later this afternoon with the boss.'

I think it's time for the two top men to have a chat about this. I don't think I'm going to get anywhere with the Deputy.

He unpacked his briefcase and waited for the call.

Southeast Kenema, Sierra Leone

It was dark. Sam was on her side, her mouth gagged and her feet and hands tied together. She didn't have a blindfold on, but it was too dark to matter. She knew Henry was behind her. They had grunted to each other. Her hands, which were behind her back could feel his shoulders. And she felt what she assumed were his fingers behind her knees. She couldn't imagine what position they were in. At any other time it would be comical.

Her stomach was agony. It was if though someone had stuck a blunt knife into her old wound and was moving it around. It took all her effort not to scream out through the gag. But when she closed her eyes she couldn't stop herself crying due to the pain.

Through the tears she thought *what a mess*. She guessed they were in the boot of someone's car; she smelt a rubber smell; a spare wheel? But they were stationary. She had no idea how long they had been still for. She knew they had been brought down by a Taser weapon of sorts, the buzz of electricity still percolating through her body in aftershock. She guessed that the Americans had caught up with them.

The assault had been over so quickly. Zap, pain, blackness and then she had come round after what felt like a reasonably short space of time. Although she couldn't be sure. She had tried to break from her bindings but the pain in her stomach which ground and ground away, sapped her strength. She soon realised that any attempt to get them undone was futile. They had been very efficiently kidnapped.

Another wave of pain swept through her. She almost retched.

There was the sound of footsteps and then some shuffling. The clunk of the boot being open followed. It was dark outside, but there was a little ambient light. She couldn't make out her assailant, but it was a man and he effortlessly lifted her onto his shoulders - *God that hurt* - and carried her into what seemed to be a two storey brick building. She gave no resistance. She couldn't. From what little she saw she didn't recognise it. They were somewhere new.

A switch was thrown and a strong white light from an overhead bulb lit up the room. As she was swung round she spotted two unmade beds, a couple of chairs and maybe a wardrobe. Oh and there was a sink. It was a bunk room of some sort.

The man threw her onto one of the beds, her back hitting the wall and arresting her movement instantly. Pain shot through her abdomen and, if anything, it got worse. She scrunched herself into a ball. *Please make this end*. Tears again.

She opened her eyes and looked up. It was the black man, Wayfarer. He was staring at her. *Yikes, his face is a mess*. He smiled at her and with a swiftness that caught her completely off guard he thumped her in the stomach.

'That's for this.' He was pointing at his face.

She couldn't cry out. The gag wouldn't let her. All she could do was bend double even tighter and try and protect herself from further assault. The tears were unstoppable. They flowed and flowed.

With her chin pressed to her chest and her knees now close to her mouth, she heard a muffled noise from across the room. She opened one eye and looked over. Henry was having a fit. He was on the other bed, his eyes wide and angry staring across in her direction. He was convulsing, his body moving but not going anywhere. Gagged shouting came from his mouth. She recognised the back of Kurt, Binos man, bending over Henry, holding him down. *He's trying to get to me. To help me?*

Henry's attempts didn't last long. Kurt pistol-whipped him across the face with the handgun he held. There was a crack, a bone breaking. Henry went limp.

Sam closed her eyes. She registered all of this, but none of it.

181

Mull, Monrovia, Tubmanburg, releasing Henry, the gung-ho border crossing, death in the kitchen. And now this. The pair of them fighting evil in the jungle.

Pathetic. You're pathetic.

She was emotionally out of it; drained. The pain in her stomach was overwhelming. She had brought Henry here, probably to his death. But she had no energy to fight them. She was completely spent. The Americans had never been far behind them. She had been stupid enough to think that they could stay ahead of the professionals. *Stupid. Stupid.*

Her arrogance and recklessness had got them here. In her acute pain, and now with an overbearing sense of shame, she sobbed again. She tried to fight the blackness, but all she came up with was self-loathing; self-loathing laced with an enveloping tiredness. *It's been a rubbish eighteen months.*

She must have slept for a short while. She was woken by the two men talking. It was incidental stuff, nothing that she could make out as important. Lifting her head she spotted the pair of them sat at the table making something. Preparing something. The more she looked, the more horrified she became. Kurt had a couple of brown bottles, medicinal type bottles. He passed one to Wayfarer who was holding a syringe. Wayfarer turned the bottle upside down, inserted the needle into the bottle's silver lid and drew off some liquid. He then tapped the syringe, squirted a bit of the liquid out of the top of the needle and handed it back to Kurt.

Kurt walked over to where Sam was. He had an expressionless face, devoid of emotion. Sam could feel her eyes popping out of her sockets. She surprised herself by being bothered.

'So, you are Sam Green? It's a shame that we didn't meet that time on that Godless island in Scotland,' his accent drawing out the first syllable. 'It's also a shame that we're not going to get to know you well. I'm sure there's a lot you can tell us, but we're running out of time. I think we need to finish this.'

The finality of his last sentence smashed what little resilience Sam had left. If she could have spoken she would have had nothing to say. After the hell of what she had been through, all she now wanted was for it to be over. She'd lost the only man she'd loved at the hands of one set of terrorists. Her feelings for Henry were strong, but not strong enough to break into the cycle of violence, depression and more violence that had been her recent life. Just now all she wished for was that the needle would close it all. All she wanted was for all the pain to go away. There was nothing else that she could bear.

She looked into the Binos man's eyes, pleadingly.

Almost knowingly Kurt stuck the needle into Sam's left arm straight through her shirt into the muscle. The last words she heard was, 'Goodbye, Sam Green. And may God the Almighty and protector of our Earth love and cherish your soul.'

As Sam drifted off into oblivion her last thought was for Henry. *Sorry Henry, I really am.*

Southeast Kenema, Sierra Leone

Henry drifted in and out of consciousness. In his more lucid moments the pain in his face was excruciating. For the sake of it he tried to open his mouth (he didn't want to open his eyes) but the crunching of bone and sinew lubricated by his own blood was almost as shocking as the pain. Something was broken, but he had no idea what it was nor how it might have ended up that way. He knew he was lying down somewhere and every so often he heard men's voices, but could only pick out the odd sentence. He had tried to move his arms and legs, but they seemed to be affected by a lethargy which he couldn't understand.

He slept again. It seemed better that way.

He was awake. Startled. It had been easy being asleep. He hadn't had to think about his face. And he didn't have to think about what else was going on. It was like the choice of opening his eyes; he *really* didn't want to do that. Easier not to. There was something horrible deep in his memory which wasn't meant to be accessed. He knew that if he explored it he would be in a whole world of hurt. He didn't want to go there. Sleep was better than thinking.

But something had changed now, perceptibly so. His cocooned world with listless arms and useless legs was being invaded. By something unpleasant. He smelt it first. Smoke. Like a strong cigarette smell that catches your throat when you're having a pint outside a pub on a summer's evening and someone on the next table lights up. You know then that if they continue to puff away you're going to have to move to another table.

But it was stronger than that. The smell was more pervasive. And more putrid.

Then there was the noise. The crackling; an overlapping sound, a crackle here and more crackling there. And then a thud. Something falling to the floor.

Now there was heat. A gentle warming heat to begin with mixing seamlessly with the smoke, but all of a sudden it was dangerous heat. Heat that burnt you if you let it. Heat that tore at flesh, shrinking and warping it, and then dripping it on the floor.

Fire. That's what it was. The thing invading his sleep.

Shit! Fire!

Everything coalesced at the same time. *Liberia. Sierra Leone. Mrs Tebie's house. The hospital. Then what? What happened next? Fire....*

Oh God, Sam! Where is she?

His brain was alive now. He remembered everything apart from how he got to where he was. And now he knew he was in mortal danger. No, *they* were in mortal danger. The intense heat of the flames was close. Very close. He willed himself to open his eyes. No that didn't work.

Sam. Where are you? Come on Henry. Get your stupid carcass up and find her.

He coughed involuntarily, sending spikes of pain through his cheeks and down his spine. The pain was so sharp his eyes opened and watered. He couldn't move his head easily, but he could see. A dark room lit up red and orange with fire, most of it centred to his right in what looked like another room. But the flames were threatening where he was. Smoke was high on the ceiling and he knew that oxygen would be running out and carbon gases filling the void. He had to get out. He had to get them both out.

He looked directly across the room. There was a bed with a body on it. *Sam!* She was there, asleep? Unconscious? He must save her.

He gritted his teeth (*God that hurt*) and tensed every muscle in his body. With willpower he didn't know he had he lifted his torso off of the bed and swung his legs round so his feet touched the floor. Everything was jelly. His body was useless. A crash of timber from the next room and 'whoosh' of terrifically hot air and ash spurred him into action. He stood up, but dropped down again. He stood again steadying himself with his hand on the bedstead which was almost too hot to touch.

He knew he only had one chance. There was a door to his left, away from the fire. He tentatively shuffled across the floor, each step a guess as to where his uncommunicative feet might take him. Six steps, seven, eight and then he tumbled onto Sam's bed. She didn't move.

He wanted to check on her, feel for a pulse, but he knew he didn't have the time. They didn't have the time. The heat was stronger now, the flames alive on the wall just by his head. The heat was intolerable.

Anger took over. There was so much latent fury, none of which had surfaced since he had arrived in West Africa. Something snapped and the anger soared through his body. He closed his eyes which were watering from the smoke, straightened himself and put his limp hands under Sam's light body. With some shuffling and grunting she was a baby in his arms. She was always the strong one. Always the one with a plan. She had saved his life, but now it was his turn to save hers.

Still with his eyes closed he picked her up and turned to his left. He felt his back prickle with heat that he knew was now burning his clothes. *Quickly, Henry, quickly*. With one eye open he shuffled towards the door, every step like a new-born fawn. *Bambi, just like Bambi*. He almost laughed.

He looked with his opened eye. The door seemed a lot further away than he expected, but he shuffled on weakly every step a monumental effort.

Then, without warning, his legs gave way. There was no pain as he fell - his body had all but lost its sense of feeling; everything was a blur. He tried to let Sam down gently, but she fell from his arms. He hadn't the energy to open his eyes fully to see exactly where she was but he felt her beside him. He thought he could move his arms a bit, but his legs just didn't respond. He knew then that there was nothing he could do. This is how it would end for both of them. As his brain closed down he managed to get his arms to pull him into a position where, if nothing else, he was between Sam and the fire. When this thing came, and he knew it was soon, he would go first.

It was at that point he knew he loved Sam Green. A pointless, pitiful love. Tears ran down his cheeks as his back singed.

Chapter Twenty-One

Headquarters MI6, Vauxhall, London

David looked at his watch. It was two thirty in the morning. He had just finished walking round his staff and testing them on any last minute theories as they prepared for a night in the office. He had called a lockdown for that night. They would know tomorrow if they had been tilting at windmills. Actually it was pretty much his own theory. He guessed a couple of his staff thought it was his windmills they were tilting at.

The conversation with the Deputy at Langley had been short. They had nothing particularly new, just another intercept that spoke of an imminent threat. David thought they may be tracking the same calls? The threat warning to Reuters had been issued by one of the Deputy's staff and the man had been reprimanded. After their brief conversation David still wasn't comfortable. He was an old hand at reading people, even over the telephone. He thought there was something the Deputy wasn't telling him.

He'd met his own boss just before midnight. His boss had spoken to the Director as asked but had nothing to add. David knew the Director would be much more focused on US specific threats from abroad and would delegate threats to other nations to his Deputy. He was an Afghanistan veteran and, according to some, blinkered when it came to emerging terrorist cells in places like West Africa.

'He has the greatest confidence in his Deputy,' his boss had added.

And that was that. A European threat from a West African Islamic fundamentalist cell fell to a man who David no longer trusted. He was, as he had been since the beginning, on his own.

They needed a piece of luck. He was convinced that the attack would come later today. He was pretty convinced it was Ebola based and that the target was St Paul's. In terms of casualties, unless they had got the delivery method wrong, it was a hopeless target. But in terms of reach and global repercussions it was perfect. An ISIS or Al Qaeda attack at the heart of Western European Christianity. With a weapon as horrifying, as terrorising, as had ever been used on civilians. If anyone had any doubts that they were on the brink of a war between two civilisations, this would be the catalyst. The repercussions in the UK and across Europe would be far reaching. There would be a war. The liberals and pluralists would not be listened to.

He was tired. He needed to sleep, to be at his sharpest should new intelligence come in. He walked across to his window and rubbed his eyes. *The best office view in London*. Well, if the attack came off as he thought it might, he may not be enjoying it for much longer. And if it didn't, his position might be under review in any case for wasting time on a ridiculous hunch.

SLA Brigade Headquarters, Kenema

Sam felt herself coming to. She slipped into and out of sleep but eventually felt awake enough to think. *She had been asleep for days?* No, that didn't make sense. *She was dead?* But then she felt the drumming of low intensity pain in her stomach. No, that couldn't be right.

She coughed, a barking cough. Her lungs were raw. More pain, but different. She was bored with pain. She coughed again, she couldn't help herself. Her lungs stung; paint stripper sore. But the pain in her stomach was dull. It was bearable.

She tried to open her eyes. *No! Too bright!* Her eyes stung. She tried again, blinking this time.

There was a man standing over her. She flinched and pushed her head back...into a soft pillow. She kept her eyes closed waiting for something to happen. Something horrible.

'Miss Green. Can you hear me?' It was a familiar sound. Northern European. Swedish!

She knew just then that she wasn't dead.

She gently opened her eyes and focused on Doctor Urgsmund. She blinked and then involuntarily coughed again. More burning from her lungs. And now her head hurt in a woozy way.

'Miss Green, can you hear me?'

She tried to talk but her mouth was dry and a rasp came out. It should have been a 'yes'.

'Sit up if you can, Miss Green and have some water.' He was helping her up. She was trying to keep her eyes open but the light was too strong.

She took a sip. Then some more. Then she coughed, water everywhere.

It took about thirty seconds before she could begin to operate like a reasonably functioning human being. She laid back down on the pillow and tried to find some tears to wet her eyes. She coughed again and was about to answer one of Doctor Urgsmund's many questions when she thought *Henry!*

She sat up ignoring all the fluffiness in her head, the twinge from her stomach and the burning in her lungs.

'Where's Henry?!' It was almost a scream.

Doctor Urgsmund put both hands up and motioned for her to calm down.

'Your friend is in another room. He's not as well as you, but in time he will be fine I'm sure.' His words reassuring, but only up to a point.

'I want to see him,' she was lifting the bed clothes and trying to turn her body to one side. And then the drip caught, a drip she didn't know she had attached to her - she felt the drag in her arm. She stopped herself, looked to the door. She was surprised to see a soldier stood there, a rifle in his hand.

'Easy, Miss Green. Easy. You can't see him quite yet. He's still sleeping and won't be able to talk to you...' The doctor's words were interrupted by a voice from behind him.

'Is she awake? Can I speak to her now?'

Sam immediately recognised the voice. *Good*, she thought, *my memory's still there*. It was the woman who'd phoned after Mull. On the train to London. The woman she had dismissed. The woman she didn't trust.

'Sam Green. I'm so glad you're awake and indeed alive!' The face to the voice was mid-thirties, dark hair and high cheeks. A good looking woman, Sam thought; despite the lack of makeup and the ruffled hair.

'MI6?' Sam asked. She coughed some more. Paint stripper again. *Ouch!*

'Yes, 'fraid so. Jane Baker. We need to talk now, are you up to it?' The attractive faced smiled. Sam looked beyond her to the window. No curtain. It was dark outside.

'What time is it?' Sam asked.

'About five o'clock in the morning. You've been out for four or five hours.' Jane pulling up a chair and settling herself down. Doctor Urgsmund stood back.

'Where am I?'

'You're with the Sierra Leonean Army. We brought you here to keep you safe.' Jane was taking out a notebook from her blouse pocket.

'What happened?' Sam coughed some more.

'Looks like you were both drugged and then the hostel you were in set on fire. It was made to look like an accident.' Jane looked sympathetically at Sam. Sam realised she had a maternal way, already making her feel comfortable.

'How did we get out?'

'Well the first thing you should know is that we found you in Mr Middleton's arms. He was obviously trying to get you out of the building when he collapsed.'

Sam shut her eyes for a second. She wanted to cry right now. That could wait. It had to wait. 'But how did we get out?'

'Me and the Sierra Leonean Army found you. The fire had engulfed the building, but it wasn't so far gone that we couldn't pull you out. The soldiers...' and she pointed at the lad in Army fatigues at the door, '...were very brave indeed.'

And you too, Jane Baker Sam thought. She coughed and coughed. She reached for some water. Something to douse the raw pain in her lungs.

'Doctor Urgsmund here thinks you've both got minor carbon monoxide poisoning and Henry, I'm afraid, has bad burns to his back. From what we saw it looked like he was trying to shield you from the flames.

Idiot Sam thought. She held back the tears again.

'But how did you know where to find us?'

'I know some very clever people back in England. They were able to track you to within a couple of blocks - one of you had left your phone left on, data enabled? When we got within a couple of streets we saw the flames and were able to go straight to hostel.'

Idiot Sam thought again. Then, *how lucky are we*?

Jane's maternal nature was turning quickly. More efficient now.

'Look, we can talk through the detail of this in due course, but I need to know what you've found out about Doctor Tebie. And I need to know it now. We have a potential major incident about to go live in the UK and you may have information that can help us prevent the attack from happening.' She turned to the Doctor. 'Could you leave us now please and ask the guard to stand outside?'

The Swede nodded. 'Yes, of course. I'll go and check on Mr Middleton.

Jane waited until the room was clear.

'Tell us all you know, Sam.'

In between coughing fits Sam worked backwards. She knew that if time was short the best she could do was to give the latest information first. She focused on Tebie, reciting fact not conjecture. As an analyst it was never her responsibility to amplify, only to report. Unless she were asked...

By the end Jane sat back in her chair, seemingly exhausted. Sam thought she looked resigned to some fate, as though she had failed in some way. There was no colour in her cheeks.

'Thanks Sam. And thanks for the briefing style. Very helpful. There's not a great deal new there.'

Sam hadn't finished.

'I haven't told you about Doctor Arthur Wesley.'

Jane quickly leant forward. 'Who? Go on,' she said.

Sam quickly summarised the conversation they had had with Doctor Urgsmund.

Jane stopped her abruptly. Her face was animated now. Her face starting to get its colour back. 'He must be the second operative. He's the man in London.' She was excited. 'Do you have a photograph?'

'Did my daysack survive?' Sam wasn't hopeful.

'No, sorry.'

'That's fine. Google him. There are good quality photographs available. Make sure you include Kenema in the search.' *Otherwise you get an unremarkable male model from Bradford.* Sam was about to add something, but Jane, reaching for her mobile, put her hand out to stop Sam from adding anything else.

It took a couple of seconds. Then 'David?' There was a further pause. 'I think we've found the second operative.'

Headquarters MI6, Vauxhall, London

It took David about fifteen minutes to get his team together. They turned up in various states of undress, one or two carrying folders, a couple nursing cups of coffee. His call from Jane had taken a couple of minutes. He realised that he hadn't spent anywhere near enough time discussing Green and Middleton and other niceties. That could wait. They had a new lead which required immediate attention. He would make amends later.

'Pay attention everyone. We may have the second operative.' He swiped across his iPad and the beamer threw up the best photograph he could find of Doctor Arthur Wesley.

'Here he is. A colleague of Tebie's. He's a devout Muslim, known to be a fundamentalist. But he could be doing this for money. Whatever. We have...' he looked at this watch, 'About four hours to find him. Trevor, take your team and look for Wesley on Tebie's flight from Dulles or one flying in at about the same time. Mike, get this across to the Met electronically. And follow it up in person. Let's make sure they have this image and the other four I have just emailed to you all. He's the man they need to spot in a crowd tomorrow. Sorry, today. Susan, call in all of our Muslim contacts in the local mosques - a radius of twenty miles from St Paul's. Share the photo and see if anyone recognises him as someone who has recently joined their flock. Give whatever secrets away you need to impress the importance of their attention. Everyone else, use whatever means you have, pull any contact or source - let's track him down now. We need to know where he's operating out of.'

He looked across at them. They were sat and he was still standing, but bent over the table with straight arms resting on his fists. 'Come on! Let's go!'

Chapter Twenty-Two

Brigade Headquarters, Kenema, Sierra Leone

Sam had been allowed to look in on Henry, but not to wake him. The soldier guarding him opened the door wide enough for her to poke her head round, but nothing else. Henry was lying on his side. There was a drip with two bags feeding into his arm. His face was battered, but he was breathing calmly.

Doctor Urgsmund had briefed her on her and Henry's injuries. He had given her a thorough examination when she had arrived at the Army base, especially around her old stomach wound as it was clear when she arrived she was in a good deal of pain. He didn't know if there was any damage; he'd need an x-ray. They would conduct one later in the morning at the hospital when Miss Baker gave them the all clear to travel there.

Sam had told him about her old wound and he had seemed uncomfortable that he might have missed something. He'd asked her a couple of questions about her stomach and examined her once more. He then told her to rest and had upped her Valium dosage.

It seemed that Henry was still delirious. The doc reckoned it was a combination of the head wound (Sam had told him about Henry being hit with a pistol), smoke inhalation and some shock from the burns. But he was happy with his progress and the drip was doing the job of rehydration. He reckoned he'd be fully conscious in a couple of hours. He'd then be able to assess him further.

She felt impotent lying in her bed waiting for something to happen. It was light outside. Sam was still wearing her watch. It was ten thirty. She needed a coffee. She gingerly got herself out of bed without coughing (that was a first) and asked the soldier to take her to find Miss Baker.

Jane was in the Chief-of-Staff's office. They appeared to be discussing how they might track down the two Americans. Jane noticed Sam.

'Hi Sam, come in.'

'Thanks.' She walked tentatively into the office. Her stomach was a little bit sore just now. 'How's it going?'

'Nothing from London.' Jane stopped herself. She turned to the Chief-of-Staff, 'Major, do you mind giving me and Miss Green use of your office for a few minutes?'

The Chief-of-Staff stood up immediately, gave a short bow and left.

'Sit down Sam. I know we discussed some of the detail last night and I have to remind you that everything we discussed is secret?' Jane looked for a response.

Sam nodded.

'They think they've found where Wesley worshipped. A mosque in Wandsworth. But they've not yet been able to track him down. All eyes are now on St Paul's. It's a waiting game unless anything new comes up.' Jane sighed. She looked at her watch.

'Oh,' Sam said. 'And what about Kurt and the other guy?'

'Well that's an altogether more difficult situation. The Sierra Leone police have their details and will arrest them on sight, irrespective of immunity or whatever they try to pull. But these boys are expert. I think they'll be out of the country by now.'

'Oh.' Oh again. Sam's response was flat. She had started the conversation and now thought she probably didn't want to continue. But she couldn't stop herself. 'What about speaking to their people in the US?'

'That's not my call I'm afraid Sam. We know who Kurt is and we know he works for the US government. We don't have anything on the other guy. I've checked the appropriate staff lists and can't find his name anywhere. But in terms of talking to the States, when and how that happens will fall to my boss.' She waited, looking at Sam. 'You understand it's a very delicate situation.'

'I see,' said Sam. That was better than 'oh' she thought. 'When will we know whether or not your people have prevented an attack?'

'My boss thinks it'll all be over in a couple of hours. Terrorists are morning people. They don't like to hang around.' Jane was trying to smile.

'Urgsmund says he'll be taking us to the hospital mid-afternoon after the hullabaloo has all died down and Henry has regained full consciousness. What happens to us then?'

'I've spoken to the High Commission. They're sending a small convoy up here now. They'll pick us all up and take us down to Freetown. I can't move until the end of the day and I know whether or not there's more we need to do here with regard to Tebie. And we can't move you until Doctor Urgsmund gives us the all clear. I'd resign myself to another night in the barrack room.' She had that maternal approach thing going again, the one she showed last night. 'You're safe here. All the guns are pointing outwards.' Jane now managed a broad smile.

Sam stopped herself from saying anything, not that pressing Jane for anything else would have got her very far.

'I think I'll go and see if Henry's awake. Thanks for your honesty.' She smiled, stood and walked out.

Sam made her way as quickly as she could to Henry's room. The door was open and the guard let her in. Henry was sat up in bed, twisted slightly, favouring his back. Doctor Urgsmund stood beside him taking his blood pressure. She stood still. Henry smiled at her, a crooked smile bent by the bruising around his eye and mouth. She smiled back.

'You idiot,' she said.

His smile broadened further until it obviously hurt; he winced.

Doctor Urgsmund offered her a seat by Henry's bedside and she sat down. He then left the room. She held his hand and they talked. It was aimless stuff about him leaving his mobile on and how Doctor Urgsmund looked like Beaker out of the Muppets.

After about fifteen minutes Henry asked, 'And what is this all about? Why were we so special to those two American bastards?'

Sam knew that a lot of what she had been told was not to be divulged to anyone, so to begin with she tried her best to tell Henry what she knew without really telling him anything. It wasn't going to be easy and she really didn't care that much.

'They think Tebie and Wesley were, or are, part of a team trying to attack London - in the name of Islam.' She had already given too much away.

'When, where?' Henry coughed. He flinched in pain.

'Today? St Paul's Cathedral, London.' Oh well, in for a penny in for a pound.

Henry stared intently at her. He seemed set to ask a number of follow on questions, but instead he closed his eyes. He said nothing.

'Are you ok Henry?'

He raised his free hand stopping further conversation. Sam assumed he was getting through some pain. She waited, turning to look out of the window. It had started to rain accompanied by the patter of drops on the tin roof. It would soon be a deluge and the roof would become a symphony of percussion.

Henry opened his eyes.

'Sorry. Something caught in my mind, something jarred. I have no idea what. Where were we?' He scrunched his eyes together this time obviously fighting a new wave of pain.

Sam smiled at him and squeezed his hand. 'I was explaining that Wesley might just now be about to attack St Paul's.'

Henry gently shook his head. He looked perplexed. 'That can't be right. There's something here which doesn't make sense. And I don't know why. What are they going to attack it with, it's a pretty big target?'

'Apparently Ebola.' She had now sold the Crown Jewels and would be locked up in the Tower forever. Oh well, these things happen.

Henry went quiet again looking dead ahead. After a couple of seconds he turned to her. 'Wow. That would be something. But St Paul's? No, I don't get it. It's not right. Yes it's a fabulous target for Islamic extremists; you couldn't pick a higher profile place. But you wouldn't infect anyone. I did A-level chemistry and even if you could throw a whole load of Ebola about you'd be wasting your time in such a large space.' He looked at Sam and half smiled, the bandages creasing at the corners as he did. 'Although, I grant you it's a good target if you want to cause major upset and unleash a religious war'. He paused, so deep in thought it seemed to hurt.

Sam began to see why he was high up in the United Nations. His political mind was far more attuned than hers. 'Maybe you should rest Henry?'

'No. No. There's something else here.' He was insistent. 'Something's really bothering me. Give me a couple of seconds.'

Sam waited, glancing around the room. She opened her mouth to say something but Henry's look was withering. She shut up and stared out of the window again. The rain was now coming down in stair rods and the roof was being drummed by a thousand gorillas. Phil Collins would be pleased.

'I heard stuff last night. The whole thing is a blur, but bits are coming back. I seem to remember men's voices. The odd word echoes, but I can't quite piece anything together.' Henry was looking out of the window, talking to himself almost. 'God, the rain is blooming noisy.'

'Can I help?' Sam asked.

'No.' He was too sharp. 'Sorry. I know they were talking about an attack. An event that would kill thousands, maybe more. And that's why St Paul's seems an unlikely target.'

'Maybe the number of deaths is a consequence of the attack. The religious war you've just mentioned?' Sam replied, always the analyst.

'Yes, maybe, but there's something else up here,' he pointed to his head with his free hand, 'something that's more immediate, more now.'

'If you have something Henry, we need to find it in the next few minutes if it's about the attack.' Sam was pressing him. She gently squeezed his hand.

He closed his eyes. And nodded his head as his mind sketched out his thoughts.

'Something to do with beneath, or underneath. Maybe in the crypt? But how would they infect thousands by letting Ebola off in the crypt of St Paul's? It doesn't make any sense.' Henry was grimacing, frustration rising to the surface. His face red and covered in sweat.

'Henry, you ought to...'

'No! It's here. I know it is. There's a word that I heard that will unravel this.' He turned his head to her. 'Help me Sam. Help me find it.'

Sam closed her eyes. She could see the thought process, the disregard for St Paul's as a target. But sometimes terrorists aren't the most intelligent of people. And the media impact of an attack there would be enormous.

She concentrated on what she knew. St Paul's. Beneath. Under.

Then it came to her.

'Did they mention 'underground'? Or even metro?' Sam's words were sharp, immediate.

Henry opened his eyes and looked across at her. He said almost in a whisper, 'Yes, that's it. They said something along the lines of *kill thousands in the metro, it'll be like poisoning an ants nest.* Yes, that makes sense.'

Then they both said together, 'St Paul's underground station.'

'Of course!' Henry face alive now. 'It's perfect. You would easily infect hundreds, who would infect hundreds more. And the world media would report the key words *Saint Paul.* Islam strikes at the heart of Christianity. The fact that it's a tube station is irrelevant. It's a double whammy. A perfect target.

Sam sprung up. 'Wait there.' She stopped and smiled at him. 'Well, let's face it you're not going anywhere tied up with all those drips. This has got to be key. I'm going to see Jane.' And she rushed out of the door.

Chapter Twenty-Three

Order, counter-order, disorder. That was Police Sergeant David Trainer's view of where they were with the current threat. His boss, him and his team had the Cathedral nicely sewn up. There were twelve of them. Six taking the north segment led by his boss, and he had taken the south segment with five other lads. A further on-call team was thirty minutes away. They had spent twenty-four hours getting this right, including recess and building acquisition - nobody seemed to mind if a member of the Met's anti-terrorist squad turned up and said 'do you mind if we use your window for a day or so?'. They always ran a wager on the quality of the cake that followed shortly after their arrival. One or two of the younger lads probably had a different sort of water, but every one of them was the best the Met had and he trusted them implicitly.

Best laid plans. About twenty-five minutes ago their Super had been in touch and ordered an immediate reconfiguration to cover all entrances and exits of St Paul's Underground as well as the cathedral. They hadn't planned on that. But he knew there were no more Bobbies available at such short notice to oversee the additional target. Within a minute his boss had selected two men from the northern segment (one of whom was already in a trigger position covering the Cheapside exit of the station) and one from the southern segment and told him to make it up as best he could.

That's what he did. A box cover, with one man on each corner. He had checked his map and issued orders over the radio. Five minutes later they were in position, albeit in deterrent rather than ambush mode.

Within fifteen minutes Sergeant Trainer spotted someone he thought looked like the mugshot that was sellotaped to the butt of his Glock semi-automatic. He had another quick look at the photo and then back down the street to where the man stood. The guy looked in his direction and quickly turned away. As he did so Sergeant Trainer spotted the tell-tale signs of a bulky rucksack.

He reached for the radio pressel on his belt, moving towards the target as he did.

'Mike Alpha Three this is Charlie Two. I have visual. Ten yards south of Cheapside. He's turning the corner and will be in the north entrance any moment now. Blue jacket, black beanie and a bulky green rucksack.'

Short pause. 'Roger, got that Mike Alpha Three. Mike Alpha Six do you have visual?'

Click. 'Wait...wait...got him. Moving in now. Mike Alpha Eight follow me.'

Then from his boss, 'Charlie One roger. We're staying put here.'

Police Sergeant Trainer didn't register his boss' acknowledgement as the blood was pumping round his head filling his ears with noise as he sprinted down Payner Alley, barging people of out his way. 'Sorry, Police. Sorry.', to a man in a smart suit who toppled from the pavement. As he turned the corner into Cheapside and within a few yards of the St Paul's Underground sign he heard the unmistakable loud crack of a single gunshot. Around him the countless people entering and exiting the station collectively flinched, some already starting to run; others bent down, turning their backs to the focal point of the sound.

He continued to run. It was a few yards, but in the seconds it took him to reach the main north entrance, people were already screaming, running and shouting.

He pushed his way past the stampede into the station; the entrance lobby was emptying quickly. He continued to force through the wave of people and soon saw what he needed to see. The man he had spotted outside, the man they had been told to arrest, or shoot to kill if he looked like preparing to use the weapon on his back, was lying on the floor face down. His oversized rucksack like a tortoise shell on his back. Charlie Four was stood over the body checking for a pulse.

He paused a few feet from rucksack man, his mind racing. Nobody should interfere with the body now. No contamination of the scene. But they needed to secure the weapon. Deal with potential leakage from what he assumed was a cylinder in the rucksack. A cylinder full of a dangerous liquid. That's all he knew.

They had to work fast.

'Charlie One this is Mike Alpha Three. Suspect is down. We need an ambulance and the decontamination team here as soon as possible.' He had a quick glance round and added, 'All secure here.'

As he waited for a response he reached behind his back and, with one hand, opened a small satchel that he had been issued with yesterday. He took out a very modern black gas mask, removed his hat and started to put it on.

Chapter Twenty-Four

McDonald's, just off Trafalgar Square, London

Sam took a sip of her coke. She looked across the table at Henry. His face was getting better, the swelling gone but the bruising still looked raw. She noticed that when he walked into the Foreign and Commonwealth Office he walked uncomfortably as though his back was still playing him up. She'd not had chance to speak to him since they'd left RAF Brize Norton, and certainly not much opportunity today. It had been a bit of a whirlwind and she was glad to be out of the FCO and back into the normal world.

'How's your back'. She took a handful of fries. God, they tasted good.

Henry put his burger down and felt his back. 'It's still a bit sore, but the Doctor said yesterday that I'm unlikely to need further surgery. So that's a positive.'

Sam took another slurp of her coke. She was famished. 'Did you get David Jenning's line about Tebie?'

'What, that he took his own life rather than go through with, what did they euphemistically call it, *the event*?' Henry gently raised his eyes to the ceiling.

'It's a neat fit, but it does take some believing. Especially as they reckon his lad in the States is making a good recovery from his op.' Sam reached for her coke again.

'I don't know. If he knew his boy was going to be ok, maybe he didn't want his lad to grow up knowing his Dad was a mass murderer?' Henry pursed his lips and tipped his head to one side.

'Could be.' Sam chomped at a few more fries. 'Did you sign the Official Secrets Act with your own name?' She was teasing him now.

'No. I used yours.' They both laughed.

Henry finished his burger and wiped his mouth with a paper napkin. 'I'm glad you brought up about Kurt and Ralph. If you hadn't I probably would have.'

'It's not going anywhere Henry, we both know that. And even if it were, we'd be the last to know about it. Even though you've signed the OSA!' Sam smiled cheekily.

'In your name...' They both laughed, raucous laughter. Sam held her side and Henry raised his hand to his chin. His face is obviously still very sore.

'How's your stomach?' It was Henry's turn to press on their collective injuries.

'It's fine, thanks. No permanent damage that wasn't there in the first place. St Thomas' reckon that the Taser sent the muscle into spasm which trapped an already exposed nerve left over from the operation. Dr Urgsmund's prescription of Valium was an inspired choice.' She was holding her coke with both hands. 'I've asked for a year's subscription. Do you want some?' They both laughed again, the enduring pain of their injuries brought tears to both of their eyes.

'Did you get anything on what happened to the clinic and the outbreak of Ebola? Everyone avoided the question when I asked it.' Sam still needed answers.

'No, not really. I spoke to Jane and she was pretty evasive. She was convinced that the clinic existed and that it was torched, either by accident or design. But, as to the outbreak of the Ebola pandemic, she was shtum. I think gestation of the disease will always be linked to a remote village in Guinea and those bats.' Henry had his serious face on now. After the initial bout of energy he looked tired. She couldn't blame him. She wouldn't ask more questions.

She nodded and raised her coke to her mouth looking beyond Henry to the traffic moving slowly down Whitehall.

That was that. It was over. Tebie killed himself rather than let Ebola loose on the world. He embarked on a futile journey that enabled him to raise enough cash to save his child, but in the end brought death to himself and his wife. Wesley was a fanatic, who enjoyed the trappings of extra cash and, she guessed, wanted the stardom and fame of being central to a major terrorist incident. His reward would come in heaven? That's what he probably believed.

And the two Americans? Who knows? They were central to this somehow, maybe even leading it. But why? She had no answers, but she sure hoped that her new pals in MI6 had some.

Her new pals. Once they had both been given their commendations by the Home Secretary, commendations they weren't allowed to publicise, David Jennings had taken Sam to one side and given her his card.

'If you want a job, give me a call. We'd need to run some background checks and the work would be dull, office stuff, but I need people like you.' He'd stood expecting a reply, but Sam had just taken the card and said 'Thanks.' After a short embarrassing silence he'd bowed his head a little and walked away.

You never know Sam thought. She looked back at Henry and a thought came to her.

'Your flight is later this afternoon. Have you still got a job?'

Henry was wiping the last of the tomato sauce up with his few remaining chips. 'Apparently the UK's Ambassador to the UN, a man I have never met, spoke to the Secretary General, and my job is secure.' He finished his mouthful. 'The thing is, I'm not sure I want it anymore.' His expression had changed just slightly. There was a real warmth in his face as he looked at Sam. He reached across and took her hands in his.

'Look Sam, it's been a helluva ride', he was looking down at the table now, his head shaking gently. 'And I was just wondering...'

'Henry', she interrupted him. 'Don't do this, not now.' She felt the tears rising. 'We both nearly died back there. The emotions, the buzz, the fear, the rubbish. It's all still here, with us.' She'd taken one of her hands and pressed it against her chest. 'I know about trauma and what it does to people. It doesn't help with decision making. Not these sort of decisions. Trust me.'

Henry's expression didn't change but he sat back, taking his hand away. He kept looking straight at Sam. She thought she saw dampness in his eyes.

'That's fine Sam. I think I understand. Can I come back and see you in a couple of months and we can talk again?'

'Better still, if you invite me I'll come to you. I've never been to New York.'

She knew she'd done the right thing. It was too early. Too raw. Neither of them were ready to explore anything new. Not yet anyway.

'I'll give you a ring in a couple of weeks then.'

Then it was time to go. Henry had a flight to catch and Sam, well she needed to buy a new campervan. *Continental Europe this time* she thought. *Yes, that would be great.*

As they left McDonald's, sat in a distant corner, a medium-build black man took a swig from a can of Diet Pepsi. Neither of them had noticed him.

Epilogue

'Are we on a secure line Kurt?' The Deputy Director asked.

'Yes sir, we are.' There was a slight crackle on the line from the US to Liberia.

'And are you alone?'

'Yes sir, all alone.'

'Good. Have you heard that the Limeys caught Wesley just before he was about to carry out the attack.' The Deputy Director paused for acknowledgement.

'Yes sir, I'd picked that up on the wires here. They shot him, I understand. I suppose there will be no announcement as to MI6's success?' Kurt had a relationship with the Deputy that allowed him to press for answers.

'No. The last thing they want to do is to fan the fires of this religious war. They will report that a terrorist attack has been thwarted in their private quarterly summary of incidents to their Commission. The police will probably attribute the killing to a drug's bust or something similar. But no details will be released to the press. Unfortunately.' The Deputy's voice was almost monotone - slow, calm and clear. 'You did the best you could, but as you know there is no longer work for you here.'

There was a pause. It could have been the satellite link or the various electronic algorithms encrypting their speech, but the Deputy assumed it was Kurt coming to terms with his fate.

'Yes sir, I understand that.'

'So I'll have your resignation by the end of the day? It will, of course, be followed up with an unattributable payment of five hundred thousand dollars to the account in Luxembourg which is in your name.' A small price to pay, the Deputy thought.

'Yes, sir. I've started drafting it already. It will be with you in an hour.'

'Good. And I'm hoping that as we discussed at the beginning of this you have dealt with Mr Bell and he should no longer be a concern of ours?' Still monotone despite the gravity of the discussion.

There was a longer pause.

'Yes sir, that has been dealt with.' Kurt cleared his throat at the end of the sentence.

'Good. He had no further use to us. And after he allowed Middleton to escape from the compound there was an inevitability about that particular outcome.' The Deputy changed the subject. 'Well, all I can add is to thank you for your support in this operation. I have closed down the two-man support team here and the file and all other transcripts have been destroyed. It is, as of now, a non-operation.' The Deputy almost waited for acknowledgement from Kurt but with nothing forthcoming he decided to close the whole thing down with a final statement.

'God is on yours and my side Kurt. He has been with us throughout. But for whatever reason He didn't want us to succeed - this time. I am in no doubt that this is a conflict which we will inevitably win and He will prevail. The scourge of three millennia will be defeated and we must use whatever methods at our disposal to hasten their demise. You should be proud of the part you played in this battle. God bless you Kurt.'

By the time the Deputy had got to the end of his short monologue he was standing up, his eyes looking skywards.

A short silence

'And Amen to that sir.'

'Goodbye Kurt.'

'Good bye sir'

The line went dead.

About the author:

Roland Ladley draws upon twenty-five years military service, including complex tours of Bosnia, Afghanistan and Sierra Leone, to bring realism to his thriller writing. Subsequent work as a teacher enables him to communicate lucidly to a wide audience, and two grown up daughters ensures he can laugh at himself and find comic moments in his writing when the tension is at its greatest.

Now a full time writer based in Bristol, UK, he lives an itinerant lifestyle with his wife in their motorhome, posting a daily blog under the title of 'The Wanderlings' and penning his second novel.